BAD HABITS

A Tampa Bay Tropics Thriller

George L. Fleming

ST. PETERSBURG
—— PRESS ——

For Linda, the love of my life, the most extraordinary person I have ever met, and, of course, the inspiration for Ms. Reed O'Hara.

Je t'aime, mon beau guerrier.

Chapter One

Father Bob walked unsteadily outside of his modest ranch house in Temple Terrace, a small community just a few miles north of Tampa, Florida. He walked unsteadily because he had been drinking cheap vodka and watching television late into the night. He had had only three hours of sleep — he always awoke at dawn. And he couldn't get out of his head the priest jokes he heard on an HBO comedy special.

"If you're stranded on a desert island with Adolf Hitler, Attila the Hun, and a Catholic priest and you have a gun with only two bullets, what do you do?" the comedian said. "You shoot the priest twice!"

Yeah, that's real fucking funny, Father Bob thought. Why can't people just let bygones be bygones? There's a reason they call it *ancient history.*

Another joke really stung him:

"How do you get a pedophile priest out of a tree? Cut the rope."

So a few priests had sex with children, Father Bob thought. Big fucking deal. After all we've done for those unappreciative little shits and their parents. We have needs after all, and kids are the perfect vessels for filling those needs. Besides, how does this piddly little shit compare to ethnic cleansing or carpet bombing? We need a proper perspective, is all.

Though it was early February, Father Bob was gardening furiously. Tampa Bay is in a subtropical zone, so he figured a hard freeze was unlikely. And when he moved into his new home in January, there were no flowers in his front yard.

No, he thought, my delicate little flowers will thrive. And the broad live oak will help keep them safe. Same way the Church has kept me safe.

Father Bob was short, overweight, and seventy-two years old. So he was glad to get this cool morning, though he was already perspiring.

He had planted a hedgerow of thryallis, which were covered in tiny yellow blooms. An elegant areca palm was the centerpiece plant surrounded by variegated bromeliads. The live oak, about two hundred years old, was on the west side of his property, its long horiziontal limbs stretching out across the front lawn. The oak allowed Father Bob to plant a variety of flowering plants that required shade.

But that also meant that when he replaced the original crazy quilt lawn, really only a sandy patchwork of bahia grass, weeds, and sandspurs, he had to lay down the much more expensive variety of St. Augustine sod that thrived in shade.

Replacing the lawn was a huge job. He was too old and obese to do it himself, so he hired a crew of young Mexicans – or maybe Guatemalans or Columbians or Dominicans, he truly didn't care – to till the old lawn, clear the debris, lay down several yards of top soil, and finally carpet the yard with St. Augustine sod, using machetes to cut the rectangles of fresh sod. Pretending to watch over their work, Father Bob instead admired the teenagers with their shirts off, their sweaty arms and chests heaving to the hard work.

Probably Catholics, Father Bob thought, I'll bless them when they're done. Goodness, such tight little brown bodies. Ah, the good old days. I do so miss Ecuador.

As a result of the lawn crew's considerable effort, Father Bob's lawn now was a luscious, dark green carpet, perfectly edged and mowed, and without a single weed. All he had to do was water and fertilize.

On this particular February morning, all sunshine and cloudless blue ski, Father Bob's plan was to plant red wax begonias in front of the thryallis hedgerow, then plant red and white geraniums around his mailbox at the end of the driveway.

On his knees, Father Bob carefully scooped out the reinforced soil, making neat pockets for the starter begonias.

Must be delicate with these helpless babies, he thought.

As he worked, he thought of the priest joke from the comedy show that he actually liked:

> *"A priest and a rabbi are walking down the street. They see a young boy approaching. The priest says, 'Hey, let's screw him.' The rabbi says, 'Out of what?'"*

At least the kikes also take it on the chin with that one, Father Bob thought.

Still on his knees and with his back to the street, he never knew what hit him.

There was a slight swishing sound, and a black arrow shattered into his lower spine.

He instinctively reached around and grabbed at the arrow half way sunk into his body. The priest couldn't dislodge the arrow.

"What the fuck!" Father Bob exclaimed.

Almost immediately, there was another swishing sound. A second arrow struck dead center between his should blades.

A third and final swish.

A third and final arrow.

This arrow pierced the base of his skull. About six inches of the arrow protruded from his mouth. He looked as if he were pointing to the nearest restroom.

Father Bob sat straight up, still on his knees.

His last words were, "Well, fwok me."

His last thought was recalling the most foul of the priest jokes he heard last night:

> *"How do you get a nun pregnant?*
> *Dress her up as an altar boy."*

Now dead, Father Bob fell forward, crushing the tray of red wax begonias.

Chapter Two

"Lean forward, arms straight, then pull the chain as if you were starting a lawn mower," Jake Dupree said.

Jake was assisting a beautiful young woman on the rowing machine at his executive athletic club in West Tampa. The rower was his favorite exercise equipment.

Though she looked the part, dressed in a new tank top, yoga pants, and gym shoes, Tatiana struggled to row gracefully. She appeared frustrated.

"Take your time, Tat," Jake said. "Knees forward, push off your heels, and pull back as far as you can."

The woman appeared to acknowledge Jake's advice.

Jake was on the rower next to Tatiana's. His movements were fluid; he barely exerted himself. Yet with each pull, his massive arms flexed tellingly. At six foot two inches and weighing two hundred pounds, he was in superb condition for a forty-year-old man.

"Jake, this much sucks," Tatiana said. She made a small child's pouty face.

"Cut it out, Tat. And watch your syntax — your word order. You meant, 'Exercising on this rowing machine truly sucks.'"

Tatiana, still rowing in a herky, jerky fashion, frowned at Jake, paused, then broke out her most alluring Ukrainian smile.

"Okay, Jaky, how is this for the good syntax — in my opinion, rowing sucks a big cock."

Jake stopped rowing. He looked around the club to see if anyone heard her coarse comment.

"Tatiana, you're my guest at this club. Keep talking like that and you'll get us both banned. And I really like working out at this club."

Jake started rowing again, pretending not to acknowledge Tatiana's presence next to him. Which was not an easy feat to accomplish, as Tatiana was a Slavic beauty, all of twenty three, tall, with dark brown eyes, long brunette hair, and a figure ideally centered between slender and voluptuous.

Not admiring her is a Crimean shame, Jake thought.

But Jake kept rowing, his rhythm powerful and steady.

"Please, Jaky, I'll be good. I promise," Tatiana said.

He ignored her while continuing to row. He also looked around the fitness floor, hoping no fellow members were making a hairy eyeball. They were not.

"See, I can do it," she said. "I will row and row and row. The right way. And no more bad words."

Finally Jake nodded approvingly. He would not make her beg for his approval, as if he were some low forehead alpha male.

Jake and Tatiana were not lovers. They were more acquaintances than friends. Their relationship was strictly professional, but it was not, as some might suspect, one of pimp and prostitute. Though Tatiana did indeed work for Jake and his wife, Reed O'Hara.

Two months ago, Tatiana walked into Namaste, Jake and Reed's cabaret nightclub on Lois Avenue in West Tampa. It was noontime. On a Monday. Tatiana was reed thin, sickly looking, and her hair disheveled. Her four-inch heels made her well over six-feet tall. She wore a wrinkled, dirty tee shirt and ragged jeans. She hadn't bleached her hair in months, so her brunette roots stretched a good four inches from her scalp.

Jake was sitting at a grand piano in the center of the nightclub. He was busy working on a new composition. He sipped from his second and last *café con leche* of the day. He wished, after all, to be alert, but not wired.

He hit a few notes on the piano keys, stopped, then made musical notes on the composition pages in front of him.

Jake looked up to see the young, beatific blonde make her way awkwardly toward him.

Andre, head of security at Namaste, blocked the woman's path to Jake. Andre was six-foot five-inches, a chiseled two hundred fifty pounds, and one of the kindest people on earth. Except when it was time not to be kind.

"Miss, we're not open until seven p.m.," Andre said. "How can I help you?"

The young woman dropped her overstuffed gym bag on the floor. She didn't seem particularly frightened or intimidated by Andre. She just seemed very, very tired. She seemed almost ready to fold a totally lousy poker hand.

"Please, I must to speak with that man," she said. "He's boss, yes?"

"Yes, Mr. Dupree is co-owner of Namaste. Only he's busy right now," Andre said.

"I must to speak with Mr. Dupree. I want to be a dancer here."

"Andre, I'll talk with her," Jake said. "Have her come over."

Andre escorted the young woman to Jake and his piano. He then pulled a chair from a four-top table and placed it next to the piano.

The young woman might have bolted at any second.

"Please sit down, miss," Jake said. "Would you like a coffee or juice? Perhaps something to eat?"

"Yes please, all of them?" she said tentatively. Though she wanted to, she would not permit herself to smile.

"Of course. Andre, have Glenn whip up an omelet with bacon and toast. And coffee and orange juice, all right?" Jake said.

Andre nodded warmly. He walked in the direction of the kitchen.

"Come on, let's go sit at that table," Jake said.

"Thank you," the young woman said.

She and Jake sat across from each other at a nearby table. For a solid thirty seconds, neither person spoke.

Jake finally broke the silence.

"I'm Jake Dupree. I believe Andre told you that I co-own Namaste. My wife Reed O'Hara is the other co-owner. She's also an attorney who practices in Tampa."

"I am very pleased to meet you, Mr. Dupree. I am Tatiana Smolenkov."

Just then, Chef Glenn brought Tatiana her omelet with juice and coffee.

Tatiana thanked the chef, then picked up the glass of orange juice and drank all of it. Then she held the mug of coffee with both hands, taking several quick sips. Her thirst satisfied, she tore into the omelet, showing off impeccable table manners despite being obviously famished.

"Is better now, Mr. Dupree. That was so good. Um, okay, I dance here, yes?"

"I like your directness, Tatiana. But first things first. I need to ask you a few questions. And at any point where I think you're lying, our interview is over, and Andre will see you to the door. You can trust me to be completely discrete. What is said here stays here. Is that fair enough?"

"Yes . . . fair enough," she said.

"First, an easy one: how old are you?"

"Twenty one, no, twenty three."

"You're sure?"

"Yes, twenty three."

"All right. Do you dance well?"

"Yes, most absolutely. I was ballet dancer for long time."

"Where did you study ballet?" Jake asked.

"In Kiev. In Ukraine. I started when I was little girl, but had to quit when I was fifteen. I went to work in truck parts factory to help my family," Tatiana said.

Totally out of character, Jake asked Andre for a third *café con leche*. He was committed to seeing through this interview.

"So you're an experienced dancer, but you haven't trained for eight years, correct?" he said.

Tatiana nodded yes.

"If you got back to it, and worked very hard, could you return to form?"

Tatiana nodded yes very eagerly. She sat straight up in her chair.

"Now some tough questions," Jake said.

"Okay. I be very honest," Tatiana said.

"Fine. Do you smoke?"

"Yes. Cigarettes. And weed."

"Do you drink alcohol?"

"Of course."

"Any illegal drugs other than marijuana?"

"Well, I do coke when I can afford it. Sometimes I have to smoke crack."

"Married? Children?"

"No married. No boyfriend anymore. I have little girl. Katarina. She five. Good girl," Tatiana said.

"Where is Katarina now?"

"Friend watch her at shit motel where we live."

Jake finished his coffee, then sat in silence for a full three minutes. He rested his chin in his right hand. Finally, he spoke.

"Tatiana, I believe you've been honest with me. I appreciate that. So we'll take you on as a dancer. But Namaste has a lot of strict rules for all of its employees. And for the employers, for that matter. I'll explain the rules to you, then you decide if this program is right for you, okay?"

"Yes, Mr. Dupree," Tatiana said.

"Here we go then. Some of our dancers perform topless. But not full nude. We expect you to be sensual, not nasty. It's your decision to go topless. Are you all right with this?"

"Yes, I am. So some nights I go without top, and other nights I keep clothes on?"

"That's correct."

"Is good for me, Mr. Dupree."

"You'll be a Namaste employee, not an independent contractor, so you'll draw an annual salary of $50,000 and have full benefits, including health insurance for you and Katarina."

This time, Tatiana nodded with great enthusiasm.

"And tips?" she asked.

"You keep all of your tips. We make our money with admission charges, membership dues, drinks, and food," Jake said.

"Okay. Is good. Is all good."

Jake leaned forward. He became very serious. His polar blue eyes beamed directly at Tatiana.

"Now for the hard part, Tatiana. You have to quit smoking. You have to quit drinking alcohol. And you have to quit using illegal drugs. And don't let us catch you abusing prescriptive drugs," Jake said.

"Okay, it'll be hard, but I can do it. At least I hope I can," she said. A look of quiet determination came over her face.

"To keep you honest, we'll drug test you periodically. If you fail, you get one warning. The second time, you're out of here."

"Is fair," Tatiana said.

"Are you willing to take yoga and meditation classes? They'll help you get over your addictions," Jake asked.

"Yes, I will do it."

"There's one more thing. And you're going to like it. We'll get you a one-year lease at the nearby Cove Apartments. So we pay for the first year, up to you after that."

Tears welled up in Tatiana's eyes.

"I take it that you accept our offer?" Jake asked.

"Yes, thank you very much," Tatiana said.

"You're welcome. Now, we want you exercising strenuously each and every day. Starting today. You'll join me at three p.m. at my athletic club at International Plaza. I'll get you a guest membership."

Which is how, two months later, Tatiana came to be rowing with Jake at his athletic club. Though still new at the rowing machine, Tatiana was expert at the elliptical machine, the stair climber, and battle ropes. She couldn't get enough of Pilates, yoga, and meditation. She was even taking ballet classes at the YMCA in Ybor City. She had become toned and muscular, and she strode around the club in assured confidence.

Tatiana had regained her health and swore off all intoxicants. She and her daughter were settled into their new home at the Cove. Her dancing was pure double diamond at Namaste, and she was making a very good living.

I like it when a good plan comes together, Jake thought, as he continued to rip it at level ten on the rower. The turbine fan roared with each pull.

Jake looked up from the rowing machine at the bank of large flat-screen televisions on the wall in front of him. One screen was showing a local news special report about a retired priest having been murdered outside of his home in Temple Terrace.

Christ, now we're killing our old priests, Jake thought.

The rower's turbine fan kept roaring.

Chapter Three

Father Jules was having a fine Saturday afternoon. He had driven from his condo in South Tampa, traversed the Howard Franklin Bridge across Tampa Bay, and arrived in downtown St. Petersburg, an area that had transformed itself from being called "God's Waiting Room" to the "Gulf Coast Riviera."

While trying to find a parking space, Father Jules marveled at the variety of upscale restaurants, bars, and boutiques on and around Beach Drive. Sometimes, he enjoyed a classic mojito at the lobby bar in the Vinoy Hotel. Occasionally, he sat at one of the several open-air cafes on Beach Drive, feasting on a grouper sandwich with sweet potato fries.

St. Pete reminds me of San Diego, he thought.

Today, though, he was bound for the Dali Museum, where it was the last day for the Pablo Picasso and Salvador Dali dual exhibit. He expected a large crowd.

Those pussy impressionists can't hold a candle to the abstract genius of Picasso and Dali, Father Jules thought.

And today, I get to see these artistic titans side by side, he thought.

Such brilliance. Such bravery. They gave in completely to their primal creativity. There was no shame in what they envisioned. There was no shame in what they painted. Pure originality.

And I have no shame in expressing my primal desires, my unbridled creativity, Father Jules thought. In some ways, I, too, am an artist.

Really, if I thought about it carefully, those boys are my canvasses. What I do is create sensual and outrageous performance art. Ephemeral, yet somehow eternal.

How am I any different from Dali and Picasso? I'm not. I am their peer, he thought.

Father Jules found a parking space in the bay marina, which was filled with yachts and sailboats.

He walked by the old Al Lang Stadium, where the St. Louis Cardinals and New York Mets used to play spring exhibition games, as part of Florida's Grapefruit League. Father Jules saw Daryl Strawberry and Dwight Gooden make their rookie debuts at Al Lang Stadium.

Today, the venerable, cozy ballpark is a soccer stadium, home of the Tampa Bay Rowdies. Father Jules had been to a few Rowdies matches. Soccer didn't really hold his interest; he actually went to the matches to gawk at the plethora of young boys running around with wild, innocent abandon.

As Father Jules walked toward the Dali Museum, he felt a slight breeze coming off the bay. There was nary a cloud in the soft blue sky, meaning humidity was low. The sunshine warmed the aged priest. He was in a good place in his mind.

Just as he was about to ascend the steps to the museum entrance, Father Jules spotted something in his peripheral vision. Something quite wonderful.

A boy, a beautiful, beautiful boy, was sitting by himself on a bench across the street. The bench faced out to the marina, so the boy sat with his back to the priest.

Probably sitting out here while his parents view the Picasso/Dali exhibit, Father Jules thought. What could it hurt to have a chat with this tasty treat? My god, he can't be but twelve! He truly could benefit from my hard-earned wisdom and expertise. Why, I'd make him a veteran heading into that most foul of stages, puberty.

And I haven't practiced my art in a very long time. Too long, really.

Perhaps just a taste, a dabble, before I view the exhibit, he thought.

Father Jules waited for several cars to pass, then started to cross the street, heading toward the boy on the bench.

The boy was wearing wireless headphones that were so popular among young people. The boy's head, covered in strawberry blonde hair, seemed to bob to the music playing in the headphones.

Strangely, the boy's head also bobbed with each step Father Jules made toward him.

The old priest made it to the middle of the asphalt street and stopped suddenly on the street's double center line. A motorcyclist flew by, nearly striking him.

"Asshole!" Father Jules yelled at the motorcyclist, who promptly shot his gloved middle finger at him. Father Jules noticed a black ponytail with red tips hanging out of the motorcyclist's helmet. Bending forward, the motorcyclist exposed part of her waistline; Father Jules noticed a butterfly tattooed on the small of her back.

Jesus, Mary, and Joseph. I almost got run over by an inked bitch on a bike, he thought. What a horrid way to go — and only feet away from my prize.

Then, just as he was about to resume stalking the boy on the bench, he heard a faint swooshing sound.

It was the final sound Father Jules would hear.

The arrow struck him between his eyes, shattering his black frame glasses.

His right hand grabbed the arrow, a strictly bio-mechanical move by his body, as his brain was no longer in his control.

A second arrow pierced his chest, exactly on the left side over his heart.

Blood sprays emanated from the priest's head and chest. Father Jules stiffened straight up, then fell backwards off his heels onto the asphalt. His fall was almost cartoonish, resembling Tom the cat getting knocked out by an oversized mallet swung by Jerry the tiny mouse. The only thing missing was the sound of a gong.

But unlike a Tom and Jerry cartoon, Father Jules was dead — very,

very dead.

A white Mercedes Benz sports sedan slammed on its brake, narrowly missing its driving over the dead priest's head. The Mercedes Benz driver, an elegant, attractive middle-aged woman, looked down at the dead man on the street in front of her and crossed herself. She reached into her coat pocket and pulled out her smart phone as well as her rosary.

The boy on the bench, still listening to his music on the headphones and staring out over the marina, was oblivious totally to the carnage behind him.

Chapter Four

"Morning, cutie pie. Reed O'Hara around?"

A short, squat older man stood in the doorway of the front office to the O'Hara Law Group, which was situated on the top floor of the Gulf Bay Bank skyscraper in downtown Tampa. It was no coincidence that the O'Hara Law group chose the highest office in the tallest commerce building in Tampa.

The man was dressed in a wrinkled charcoal suit, an open collar white dress shirt, a gold chain hanging around his neck, no socks, and black Teva sandals. His uncut toenails were green and black.

He wore on his wrist a gold Invicta watch, monstrously large even for Invicta standards.

He held in his right hand a yellow legal pad with a plastic pen clipped to it.

The man was perspiring heavily. He exuded an unpleasant body odor.

The woman he had addressed as "cutie pie" was standing with her back to him. She was gazing out the large panel window at the city's Channelside district. A Carnival cruise shop was preparing to depart, most assuredly for Cozumel, Mexico.

"Hellooooo . . . . .anybody home in that pretty little blonde head? I'm Jasper Conway. Is O'Hara in or not?" the man said.

Finally, the woman turned and looked at the perspiring fat man.

She was barely five-feet four-inches tall.

She weighed maybe an Irish scone over one hundred pounds.

Her blonde hair was mid-length. Deep golden streaks rippled through her hair.

The woman's eyes were a crystalline blue with a slight emerald green hue.

Her figure was lean and athletic. She clearly exercised often.

The décolleté of her blouse showcased perfect pert breasts.

She wore a black and white Naracamicie blouse, black slacks, and woven Italian slipper shoes.

The woman wore no jewelry, other than a gold Rolex on her left wrist and a large diamond ring with a wedding band on her left ring finger.

Her nails were exquisitely manicured.

She appeared to be in her mid-thirties.

"Do you have an appointment with Reed?" the woman said. She neither smiled nor frowned at the man. A complete poker face.

"Nope. It's just past lunchtime, thought I'd drop by," Conway said. "I'm an attorney, too, you know."

The woman sat back against the large desk in the center of the room. She laid a brown leather bound notebook on the desk, though she kept the Mont Blanc pen in her right hand.

"What do you want to discuss with Reed?" she asked.

"I represent a businessman who wants to make a very nice offer for one of O'Hara's companies," Conway said. "Hey, why's this place so fucking empty? Just you and me here?"

The man edged closer to the woman, who stayed perfectly still. She maintained her poker face.

"My colleagues haven't yet returned from lunch. But don't get any ideas about you and me, Conway," the woman said.

"Please, call me 'Jasper.' And no worries, lil' sweet potato pie, you and me can talk later after O'Hara and me take care of business," Conway said.

The woman glared ice-blue darts at Conway.

"You and me? That's not happening. Ever," she said. "And just for the record, you fat fuck, I'm Reed O'Hara."

Chapter Five

Conway's eyes rounded. His facial expression connoted both fear and hatred.

He appeared caught between assaulting Reed O'Hara or backing down completely.

Fortunately for Conway, he decided to back down, as Reed was prepared to punch multiple holes in his broad chest and ample belly with her Mont Blanc pen.

"Look, Counselor, I didn't know Reed O'Hara is a woman. I guess I shoulda called for an appointment," he said. He gave off an air of faux submissiveness.

"Yes, you were trying to ambush me, Mr. Conway. Highly unprofessional," Reed said.

Conway pursed his lips and lowered his large head.

"Enough of the puppy dog routine, Mr. Conway. I can give you a few minutes. At least then I will be done with you," she said.

Conway lifted his head and gave Reed his very best slime ball smile. Curiously, he bore the whitest teeth that Reed had ever seen.

"Thanks, counselor, like I said, my client is very much interested in buying outright your, how shall I say, gentlemen's club," Conway said.

Reed laid down her pen on her assistant's desk, folded her arms, and once again leaned against the desk. Conway had no way of knowing that this was Reed's crypto fighting stance.

"If by gentlemen's club, you mean Namaste, then your client should know right up front that it's not for sale. Period. End of *rapprochement,*" Reed said.

"End of what?" Conway asked.

Reed shook her head ever so slightly, ever so derisively.

"End of pleasant discussion. Where exactly did you get your law degree?" she said.

"Stetson, why?"

Reed smiled a Mona Lisa smile.

"Never mind," she said.

Once a Hatter . . . , Reed thought.

"Would you at least sit down with my client? You know, just to talk, uh, just to 'rapprochement' the subject at hand. I mean, he really likes Namaste. He wants to make it part of his chain of titty — I mean, strip — bars."

Reed turned away from Conway, returning to her studying the cruise ship at Channelside.

It's in Carnival's Fantasy class, an older ship, got to be the *Paradise,* she thought.

"Your client is Victor Petrov, isn't it?" Reed said.

Conway seemed to close in on himself, as if he were an immense sphincter muscle contracting.

"Maybe," he said.

"There's no maybe about it. Petrov is just the kind of Russian mobster that would hire a guttersnipe lawyer like yourself to act as his front man."

Conway's face reddened. He moved slowly toward Reed.

"That's a shitty thing to say, O'Hara. If you weren't a cunt, I'd . . . ."

Conway didn't get to finish his obscene threat. Reed gracefully spun around, took two quick steps, and, with all deliberate speed, front kicked Conway in his crotch.

Conway hunched down, grabbing his genitals and exhaling loudly.

Frazier was about to go down.

Reed took hold of Conway's shoulders, then punched her right knee into the man's lower belly.

Conway dropped to his knees. Only the extreme paint kept him conscious.

It was the ideal takedown. The man was totally incapacitated. And no blood or broken bones.

Fly like a butterfly, sting like a bee, Reed thought.

Maybe a little soft-tissue damage, Reed thought, but chubby had it coming. What is it about the c-word that sets me off?

"Why'd you do that, you bitch!" Conway grunted.

"I like a lawyer who asks and answers his own questions," Reed said.

Conway's breathing became steadier, though he still grimaced in pain.

"Fuck that mean?" he asked.

"You behaved in a threatening manner, Mr. Conway, and I merely defended myself. By the way, I am a third-degree black belt in tae kwon do. Now get up off your knees, collect yourself, and get the hell out of my office."

Conway struggled to his feet. As he rose, he emitted ferocious flatulence. Though he didn't apologize, he at least looked sheepishly at Reed.

"Victor Petrov isn't going to like this," Conway said.

"What, my turning down his overture to purchase Namaste, or my kicking your ass?" Reed said.

"You damn well know what he'll be pissed about, you fucking . . ."

Reed stepped quickly toward Conway.

"No, no, no more. I'll leave," Conway said.

Conway started running out of the office, not Usain Bolt style, yet surprisingly agile for a fat man.

Reed heard the elevator ring and its doors sliding open.

"Fuck you, O'Hara!"

Reed O'Hara again struck her Mona Lisa smile.

Chapter Six

Father Dave always thought of the north end of Clearwater Beach island as a self-contained paradise within a much larger Eden. The barrier island's northern tip was entirely residential and very exclusive. A string of sand dunes separated the homes and the white sand beach. Most of these sand dunes were inaccessible, as they were protected sanctuaries for seabird nests.

Of course, that didn't stop the occasional couple from making love or sunbathing nude while hidden in the dunes.

Very few people, though, knew about this length of pristine beach on the Gulf Coast.

But Father Dave knew about this beach. And he never shared this place with friends or family.

Every chance he got, which was often since he was retired, Father Dave drove across the causeway to Clearwater Beach, turned north on the barrier island, passed through the tourist district crowded with hotels, restaurants, and ersatz surf shops, and drove until he ran out of road.

He always parked in front of one of the residences, comporting himself as if he lived in the neighborhood. Really, no one cared about an old man strolling down their street.

Father Dave liked to use the long boardwalk at the Carlouel Yacht Club to get onto the beach. He didn't care about the club's swimming pools or tennis courts or bungalows — he focused on its boardwalk.

He was elated that only a few people were walking on the beach.

Father Dave enjoyed these near-solitary walks on the beach. There were no children, especially boys, to distract him from his purer, more refined thoughts of confession and absolution and redemption. The North End was his sanctuary.

The priest recently had become a born-again Christian by way of a Texan television preacher. Father Dave knew full well that the evangelical preacher amounted to little more than cotton candy Christianity. Yet the preacher's soothing pitch for a personal relationship with Jesus appealed to the old Catholic priest. Especially the part where he could confess his onerous sins directly to Jesus Christ, bypassing altogether confessing to a fellow priest, who might very well turn him in to the Diocese. Besides, switching to Protestantism was like being traded from the Boston Red Sox to the Yankees, strictly a lateral move.

As he walked on the beach, Father Dave confessed more of his pedophilic sins directly to Jesus Christ. He understood that, once he had taken Him into his heart, all of his sins were forgiven. Still, it felt comforting to describe all of his horrific sins, though he suspected the ulterior motive was to become aroused over re-visiting his diabolical acts.

The wind started to come in from the Gulf of Mexico. Father Dave became concerned.

The air was quite cool, a sign that a rain storm was brewing. Indeed, a good thirty miles out, there was an impressive thunderstorm gathering its way eastward to the Gulf shore.

Father Dave pulled up the collar on his black nylon windbreaker.

He thought it best to turn around and head back to his car.

The other beachcombers already had retreated from the beach.

After all, a Florida thunderstorm can swallow you up in minutes, he thought, and safe shelter was three-hundred yards away.

As he turned around, Father Dave saw a lone figure standing in the dunes at least a hundred yards away.

The stiff wind coming off the water started swirling around Father Dave.

He used his left hand to block sand from getting into his eyes.

He could barely see the figure who was still standing in the dunes. All he could make out was that the person was covered head to toe in black.

Suddenly, an object flew by him, grazing his neck and causing him a severe stinging pain. It felt like a severe paper cut.

"Sweet Jesus! What was that?" he exclaimed.

Instinctively, Father Dave dropped flat onto the sand.

Rain fell in gray sheets.

The wind roared across the beach.

Waves crashed on Father Dave, who remained prone on the sand.

After waiting for a minute, Father Dave looked up and saw that the figure, now no more than a black silhouette in the worsening storm, had moved to within fifty yards of him.

Father Dave jumped to his feet.

"Come on, you demon," he screamed. "You want a piece of me?"

He started charging toward the black figure. A major mistake on his part.

This time, Father Dave was struck in his right thigh. The old priest collapsed to the sand, writhing in pain and bleeding profusely from his wounded leg.

"An arrow, I can't believe it, I've been shot by an arrow!" he yelled.

Father Dave sat up and tried to stanch the substantial bleeding.

Musta hit an artery, he thought.

He was starting to go into shock.

A third arrow put Father Dave out of his considerable misery. It struck him right between the eyes.

The dead priest fell back on the beach. His windbreaker made loud popping sounds in the wind.

The black silhouetted figure disappeared.

A group of seagulls huddled nearby. The gulls would wait until the storm passed to peck and poke at the dead priest's body.

Chapter Seven

Victor Petrov and two other men entered Namaste on a busy Wednesday evening.

A tall, attractive young woman, wearing a very short little black dress and black high heels, stood behind the club's front desk.

"Good evening, gentlemen," she said. "Welcome to Namaste. Admission for the three of you comes to three hundred dollars."

Petrov pulled out a thick wad of bills, and tossed three hundred-dollar bills on the desk counter. The woman did not acknowledge Petrov's rudeness. She simply smiled at Petrov, who did not return her smile.

"Thank you. There's a two-drink minimum for each of you. We'll expect you to order a full dinner for each of you. And, of course, we want you to be on your very best behavior," the woman said.

"Of course, no problem," Petrov said. Still no smile from the Russian gangster.

The other two men stood silently. If it were possible, they were more deadpan than Petrov.

A short blonde hostess, also wearing an LBD and black four-inch heels, led Petrov and the two men to a table near center stage. It was by no means the best table, but it was among the best.

Namaste had forty four-top tables; on this night, almost all of them were occupied.

Much of the crowd was male, gathered in groups of two, three, and four. One male couple was holding hands and speaking quietly to each other.

There also were several single women at the tables. They, too, were scattered in groups of two, three, and four. Some of the women were romantic couples.

Almost half of the crowd consisted of male and female couples. All of the men wore tailored suits; their female companions wore designer dresses.

There were Asians and Hispanics and Europeans throughout this evening's audience. A variety of languages were being spoken.

A tall brunette approached Petrov's table. She was wearing a brightly colored yoga outfit with sandals. She appeared very fit and very zen.

"Namaste, guys," she said. "How about some drinks? Our first dancer comes out in ten minutes. After her performance, you can order some dinner, okay?"

"Yeah, sure, whatever," said Petrov, who was not even looking at the server. "Bring me a Johnny Walker Blue. Neat. Get these guys some water."

The server said to the two men, "Do you want Fiji, Voss, or Evian?"

Petrov spoke up.

"Which is the cheapest?"

"They're all the same — fifteen dollars a bottle," the server said cheerfully.

"And what about my scotch?"

"Thirty-five dollars," said the server, still smiling, though she was getting nervous.

"Jesus Christ. Okay, whatever. Bring them Voss," Petrov said.

The server nodded, then walked to the bar.

One of the two men said to Petrov, "*Spasido*, boss."

"*Bez raznitsy*," Petrov said.

Petrov scanned the club's interior.

There were lit water walls in each corner of the large room. Floor-to-ceiling sheer drapes covered the beige walls.

The center stage was about four hundred square feet. There was a grand piano to the left of the stage. Ambient light flooded the stage.

Much to Petrov's disappointment, there was no stripper pole on the stage.

New age music, ethereal and joyful, was playing over a Bose sound system.

A small booth held a DJ dressed in white linens. She did not take requests.

The long bar was behind Petrov. The kitchen entrance was to his left.

Though some guests were having dinner, many were sipping on martinis, wine, and Champagne. A few tables had pita chips and humus.

Probably charge fifty bucks for those goddamn chips and dip, Petrov thought.

"Nice place. Lots of potential," Petrov said in Russian to the two men, who nodded in agreement.

The music stopped suddenly. Then it began again, this time producing a more pulsing, dramatic soundscape.

"Ladies and gentlemen, please welcome Elena, our first performer of the evening," the DJ announced over the sound system.

"Okay," Petrov said. "Now we get down to the meat and cabbage."

Chapter Eight

Elena stepped onto the stage to Keiko Matsui's "Black River," an ideal composition for Elena's dance routine since it fuses jazz with classical music, Western sensibilities with Asian.

Elena was quite tall — just under six feet. She wore her long brunette hair in a braid. She had on a small white tee shirt, white yoga pants, and was barefoot.

She moved gracefully and with great confidence on the stage floor. Her modern dance moves were fluid and elegant. She was sensuality in motion.

The audience appeared entranced.

At one point, she struck a tree pose, then clasped her hands over her heart, uttering "Namaste" to the audience. A few people in the crowd returned the greeting.

About a dozen people walked up to the stage and politely placed fifty —and hundred — dollar bills into a brass bowl.

"That's a lot of fucking money for keeping her clothes on," Petrov said.

His two companions didn't respond. They drank their Voss directly from the large plastic bottles while continually scanning the room.

With the lights dimmed slightly, Jake Dupree walked over to the grand piano and sat on the black leather bench. He placed his large hands on the piano keys and waited. He wore a white long-sleeve *guayabera* and black slacks.

When the lights came back up, the audience saw Jake at the piano and began clapping.

Jake opened with his own composition, a tone poem that was elegant and harmonious. Very zen. He didn't use sheet music. His fingers progressed lithely across the piano keys.

Elena absorbed the gentle rhythms of Jake's piano playing and started with a series of yoga moves — downward and upward facing dog, cat and hare, cobra and camel, chair and bow, Bikram triangle and chair, finishing with warrior.

Sitting in a full split, she slowly removed her white tee shirt, revealing a tiny white sports bra.

Elena then went into a headstand, forming a perfect upside-down five-point star, an extremely challenging yoga move.

Then she slowly collapsed into child's pose.

The audience clapped and cheered.

More people came to the stage and placed money in the brass bowl.

Petrov was working on his second Johnny Walker Blue.

"Come on, come on, it's time to see the titties," Petrov said too loudly.

The two men at his table simply continued to watch the other tables. Clearly, they were Petrov's bodyguards, and they weren't going to admonish him.

Some people shook their heads and scowled at Petrov for his crass remark.

The bodyguards scowled back at them. Petrov simply ignored them.

Andre took notice of this negative energy potentially upsetting Elena's performance.

As Andre watched over Petrov's table, Elena began her third and final performance by taking off her sports bra.

She stood on the stage with her hands on her hips and her legs apart, happily showing off her beautiful breasts.

The audience clapped its approval.

Jake had gotten up from the piano and walked over to Andre.

Euge Groove's "Chillaxin" came on over the Bose speakers. The smooth jazz saxophone sound was both chilled and relaxing, ideal for Elena's dance routine.

She swirled across the dance floor, moving her hips rhythmically with the smooth jazz beat. Her precise, sensual moves suggested a ballet influence. Two minutes into her routine, her breasts and abdomen glistened in the stage lights.

Most of the audience stood, swaying in harmony with Elena's dance moves.

Finally, the music receded. The stage lights dimmed slightly. Once more, Elena melted into child's pose.

Several guests came to the front of the stage and placed more money into the now-full brass bowl.

Elena left the stage to enthusiastic cheers.

"Not bad, not too fucking bad. I wouldn't mind the owner's cut from that tip jar," Petrov said.

Jake approached the table.

"Victor, you Russian cretin," Jake said. "I'm always impressed with how you class up a joint."

Chapter Nine

Petrov gulped the rest of his scotch, then banged his crystal tumbler on the table.

He glared at Jake.

So did his two bodyguards.

"Jake, how are you, you big French prick?" Petrov said.

"I'm fine, Petrov. And I'm not French. I'm French-American," Jake said.

"Whatever, Jake. From my standpoint, if you're not Russian, then you're shit. And there's no such thing as a Russian-American. If you're Russian, you're Russian. If you're American, you're shit," Petrov said.

Jake smiled benignly at Petrov, who signaled the server for another scotch.

"That'll be your last drink here. And because you framed your severely ethnocentric tautology in such coarse terms, I think it best that you come to my office. This way, we can chat without offending the guests," Jake said.

The server brought Petrov his third — and final — Johnny Walker Blue, as well as bottles of Voss for the bodyguards.

"Comp Mr. Petrov and his friends," Jake said to the server. "And don't worry, they won't be around to order dinner."

Petrov raised his glass to Jake.

The two bodyguards continued to stare menacingly at Jake.

Andre hovered near the table. He was trying to out voodoo-eye the bodyguards.

"Come along, Petrov," Jake said. "It's not as if I'm taking you to Lubyanka. And leave the meatheads out in the lobby."

Petrov gulped down his twenty-five-year-old scotch, then banged his tumbler again on the table.

"Sure, Jake, why not?" he said.

Petrov spoke curtly in Russian to his bodyguards, who got up and walked to the lobby.

Andre trailed behind them. He prayed that the bodyguards would start trouble — he was ready to hurt them.

As the DJ started to announce the evening's second performer, Jake and Petrov entered Jake's expansive office, which was more study than office.

Bookshelves, filled with volumes on literature, history, music, and art, covered three walls. Several frameless French Impressionist prints covered the fourth wall.

Jake's long Scandinavian oak desk faced towards the Impressionist prints.

A Bose sound system was playing Arcangelo Corelli's *Concerti Grossi*.

"Nice office, very nice," Petrov said. "Music is a nice touch. Soothes the savage beastie in you, right? But you listen only to the old farts?"

"I prefer Bach, Handel, Vivaldi. The way I look at it, if it ain't Baroque, then fix it," Jake said.

"Huh?"

"Never mind," Jake said.

Petrov plopped down into a large leather chair. The Russian thug appeared out of place in this cultured setting.

Jake sat down at his desk.

"So, Petrov, what's on your mind besides a bald pate?" Jake said.

Petrov laughed.

"I'm taking your shit right now, Jake, because I want to be your equal partner in Namaste. I'll give you a million in U.S., all cash."

"Really, you want to be my partner?" Jake said, truly incredulous at Petrov's proposal.

"Well, yes," Petrov said. "You and Reed O'Hara's partner."

Petrov smiled impishly at Jake.

Most people thought that Jake Dupree was the sole proprietor of Namaste. Only a discreet handful of trusted friends, as well as the equally discreet Namaste employees, knew that he and Reed O'Hara were co-owners, equal partners in marriage and in Namaste. Reed preferred to keep a low profile, while Jake played the front man. Jake didn't mind the attention; Reed loathed it.

"Namaste is not for sale in any form or fashion," Jake said. "I sure as hell am not going to take on a partner of your low caliber."

"Jake, Jake, Jake. Don't make such a snappy tap decision. Think of me as a strategic partner. I could put a lot of cash into this business. We could expand. Sell franchises. Go full nude. Have the girls pair up for some lesbo dancing. We'd be fucking rich, Jake. Just think of the possibilities. We could call ourselves the Dirty Disney Empire."

Jake sat in silence. He studied the superb print of Monet's *Irises in the Artist's Garden.*

Finally, he spoke.

"Petrov, you're a pimp and a drug dealer. Your clubs are rat holes where dancers go to die. You force them to be prostitutes, you keep them hooked on meth and crack and heroin, and your customers are genuine bottom feeders. There's no way that we — yes, me and Reed — would ever partner with you."

Petrov jumped up from the leather chair and leaned over Jake's desk. His face had reddened like a Georgian beet. Petrov's beefy, powerful hands gripped Jake's desk. He was a portrait in Slavic menace.

"You think you're so pure and holy," Petrov said. "You think you're saving these bitches. Well, you're not. You're only keeping them from what they really want to do, what they're really meant to do. I give them what they need. And I don't apologize for making money off of them. It's give and take, asshole — they give and I take."

Petrov turned toward the office door. His inner tempest had already subsided.

"This isn't over, motherfucker," he said. "If you don't go into business with me, then I will make you and that bitch O'Hara eat shit and die!"

Petrov left, leaving open the office door. Corelli now competed with Boney James.

Jake got out his smart phone.

"Andre, escort Petrov and his security detail out of the building. Please see that they get in their car and drive off the property," Jake said.

"Yes, sir, will do." Andre said.

Petrov, please, please, please, give me a hard time, Andre thought.

Chapter Ten

Father Angel sat on the verandah to his Vatican office. For a winter morning in Rome, the sunshine was ample and bright. In fact, Father Angel was becoming a bit warm on the verandah. He considered getting up to retreat to the cool indoor shade.

The call came in via his smart phone. The priest recognized the caller's phone number. He was not surprised by the call; in fact, he was expecting it.

"*Buongiorno*, Cardinal Liga," Father Angel said. "How may I assist you?"

Cardinal Liga respected how Father Angel, who was in charge of special security projects for the Vatican, avoided mindless chit chat; instead, he got straight to the heart of the matter, a rare approach in the Vatican.

"You're aware, of course, of the three brothers in Christ murdered in Tampa Bay, Florida," Cardinal Liga said.

"I am," Father Angel said. "It is most disconcerting. I am praying continually for our fallen brothers."

"The local police authorities are investigating, and as of yet, they've made no progress," Cardinal Liga said.

"I sense you are not disappointed over the lack of progress on law enforcement's part," Father Angel said.

Time to get my fishing line wet, Father Angel thought.

"How observant of you," Cardinal Liga said. "Indeed, we prefer that

33

this matter be resolved within the confines of the Holy Church, as it is a very sensitive situation."

Father Angel took a sip of espresso, then lit a Dunhill.

"I completely understand, your Grace," Father Angel said, expelling cigarette smoke.

"You are to make this a very special project," Cardinal Liga said. "May I assume our conversation is not being recorded?" The Cardinal had not asked a question so much as made a command.

"You assume correctly. We are speaking on a totally secure line, no recording allowed," Father Angel said.

He, of course, was lying to the Cardinal: even though technically theirs was a secure phone line, his staff in the Office of Special Security was recording the conversation. Just in case.

"You may speak candidly, Cardinal Liga," Father Angel said.

Said the mongoose to the cobra, Father Angel thought.

"Good. Now I want you to travel to Florida. The Diocese of St. Petersburg in Florida will provide you an office and whatever staff you need," the Cardinal said.

Father Angel lit another Dunhill.

As if I need those morons' help, he thought, they're such inexperienced fools, not even approaching the level of my professionalism.

"We cannot have our program in the United States in any jeopardy, Father Angel. So consider your resources limitless and unquestioned. You may use whatever means as you see fit. I will send you the appropriate documents that will enable you to operate independently of Vatican oversight. Do we understand each other?" Cardinal Liga said.

"Of course, Cardinal Liga," Father Angel said.

Say his name enough times on this recording and the Cardinal will not be able to fall back on plausible deniability if anything goes wrong, Father Angel thought.

"If you need to use local resources, be certain they are reliable and discreet," Cardinal Liga said. "Do not allow local authorities to be aware of this assignment."

"Yes, your Grace."

"Find this priest killer as quickly as possible. And Father Angel...."

"Yes, Cardinal Liga?"

"Once you have found him, send him straight to hell."

"With pleasure, your Grace."

Father Angel stubbed out his Dunhill, finished his espresso, and immediately began mapping out his hunting expedition in the New World.

Chapter Eleven

It was about two a.m. on a Saturday night in Tampa's Ybor City, a community rich in Spanish and Italian history that had turned into the equivalent of New Orleans' French Quarter — lots of bars, restaurants, strip clubs, cigar shops, and vintage clothing boutiques. Where there was once a community of cigar making factories and neighborhoods of shotgun houses and casitas, there now was one big party zone.

And there was El Castillo, which took up the entire four floors of what once was a flourishing hotel over a century ago, back when Teddy Roosevelt and his Rough Riders occupied Ybor City and most of Tampa in preparation for the invasion of Cuba in 1898.

Father Andy loved El Castillo, though he couldn't care less about the building's history.

El Castillo's first floor, which once was the old hotel's stately lobby, featured a large bar, tables, and sofas.

Father Andy looked into the dimly lit great room. The crowd consisted of men and women of all ages and ethnicity. Many of the patrons were dressed in black tee shirts, black jeans, and black boots. Some wore elaborate domination and submission outfits, complete with whips, chains, leashes, and leather masks with gag balls.

The priest was amused especially with one submissive who pulled the ball gag from his mouth in order to drink water through a straw in a plastic bottle. Of course, the sub had sought permission from his dom before drinking the water.

No one paid any attention to Father Andy, even though he was wearing priest attire, including a white collar and gold cross.

He walked right past the bar and approached a woman sitting at a desk with a placard that read, "Shore Excursions."

The woman wore a fluorescent pink bra and panties with white pleather go-go boots. Atop her head was a tattered white sailor's cap.

"Father Andy, how delightful to see you again," the woman said. "Off to the Little Boys Room, are we?" She gave the priest a jaunty tip of her sailor's cap.

"Yes," Father Andy said. "Is it still five-hundred dollars?"

"Yuppers," she said. The woman raised an eyebrow, suspicious that the old man wasn't going to pay.

"Any chance I can get a discount, you know, being a repeat customer and all?" the priest asked.

"Absolutely not," she said, as she raised her chin defiantly toward him.

"Take off a hundred bucks and I'll hear your confession, absolution included, no matter the sin," Father Andy said.

"Fuck off, priesty. Five hundred right now or take a hike," the woman said.

"Fine, fine. Here, you filthy whore," Father Andy said. He handed her a Cuban bank roll of singles, fives, and tens.

"Thanks, priesty. And don't think you're currying favor with me by complementing me so lavishly," the woman said as she saluted him, then shot him a middle finger.

Since the elevator hadn't worked for years — an obvious code violation overlooked with a modest payment to a city inspector who also was an avid club member — Father Andy began walking up his personal stairway to heaven.

The second, third, and fourth floors of El Castillo consisted of the old hotel rooms. All of the doors had been removed. Electric candles lined each side of the red carpeted hallways. Each room was lit by a single Sponge Bob night light.

Father Andy bypassed the second floor, as it was designated for group sex – not the priest's avocation.

When he reached the third floor, he stopped to catch his breath.

So out of shape, I'm going to die from a heart attack, he thought.

The third floor of El Castillo consisted of various torture chambers.

Father Andy peered into one chamber where a shirtless man, perspiring heavily was wielding a whip and screaming at two naked women strapped to black crosses.

Two men in business suits sat in small chairs. They both seemed indifferent to the scene before them.

The bare-chested man with the whip first lashed the naked, bound woman to his right. Only when the woman began screaming did the man turn his attention to the other naked, bound woman. After several lashes across her chest and hips, this woman whimpered and cried for mercy.

Whip man showed neither woman any mercy.

Father Andy shuddered at this gory scene.

He had no way of knowing that it was Victor Petrov delivering this horrific punishment to two foolhardy participants.

His bodyguards gave him the heads up that Father Andy was standing in the doorway.

Petrov faced the priest and frowned at him.

"Hey, asshole," Petrov said, "You want to watch, you pay up."

"No, no, no, I'm sorry, this is not my . . . concern," Father Andy said.

The priest moved quickly toward the stairway.

He spotted three women walking towards him in the hallway. They wore hooded, floor-length black robes. Father Andy couldn't see their faces, which were obscured by the hoods. He did notice a few strands of black hair with red tips peeking out of one of the hoods.

Father Andy could not resist speaking to this medieval trio.

"Hello, ladies, are you here to give or receive tonight?" he asked.

The women did not respond; they simply passed by the priest and entered an unoccupied torture chamber. However, the hooded woman with the red-tipped black hair did extend a backwards middle finger to Father Andy.

That obscene gesture twice in one night, certainly a bad omen, Father Andy thought.

Petrov had been standing in his chamber doorway and watching this scene unfold.

"Hey, priest, you sure got a way with the bitches," he said.

Petrov chuckled and his bodyguards followed suit. The two tortured women did not make a sound.

Father Andy laughed nervously, then ascended the stairs to the fourth floor.

The right side of the fourth floor was designated as the "Little Girls Room."

Young women, no more than eighteen or nineteen-years old, were dressed as little girls and, with a generous gratuity, would engage in virtually any ersatz pedophilic passion play.

Each woman was in her own baby crib.

Father Andy, though, was interested only in the left side of the fourth floor, which was designated the "Little Boys Room." These young men, mostly Indonesians and Filipinos, performed the same role playing as their female counterparts across the hallway.

As with their female counterparts, each young man reclined in a baby crib.

Father Andy paused to utter a pre-emptive prayer seeking forgiveness for his debauchery. He then began looking in each room to find his ideal man-child.

This isn't Bangkok, but it'll do, he thought, this'll do just fine and dandy.

Suddenly, Father Andy felt incredible pain at the base of his spine.

He reached around and grabbed a hold of the shaft of an arrow sticking into his back.

He turned and faced the stairwell.

Out of the near blackness, another arrow pierced his chest.

A third arrow shattered into his forehead.

Father Andy's lifeless body crumpled to the floor, knocking over several electric candles.

Nervous giggles emanated from the baby cribs.

Chapter Twelve

Father Angel sat in a comfortable brown leather chair directly in front of Reed O'Hara's desk in her office. Though exhausted from his long flight, he knew it was wise to be totally alert with regard to Reed O'Hara.

"Counselor, thank you very much for seeing me on such short notice," Father Angel said. "I am certain you are quite busy."

Even though, Madame Attorney, I happen to know you're not busy at all right now, Father Angel thought.

Reed sipped from her espresso, then smiled at Father Angel.

"I am only somewhat occupied with the law right now, Father, but other ventures demand my attention," Reed said. "However, my assistant told me you sounded quite anxious over the telephone."

Father Angel nodded.

"I am quite anxious, Counselor. The matter at hand is very serious," he said. Sitting with his hands in his lap, Father Angel resembled a very earnest choir boy.

Reed held her Mont Blanc pen in her right hand. A leather bound notebook lay open on her desk in front of her.

"How can I help?" she said.

"I seek legal assistance, but not in your capacity as an attorney. Rather, in your capacity as a private investigator," Father Angel said.

Reed raised her blonde eyebrows at the priest.

Looks as if this guy has done his homework, she thought.

Indeed, Father Angel had arranged for his staff from the Vatican to do extensive research on Reed O'Hara. His assistants did extensive hacking, yet eventually got the information Father Angel sought.

He knew that Reed's legal practice focused almost exclusively on women's issues.

After graduating from the University of Florida College of Law, Reed started out with a large Tampa firm that defended Big Tobacco. She had grown disenchanted in a few short years with the unsavory delay tactics employed in defending lawsuits brought by plaintiffs, many of them women, who were suffering from cancer and emphysema.

So Reed struck out on her own.

Fittingly, Reed's greatest legal successes were bringing immense class-action lawsuits against Big Tobacco, joining for her, justice with irony.

Father Angel had learned that Reed amassed a personal fortune of over three-hundred million dollars, derived from successful Big Tobacco settlements and jury trials.

Today, all of her clients were women. She handled a variety of legal matters — spousal abuse, workplace sexual harassment, unfair labor practices, acrimonious divorces, and medical malpractice.

For her well-off clients, Reed charged a billing rate of five-hundred dollars per hour. Many times, she took on disadvantaged clients *pro bono*. Overall, she cleared two to three million dollars a year with her law practice.

Father Angel also knew that Reed co-owned with her husband, Jake Dupree, the Tampa cabaret nightclub Namaste, that Jake was the cabaret's manager while Reed was almost a silent partner who appeared rarely at Namaste. The couple did well with their cabaret, but wild profits was not their goal.

Despite her mercurial presence, Namaste was completely Reed's project. She wanted to give drug-addicted strippers and other beatific souls a second chance by helping them defeat their addictions, get an education, and still draw on their substantial performing skills in a much healthier atmosphere. Reed's macro view was that of using capitalism for the social good.

Father Angel was aware that Reed and Jake lived in a penthouse in a downtown Tampa condominium. The couple had no children or pets, and appeared to live a quiet life together. They traveled a lot, primarily on cruise ships. Neither Reed nor Jake used tobacco or illegal drugs. In keeping with Namaste's employee policy, they both abstained from alcohol. Both were exercise fanatics and superb marksmen, especially with handguns. Reed was a third-degree black belt in tae kwon do. Though the details were sketchy, Jake had some kind of background in intelligence operations and, Father Angel's researchers assumed, was proficient in close-in combat. Apparently, Jake's past was so much shadow and smoke and fog.

Clearly, Reed's only vice was playing slot machines. And typical of her wild Irish luck, she won more than she lost as she played in casinos all over the world. She gave all of her winnings to Planned Parenthood.

While Father Angel found useful this background on Reed O'Hara's law practice and her personal life, he was interested the most in her work as a private investigator.

His researchers learned that Reed occasionally grew tired of practicing the law. So, after acquiring a private investigator's license, she delved into investigative matters from time to time. Reed always teamed with Jake, who acted as her good and faithful second. And Reed was very adept — she never once failed to figure out mysterious dealings or to find a person who didn't want to be found. Reed was an absolute pit bull when it came to locking into an investigation.

Father Angel also surmised that Reed O'Hara liked the adrenaline rush of exploring the often unseemly shadows of sunny Tampa Bay.

He was confident that his situation would grab her attention.

"To be perfectly succinct, Ms. O'Hara," Father Angel said, "I want you to find the person who is brutally murdering our priests."

Chapter Thirteen

"Thank you for getting right to the point, Father Angel," Reed said.

She set down the Mont Blanc pen on the notebook, finished her espresso, then leaned back in the desk chair. Reed was ready to listen.

"You definitely have my interest," she said.

Thought I might, you adrenaline junkie, Father Angel said to himself.

"As director of special security operations for the Vatican, I am responsible for addressing unusual and extraordinary security matters," he said.

"But why would you be involved with the deaths of four priests in Tampa Bay? Wouldn't the Catholic Church of North America oversee the Church's participation in the investigation?" Reed asked.

"I am charged with going anywhere in the world to solve, in an expeditious and quiet manner, any unique security problems that the Holy Church is experiencing," Father Angel said. "So the horrible murder of four Roman Catholic priests in Tampa Bay constitutes a very special matter for the Vatican and, concomitantly, for my office."

Reed smiled broadly, then held up both hands. She leaned forward in her chair.

"Okay, Father, you've convinced me that you have a genuine dog in this fight," she said. "But why me, why not coordinate with local law enforcement?"

Father Angel smiled as well, though his smile bore a patrician sheen.

"I already have consulted with local authorities, specifically with homicide detectives from Tampa, St. Petersburg, and Clearwater. A Peter Langdon, of the Tampa Police Department and a graduate from the University of Notre Dame, seems a very capable homicide detective who has been most helpful to me."

Reed nodded at Father Angel, encouraging him to continue.

Like pulling teeth from a fully awake Bengal tiger, Reed thought.

"So far, all that the detectives know is that my brothers in Christ were killed by carbon-based arrows piercing their bodies. In fact, these projectiles are not arrows; rather, they are bolts, as they were fired from a crossbow," he said.

Reed raised her eyebrows.

You're shitting me, right, she thought.

"I know, Ms. O'Hara, how extraordinarily medieval, yet a crossbow has indeed been employed. The bolt head, or arrow tip, used by the killer is especially invidious — he is using an expandable blade broad head, whose blades are hidden to improve speed and accuracy, then open only when the bolt or arrow hits the prey, causing horrible damage."

Reed was both repulsed and intrigued.

Really, I can't help walking into this spider web, she thought.

"What else did you learn from the detectives, Father Angel?" she asked.

"That the killer is a superb marksman. And he is quite careful and stealthy: there are no witnesses who have seen the killer. And there are no substantial leads as of yet," Father Angel said.

Reed leaned forward and rested her elbows on the desk.

"So where do I fit in?" she asked.

"I need you to find this killer before the police do. It's that simple," Father Angel said.

"So you don't have confidence in our local authorities apprehending the killer?" Reed asked.

"Quite the contrary, I am confident that local law enforcement eventually will find this murderer. But I suspect it could be weeks, maybe months, before the police find him. Meanwhile, more priests could perish."

Reed nodded again at Father Angel.

"I want this killer found as quickly as possible, Ms. O'Hara, and I want you to find him first, so that I can deal with him on my own terms," Father Angel said.

Chapter Fourteen

"Father Angel, if you have in mind my hunting down the priest killer and delivering him to you, so that you can summarily execute him before he enters the judicial system, then our consultation ends right now," Reed said. She tapped her pen on the notebook.

Just as Father Angel was about to speak, Reed cut him off.

"I am an attorney, first and foremost," she said. "An officer of the court. I respect the law. I will not participate in some vigilante style execution, no matter how horrifically evil this individual appears to be." More tapping of her pen ensued.

Suddenly, Reed dropped her pen and began rhythmically chopping her hand into the palm of her left hand — with each chop, her fine blonde hair bounced slightly. This was her classic signal that warned a person to deal with her very carefully.

Father Angel sat back in his chair. Though he had just taken the full brunt of an Irish-American's verbal broad side, he did not appear intimidated or even upset. The man appeared to possess a kind of dark zen.

Placing together the fingertips of his hands to form a cathedral arch, he sat silently, staring at Reed.

More silence.

Finally, Reed won: Father Angel spoke first.

"You completely misunderstand me, Ms. O'Hara. And in all candidness, I am deeply offended that you think I would take a life. I would not. I respect the laws both of God and of man," he said.

Reed sat back in her chair, waiting for Father Angel to explain himself further.

There was a palatable recession of tension between Reed and Father Angel.

"Please forgive me for not being clearer, Ms. O'Hara. As I said, time is of the essence in apprehending this person. Truly, who knows how soon he will strike again. However, I do not want this person to come to any harm. I would like the opportunity to speak with him, to hear his confession, before he's swallowed up forever in your judicial system."

Reed wasn't entirely convinced, but she decided to proceed with this case, primarily because she found it so intriguing.

Care about those murdered priests, yet be very careful, she thought.

"Father Angel, let's say I agree to find this killer. I would work only with my husband Jake Dupree and possibly a small research team of my choosing," she said.

"Fair enough, Ms. O'Hara," he said.

"And, are you prepared to not interfere with my investigation in any fashion?" she asked.

"Yes, of course," Father Angel said.

"Good. We'll move as quickly as possible. I agree with you: this killer doesn't appear to be finished," Reed said.

Father Angel suddenly became serious, as if a somber cloud had passed over him.

"You're right, Ms. O'Hara," Father Angel said with sad resignation. "Who knows how many more brothers we will lose. That is why I am at present coordinating safety measures for the other retired priests living in Tampa Bay."

Reed raised her eyebrows.

This situation just gets better and better, she thought.

"The four murdered priests were all retired?" she said.

"Yes," Father angel answered.

"And just how many retired priests are living in the Tampa Bay area?" Reed asked.

Father Angel waved his hands, striking an almost casual, even cavalier, tone.

"Oh, I should think no more than two hundred," he said.

Reed's bright blue eyes widened.

"Did you say two hundred priests?" she asked.

What have I gotten myself into, Reed thought.

Chapter Fifteen

"Well, not quite two hundred," Father Angel said. "One hundred ninety three is the exact figure. Truly, it is the single greatest concentration of priests in retirement in the world. One might think Rome is the retirement center for priests, but it's Tampa Bay."

"Why Tampa Bay?" Reed said.

"Because its warm with lots of sunshine, and the Holy Church owns numerous condominiums and houses in the area," Father Angel said. "Florida's otherworldly beauty appeals to the Holy Church."

"However, Father Angel, now we have to deal with the fact that there now is a tight cluster of potential targets for the killer," Reed said.

The priest smiled.

What's with this "we" shit, Father Angel thought.

"Yes, well, Ms. O'Hara, you let me focus on protecting the priests, while you focus on finding the murderer," he said, as he raised his black bushy eyebrows and tilted his head to the left.

Reed nodded slightly — the ground had shifted as to who was in control of this meeting. Reed did not like losing control in any situation.

"Very well," she said. "Now all we need to do is have you sign an engagement letter and pay half of my fee for investigative services."

"And what is your fee?" he asked.

"Two-hundred fifty thousand dollars, plus reasonable expenses. After we sign the contract, I'll need a check in the amount of one-hundred twenty-five thousand dollars. You'll pay me the balance of my fee, plus reimbursement for reasonable expenses, upon completion of my investigation."

Father Angel knew that Reed O'Hara was expensive, especially for well-off clients. He also knew that she was thorough, relentless, and always completed her investigations.

"That arrangement is satisfactory, Ms. O'Hara. I am authorized to sign service contracts on behalf of the Holy Church, and I will be happy to write you a check today," Father Angel said.

Roman Delaney, Reed's office manager who moonlighted as a mixed martial arts fighter, brought into her office an engagement letter. After Reed and Father Angel signed the contract, Roman notarized it. He also gave Father Angel a receipt for the retainer check.

Reed and Father Angel shook hands. Each appeared impressed with the other's firm grip.

"Ms. O'Hara, I'll send over to you background files on the deceased priests, as well as copies of the police reports," he said.

"Thank you, Father Angel. Of course, I'll be conducting my own independent research," she said.

Father Angel walked toward the door. Reed noticed that the priest, probably in his early fifties and apparently in excellent physical condition, moved with confident agility.

Do not underestimate this guy, she thought.

"Before you leave, Father Angel, I want you to understand that when I find this killer, and I will find him, you're welcome to interview him, then I'll turn him over to the authorities," Reed said.

"I understand, Ms. O'Hara," he said.

Father Angel left her office.

Reed sat at her desk, idly tapping her Mont Blanc pen on the notebook.

She immediately began to wonder if she had just walked into a first-class briar patch.

Oh well, the contract's signed, sealed, and delivered, Reed thought, and so there's no going back now.

Chapter Sixteen

Victor Petrov was in a foul mood.

He paced back and forth in the living room of his large suite at the crustacean pink Don Caesar Hotel on St. Pete Beach.

Befitting his mood, he wore an all-black workout outfit. Even his Nike Air Force 180s were black.

Though in his mid-fifties, Petrov appeared to be ten years younger with his muscular build, his still-blonde — though rapidly thinning — hair, and smooth, rounded face.

But today, his flushed complexion and scowling countenance made him resemble a very angry, very dangerous, old man who had just lost a shuffleboard match at Sun City Center over in south Hillsborough County.

His attorney Jasper Conway stood in front of the suite's large picture windows that framed the shimmering Gulf of Mexico. Conway wanted to admire the world-famous view, but he knew better.

Petrov was grabbing tennis balls from a large plastic bucket sitting next to the sofa and hurling them at his bodyguards, who were trying not to flinch when the tennis balls hit them.

Just stay in front of this window, Conway thought, Petrov won't risk breaking a window if he wants to throw a ball at me.

Petrov immediately grooved a fastball right into Conway's stomach. The attorney bent over in pain.

"God damn to god damn to god damn," Petrov yelled. "Why won't that bitch sell me that club?"

Petrov bounced another tennis ball off a bodyguard's forehead. The bodyguard remained stoic, showing no pain.

"Come on, Petrov, calm down," Conway said. "You start breaking stuff and you'll get kicked out of the Don."

Petrov glared at Conway with blue-eyed menace.

"You think I give a shit," Petrov said. "Kick me out and I'll burn this place to the ground. THAT's what I should do to Club Nasty."

"'Namaste,'" Conway said.

"What?" Petrov said, clearly getting more agitated.

"The club is called 'Namaste.'"

"Fuck that mean?" Petrov demanded.

"It's Hindu. Means 'peace.'"

Conway knew it was coming after saying that.

Petrov threw another tennis ball at Conway.

"I don't give a shit about that," Petrov said. "From now on, you call it Club Nasty or I'll beat you with a belt, fat boy."

Conway held up both arms.

"Okay, Petrov, I surrender," he said. "No more corrections."

Petrov smiled at Conway raising his arms, then said in Russian to his bodyguards, "Look at fat boy, he's giving the Ukrainian military salute."

The bodyguards laughed.

Conway ignored the derisive laughter.

"So I take it that you didn't persuade Jake Dupree to sell you Club . . . Nasty?" Conway asked.

Petrov raised a tennis ball in his hand.

Conway and the bodyguards flinched.

"No, Dupree won't play ball," he said.

Conway walked gingerly to the wet bar and poured two shots of Jack Daniels into a crystal tumbler.

He held up the bottle and raised his eyebrows at Petrov, who shook his head no.

"So, what are we going to do?" Conway, taking a large gulp of the whiskey.

"Hmm, you remind me of a good joke," Petrov said.

"I'm listening," Conway said as he finished his drink.

"Lone Ranger and Tonto are being chased by Indians," Petrov said. "They get cornered in a box canyon by the Indians. Lone Ranger says, 'Well, Tonto, what are we gonna do?' Tonto says, 'What you mean 'we', white man?'"

Petrov laughed heartily at his own joke.

Though the bodyguards didn't understand a word of their boss' joke, they wisely laughed as well.

"I get your point, Petrov," Conway said, as he poured himself two more shots of Jack Daniels. He held up the tumbler and allowed the Florida sunlight to illuminate the Tennessee whiskey.

"Allow me to re-phrase: what are YOU going to do?"

"Simple, fat boy," Petrov said. "We fuck up things enough at Club Nasty, Dupree and O'Hara will sell us the place dirty cheap."

Conway nodded his approval; he was about to drink the whisky when Petrov threw a tennis ball at Conway, knocking the tumbler out of the attorney's hand.

"And stop drinking my fucking liquor!" Petrov yelled.

Chapter Seventeen

Father Angel was staying at a run-down motel on Hillsborough Avenue in Tampa.

Once a thriving retail corridor that serviced the surrounding middle-class neighborhoods, Hillsborough Avenue now was a sad sack shell of its old self.

Where once there were small grocery stores, butcher shops, diners, and sundries stores with pharmacies in the back, today there were only pawn shops, convenience stores, auto garages, massage parlors, poorly regulated taco stands, strip clubs, and dilapidated motels.

Father Angel could have stayed at any hotel in Tampa Bay — the Vinoy, the Don Cesar, the Hyatt Westshore. Yet he opted for this miserable motel on a miserable street in a rundown area of Tampa.

A bit of local dis-color, he thought, keeps one focused.

Staying at the Paradise Motor Lodge allowed him to keep a low profile while tending to the monumental task before him.

He had to admit, though, that the recently renovated Floridan Hotel in downtown Tampa tempted him. He had heard that the Floridan's martinis were all the rage.

Father Angel had returned recently from his meeting with a local security company. He arranged for thirty private security officers to monitor the three-hundred-fifty retired priests living in Tampa Bay. This expedition of his to Tampa Bay already was costing the Vatican nearly two-hundred thousand Euros.

And that's right, three-hundred-fifty priests, not the figure of one-hundred ninety-three I quoted to Reed O'Hara, Father Angel thought.

He operated under the maxim that only he needed to know all of the details of a special security project.

Reed O'Hara required only background information on the murdered priests, since her task was only to find the killer, according to Father Angel's point of view.

Father Angel was still kicking himself that he let it slip to O'Hara that a retired priest program existed in Tampa Bay.

I will not make that foolish mistake again, he thought.

Even Antonio and Bumandi, Father Angel's brilliant assistants in his Vatican office, were kept in the dark about some aspects of this project.

Father Angel suspected strongly, though, that Antonio and Bumandi, who were computer hackers first and Roman Catholic priests second, knew far more than they let on to their boss.

For computer geeks, those two are politically savvy, Father Angel thought.

Though it was three a.m. in Rome, Father Angel wanted to check in with Antonio and Bumandi.

He knew his research assistants would be awake. Their typical pattern was to sleep for a few hours during the day, allowing them to sit with their laptops all night long.

Father Angel was sitting at the desk in his dingy motel room. He was smoking a Cohiba cigar and sipping a superb California pinot noir from a plastic cup.

He turned on his laptop, went through the elaborate password protocol to get on this secured site in the Vatican's immense operations center, and keyed in a greeting to his assistants.

"Pease be unto you, my brothers in Christ. How goes the research?" he typed.

Chapter Eighteen

Father Angel's assistants responded quickly.

"And peace be unto you, Brother. Our research is progressing well. Where would you like us to start?" the assistants inquired.

Father Angel puffed from his cigar and sipped more wine.

His fingertips danced across the keyboard.

"First, inform me as to how the police investigation is progressing," he wrote.

Thirty seconds passed, then a response from across the Atlantic.

"Local authorities have gathered little forensic evidence from the four crime scenes. They have researched the background of each deceased brother: where the brothers in Christ were born and raised, their education, the various dioceses in which they performed the Lord's work. For now, the local authorities have four separate murders. For now, they have made no connections, except that the deceased were retired priests."

Another sip of wine. Another puff from the cigar. Another dance across the keyboard. Father Angel was starting to become slightly tipsy.

"There is concern permeating your matter-of-fact tone. What does 'for now' mean? Hold nothing back," Father Angel tapped out furiously.

This time, two minutes passed.

Father Angel heard an apparently drunken couple arguing loudly next door. He put on his wireless headphones and listened to Andrea Bocelli.

His researchers finally responded.

"Through a variety of covert probes, we have learned what individual law enforcement agencies in the Tampa Bay area have learned about our departed brothers' unsavory pasts. It will be only a matter of time before they share this information with each other, thereby discovering the common thread of pedophilia that intertwines among all four brothers of Christ."

This is not good, not good at all, Father Angel thought. How long before the police also discover the existence of Exodus?

Does this portend that the police will find the killer before Reed O'Hara does, he thought. O'Hara simply must move with all deliberate speed.

Father Angel poured himself more wine, then responded to Antonio and Bumandi.

"My good and faithful brothers, you have done a thorough job. Continue to keep me apprised of the local law enforcement's progress. Peace be with you," he typed.

Father Angel closed his laptop. He rose from the desk that was cratered in cigarette burns and splotched with dried hot pink nail polish.

He took off his headphones, then stubbed out his cigar in a small plastic ashtray that bore the name of a nearby strip club, a place called Twigs & Berries.

Father Angel finished his plastic cup of wine, then corked the wine bottle.

Just before beginning his evening prayers, he thought of Reed O'Hara.

"Time to put a holy fire under that Protestant heathen," he said aloud to himself.

The couple next door continued to scream at each other.

Soon, those two will either kill one another or start fucking, Father Angel thought.

Chapter Nineteen

Jake Dupree laid on his back as Reed O'Hara straddled him and ground her hips into his well-defined abdomen.

Jake was naked.

Reed wore only the green and white scarf of the Bray Wanderers, a soccer team in the premier division of the Dublin Women's Soccer League.

The scarf indicated to Jake that he was in for some passionate lovemaking with Reed, who already was aglow with perspiration.

Jake held Reed's hips, pulling her forward as she thrust. He reached under the scarf and fondled her breasts, gently pulling on her nipples.

"Your breasts are perfect, Beautiful," Jake said.

Reed smiled dreamingly at her husband. She raised her hips and very slowly lowered herself onto Jake's substantial erection.

Jake began to make the annoying facial expression that men make who are about to reach orgasm.

Reed stopped thrusting.

"Oh no you don't, mister," she said. "Ours is a civil congress, so ladies first, all right?"

"Yes, ma'am. I'll think of . . . golf?"

"Whatever works, *mon petite fromage.*"

"Reed, did you just call me your 'little cheese'?"

More hip thrusts from Reed. She quickened the pace.

"What? Yeah, I guess," she said. "It just sounded sexy."

Reed closed her eyes and tilted back her head. Her gorgeous blonde hair dangled down her arched back.

She began caressing her breasts with the soccer scarf.

Reed was thrusting her hips almost maniacally. Then she suddenly stopped grinding her hips. Her body quivered for several seconds.

Reed's orgasm peaked just as Jake came inside her.

She opened her eyes, which radiated hues of Bahamas blue and green. As she looked down at Jake, a single drop of perspiration fell from the tip of her nose onto his chest.

Reed kissed Jake, then lowered her head on his chest.

The couple hugged and cuddled, then trailed off to sleep.

Chapter Twenty

Reed and Jake awoke from their lovemaking just before ten a.m.

Jake put on a pair of boxers and went into the kitchen. He began making smoothies, using frozen tropical fruit, fresh bananas, almond milk, and a generous scoop of French vanilla ice cream. He also made coffee with a French press.

Reed stayed in bed, yet she was awake. She had thrown the green and white soccer scarf in a corner of the bedroom. She put on panties and one of her beloved NBA tee shirts — this morning, she wore a Miami Heat warm-up tee.

Reed was on her tablet, catching up on e-mail and reading news updates from the BBC World Service.

The couple's Sunday would follow in the same sweet fashion as most of their Sundays.

They always made love in the early morning, then napped briefly.

Jake would then bring into their master bedroom a tray with smoothies and a Bodum filled with freshly brewed coffee.

The early Sunday afternoon would be devoted to what Reed described "as a "center court bull session.""

First, Reed would discuss her law practice. Then Jake would talk about Namaste. They concluded their bull session by discussing matters related to their private investigations.

Typically, it was early afternoon before they finished talking.

For their late lunch, Jake often prepared them a pasta dish, sometimes linguini in a clam sauce or spaghetti carbonara or penne pasta with Kobe beef meatballs. The smell of garlic would waft through the entire penthouse condominium.

After eating, they would spend one hour listening to music together. They alternated Sundays: one Sunday, Reed would play jazz; the next Sunday, Jake would play classical music.

At five p.m. on the dot, Reed and Jake would drive in Jake's prized red Range Rover to their athletic club. It always was a vigorous workout. Jake would use the rowing machine, while Reed used the elliptical trainer. Then they would lift free weights together, finishing with a vigorous run on treadmills.

After showering and changing into casual attire, they would drive across the street to Kennedy's Steakhouse, their favorite restaurant in Tampa. Kennedy's kept reserved on Sunday evenings the couple's preferred booth in the elegant wood-paneled bar.

Reed would permit herself one virgin Miami Vice, while Jake would drink Fiji bottled water with lemon slices.

Usually, they would feast on wedge salads, tenderloin beef carpaccio, and tiny lobster tacos.

After dinner at Kennedy's, Jake would drive them back home.

They would finish their Sunday by reading and sipping raspberry herbal tea, always retiring by eleven p.m.

Chapter Twenty One

However, this particular Sunday was anything but typical.

Reed and Jake had already partaken of the smoothies and coffee in their bedroom.

It was noon. Time for their bull session. Time to re-connect.

Outside it was sunny, yet cold and windy. Typical Florida winter day — at least there was no ice, snow, and polar bears.

Inside the condominium, Reed and Jake kept warm by sitting on the leather sofa that faced the fireplace in the living room. Reed had lit the gas fireplace and it was giving off impressive heat.

There was a fresh pot of coffee set on the leather coffee table.

Reed spoke first, as she usually did.

"We have a lot to cover today," she said. "Let's get my law practice and Namaste out of the way, then we'll talk about an intriguing and challenging investigative case."

"Intriguing? Challenging? Why can't we talk about this case first?" Jake said.

"Because that's the way I prefer," Reed said, using a distinctly abrupt tone.

"Well, all right, then, boss," Jake said, feigning a petulant tone.

"Smart man," Reed said. "My law practice is going smoothly, though right now I'm not super busy. I've been focusing primarily on helping Sofia set up her nail salon franchises."

Sofia was a bona fide American success story.

She had performed at Namaste for the maximum period of five years. She made an excellent living during those five years. She also earned her GED, an associate's degree at Hillsborough Community College, and a bachelor's degree in marketing from the University of South Florida.

After her mandated retirement from Namaste, she took her substantial savings and opened a small nail salon in West Tampa.

The salon prospered, benefitting greatly from Sofia's strategy of marketing to men and women, gay and straight couples, multi-generational families.

Sofia was ready to franchise. Her goal was to open twenty five nail salons throughout Florida in the next ten years.

She had come a long way from when she first stumbled into Namaste on a blistering hot and humid summer afternoon.

Sofia was twenty-five years old with no family or friends in Tampa Bay.

An unemployed nail tech, she had hopped on a bus in Jacksonville. She wanted to start anew in Tampa.

She was a statuesque beauty, with flowing auburn hair, emerald green eyes, and long shapely legs.

Sadly, though, Sofia had become addicted to methamphetamine, a horrible street drug that was expanding quickly into a nationwide epidemic.

Her teeth were in an early stage of decay. Her skin was blotchy and a pale gray. She had lost considerable weight.

Sofia had heard on the street that Namaste sometimes offered a second chance to troubled women.

Jake was again composing at the grand piano in Namaste when he agreed to interview Sofia. He noticed that she was perspiring heavily and that she barely could hold the glass of orange juice that Andre had given her.

Don't know if I can help this one, he thought.

Jake, though, sensed the potential in Sofia. He believed she was an ideal candidate for Namaste's program of rehabilitation, renewal, growth, and empowerment.

Six years later, Sofia was a powerful and beautiful woman — well educated, healthy, financially secure, and poised to build her salon business into a veritable empire.

Jake sat up on the living room sofa and stretched.

"So you think Sofia's ready to take it to the next level of the salon business?" Jake said.

"Absolutely," Reed said. "It's smarter for her to sell salon franchises, ideally to other women. Otherwise, opening her own salons would cost her upwards of two or three million dollars, most of which she'd have to finance. This way, she avoids years of smothering debt. If we do it right with the franchises, Sofia might end up a very wealthy, independent woman."

"Which is your aim all along," Jake said.

Out came Reed's Mona Lisa smile.

"That's exactly right, my dear," she said. "Now tell me all about Namaste."

Chapter Twenty Two

"Babe, we got a problem of Promethean proportions at Namaste. First, though, let me give a rundown of the club's financial status," Jake said.

Reed nodded encouragingly to Jake. She knew not to be impatient with Jake — he had his own sense of delivery.

"Our liquor sales are way up, food sales steady," Jake said. "Admission fees are going through the roof."

Jake drank more of his coffee, then continued with his report.

"Our expenses, though considerable, remain steady. Payroll isn't a problem, even as we add more dancers."

"'Performers', Jake," Reed said.

"Yes, 'performers.' Sorry, my love," Jake said.

Reed's facial expression switched from admonishment back to encouragement.

"Okay," Jake said. "Utilities, liquor and food inventories, license fees, furniture and fixture expenses, insurance premiums — all are as stable and steady as, as . . . . "

". . .as Stef Curry splashing three's from the Oracle parking lot?" Reed said.

"That's right, babe,"Jake said.

Jake admired Reed's passion for the NBA. What he found so intriguing was that she didn't have a favorite team. She was all about the Association. This approach allowed her to enjoy the games, to admire the athleticism, without partisanship distracting her.

"So what's the bottom line, Jake?" Reed asked.

"We're maintaining a rock-sold fifteen-percent net profit, a pretty darn good bottom line," Jake said. "We're not going to get rich with Namaste, yet we'll keep the doors open for a long time, as long as we stick to our business model and nothing too crazy happens."

"You get a metaphorical cookie for that report," Reed said. "But is anything crazy happening now?"

Jake was amazed with Reed's intuition — she sensed strongly that there was something on his mind. Of course, an obvious tell on his part was overselling the good news.

Might was well get it over with, he thought.

"Yes, we have something crazy going on," he said. "Great big Russian crazy. It's Petrov again."

Chapter Twenty Three

Reed set down her coffee cup and looked at Jake with genuine concern.

"What is Petrov up to now?" she said.

"Petrov and his two Siberian huskies came by Namaste last Wednesday night," Jake said. "He started off by making very loud lewd remarks. His aim was to create a scene in order to get himself in my office and try to bully me."

Reed slowly let out her breath.

She understood that there wasn't any chance Petrov would bully Jake, making the chances for a physical confrontation quite high between the two men.

"So what happened?" Reed asked.

"Andre kept the bodyguards occupied while I chatted with Petrov," Jake said.

"And what came of this chat?"

"Flat out, Petrov wants to be our strategic partner, and turn Namaste into an upscale strip club, full nude of course. He figures he can bribe the right city officials into having Namaste go full nude and still retain its liquor license. Petrov thinks our dancers — err, performers — could get into all kinds of hinky sex acts. And he wants to go into video production."

"I take it that you told Petrov to royally piss off."

"Absolutely, though I framed my response in less classy terms," Jake said.

The Mona Lisa smile returned.

"So what do we have to worry about?" Reed said.

Jake frowned, then leaned toward Reed. He wanted her to understand that this situation with Petrov was very serious. Russian gangsters were dangerously incendiary; they also were very hard to kill.

"Petrov wants everyone to think he's the Russian Godfather, since he owns El Castillo, the Twigs and Berries Gentlemen's Club, and Lude's Adult Theater," Jake said. "But he's not. He's merely a bellicose front man for the Florida shell corporation that fronts for the Brighton Beach, New York shell company that fronts for a Cayman Islands shell corporation that's overseen by a crime syndicate in Moscow."

"You're kidding," Reed said.

"Nope. And Petrov is under a lot of pressure from Moscow to keep expanding in Tampa Bay," Jake said.

"I believe you, Jake, but how do you know all of this?"

"Let's just say I called in a couple of favors from some old friends," he said.

"Fair enough," Reed said. "Petrov's not going to play nice, is he?"

"No way. His initial overture is just a smoke screen. Petrov wants to muscle his way into owning Namaste," Jake said.

"Own Namaste? I thought he wants a partnership," Reed opined.

"These guys get even a small piece of your business, before you know it, they've pushed you out and stolen the entire operation," Jake said.

"So Petrov won't go away."

"Nope," Jake said.

"What do we do?"

"Have Andre enhance security at Namaste," Jake said. "Provide escorts home for our performers and staff. It'll be expensive, but all we can do is wait out Petrov. Only a matter of time before he makes his first real move."

"Sounds good, Jake. And thanks for being so calm and reasonable about this situation," Reed said.

"I'm trying, babe. Believe me, I'm trying," Jake replied.

"Then now's as good a time as any to fill you in about my brush with Petrov," Reed said.

Chapter Twenty Four

Jake sat up straight.

"What the hell, Reed!" he exclaimed.

"Calm down, Jake, Petrov had his useful idiot of an attorney, a chubby little slime ball named Jasper Conway, come by my office to inquire about Namaste," she said.

"Sonuvabitch!" Jake said too loudly.

"If you're going to go all primal, I won't discuss it anymore," Reed said.

Jake let out a long breath. He appeared properly chastened.

"Fine, I'll cool it," he said. "Did anything happen with this Conway?"

"Yes, but to him, not to me," Reed said. "After I shut him down about Namaste, he got threatening."

"And . . . ."

"And I kicked his ass, simple as that," Reed said. "And I didn't overdo it, since you know there's no education in kicking a mule twice."

"That's my girl," Jake said admiringly.

"Your girl'?"

"I meant my badass partner in crime and punishment and *mon beau guerrier*," Jake said.

"That's more like it. Thank you," Reed said, as she archly rolled her eyes.

"We'll need to step up security at your office, too," Jake said. "Have Roman bring in his Browning, and make certain his concealed weapons permit is up to date."

Roman was yet another rescue project for Reed. He was addicted to crack and selling himself at gay bars in Ybor City. Reed helped Roman clean up, get to community college, and earn an associate's degree, which included paralegal training. Not only did Roman become an excellent marksman, but he also traveled to Thailand three or four times a year for kickboxing and mixed martial arts tournaments. There were times when even Jake, who was a fierce warrior poet, was slightly intimidated by Roman.

"Okay, Jake, I'll alert Roman," Reed said. "He feels bad enough that he missed Conway coming by the office."

"All right, defense shields go up at Namaste, at your office, and here at home," Jake said. "Is there anything else to discuss before I fix the pasta? I'm hungry as hell."

"Actually, my dear Alfonse, there is."

"That's right — a new case came in, correct?"

"Yes, and it concerns those murdered priests."

"You're shitting me," Jake said.

"No, I'm not. And stop swearing," Reed said.

She stretched back her arms and arched her back, tightening her tee shirt across her chest and thereby outlining her erect nipples. The message from Reed to Jake was clear: speak with a civil tongue, or you won't touch these gorgeous breasts.

Message received, Jake thought.

Chapter Twenty Five

"Four retired priests have been murdered in Tampa Bay in the last two weeks," Reed said. "There's an excellent chance there will be more murders. We've been hired to find the killer."

Jake poured more coffee for the two of them.

"Hmm, 'we've been hired,' huh?" he said. "Clever use of passive voice, that. I'd like to know who hired us, but first please tell me why you're certain there'll be more dead priests."

Reed blew into her coffee mug, then took a sip. "Because these murdered priests were part of a retirement program based right here," she said. "The killer appears to be targeting this group."

Jake spread his arms and turned up his palms.

"Well?" he said. His tone bordered on childish petulance.

"I drew on some connections in the local constabulary," Reed said. "Turns out all four dead priests were forced into retirement because they were all caught molesting children ranging in age from two to sixteen."

"Holy crap!" Jake exclaimed. The petulance receded.

"And there's more. My sources are suggesting this program for retired priests in Tampa Bay may consist almost entirely of pedophile priests," Reed said.

Jake leapt off the sofa and walked over to the floor-length picture windows that framed the entire living room.

For a full two minutes, Jake stared out at the impressive Tampa skyline with Tampa Bay glittering in the background.

"So a possible scenario is that we've got a bunch of child molesters all corralled," Jake said. "I'm wondering why we even bother to find this killer, just let him pick them off one by one. Better yet, I'll volunteer to help out — I'll chop' em into chum and feed them to the sharks. We'll have predators getting fat and happy by feasting on fellow predators."

"Let me know when you're done venting," Reed said. She tapped her fingers lightly.

"All right, I'm done. Sorry," Jake said. "So how many priestly perverts are we talking about?"

"Well, I don't have an exact figure — at least one from a reliable source," Reed said. "But I think there are at least two hundred priests residing in Tampa Bay who are part of this special retirement program."

"At least two hundred pedophiles," Jake said. "Jesus Christ."

A dead calm settled over the living room. Reed and Jake stared at each other, their bodies seemingly frozen in time like porcelain figures in a Renoir painting. The Sunday bull session suddenly got very, very serious.

"Reed, are you implying that the Vatican hired us to find a righteous vigilante who is making certain that at least some of these vile priests will never again harm a child?"

Jake had spoken in such a low, hushed voice, Reed almost couldn't hear him.

"Yes, Jake, the Vatican has hired us to find the killer. More specifically, a Father Angel has employed us. He's in charge of special security at the Vatican, and apparently he oversees this priest relocation program."

Jake had returned to the living room sofa.

"Why on earth did you agree to take this job?" Jake said.

"Three reasons: because I was getting a little bored with my law practice; because I was up for an extraordinary challenge; and because this killer should be stopped from being judge, jury and executioner," Reed said.

"Then let the police find the killer. He keeps this up, he'll eventually make a mistake, and the police will get him. Guarantee it," Jake said.

"That's Father Angel's concern," Reed said, "that the police will catch him before we do. He wants the opportunity to talk with the killer, to give him the chance to explain himself, then to confess his sins and seek forgiveness. Then Father Angel will turn the killer over to the police."

Out came her Mona Lisa smile.

"And, Jake, I don't believe Father Angel for one second," she said.

"I agree, babe. This priest wants to eliminate the killer in a quiet and discreet manner." Jake said. "Otherwise, the police get him and there will be a perp walk of circus proportions, nonstop media coverage, probably a lengthy trial. The Catholic Church will be crucified — bad pun intended."

This time, Reed rose from the leather sofa, walked across the living room, and gazed out the picture windows.

"You're right," she said. "And I'm not going to allow Father Angel to dispose of this killer. We are going to find him. We will let Father Angel talk to him. Briefly. And safely. Then we will turn over the killer to the police."

Jake got up from the sofa and joined Reed.

The couple put their arms around each other's waist.

"I'm in, Reed. It's a good plan. Risky. Challenging. Dangerous, even. But you know what, if you didn't agree to Father Angel's terms, then he would have found someone else to go along," Jake said.

Reed hugged Jake, then kissed him.

"Thanks Jake, I knew you'd understand."

She held Jake in her arms.

"You're very welcome, my wild Irish rose." Jake said as he went into the kitchen to prepare the pasta dish. Soon, the lovely aroma of garlic cooking would be more than rumor.

They would still get in their vigorous workout at their athletic club and dinner at Kennedy's.

But instead of reading that Sunday evening at home, Reed and Jake strategized together as to how best to track down this priest killer. They went with green tea to sip, as the modest amounts of caffeine would keep them alert. They talked until two a.m.

Chapter Twenty Six

Dom Parnillo, an eleven-year veteran of Secure Tampa Bay and an unabashed fanatic of the Tampa Bay Lightning hockey team, sat by himself in a marked security sedan. The Lightning game was streaming on his tablet, but he wasn't paying much attention to it.

Parnillo was babysitting six retired Catholic priests who lived in an elegant apartment building just off Bayshore Boulevard in South Tampa.

Though there was a chill in the late-night air, Parnillo kept the sedan's windows down. This way, he could hear any unusual sounds, especially those from an encroaching intruder.

He wore his padded Secure Tampa Bay jacket, which kept him fairly warm.

Parnillo was a true professional. He was thorough and alert. He took seriously his assignment: on his watch, those retired priests would be safe.

Priest killer might as well take the day off, he thought.

As a Roman Catholic, Parnillo was horrified that someone would harm these men of God. He always regarded the priests in his life as figures to be respected and revered.

He sat in his sedan and constantly scanned the small parking lot and the apartment building's front entrance.

In a few minutes, he would make his rounds on foot around the building's perimeter.

Clutching his rosary in his hand, Parnillo snuck a quick look at the hockey game on his tablet. Unfortunately, the Lightning was down two – one to the Washington Capitals in the third period.

The hockey game was taking place at Amalie Arena in downtown Tampa.

Parnillo looked across Tampa Bay at the downtown skyline. He could just make out the expansive rooftop of the hockey arena.

Man, the Bolts need these two points, Parnillo thought. We're just barely hanging on to the top spot in the conference playoffs race. Home ice is crucial. Time for a comeback. Vasilevskiy gotta just stone the Caps, and Stamkos has gotta let that puck fly.

Parnillo could not resist watching the game on his tablet. The Caps tripped a Lightning forward, resulting in a two-minute penalty and a Lightning power play.

Parnillo was excited and nervous. He gripped his rosary and kept staring at his tablet.

The Lightning methodically set up Stamkos, who blasted a withering slap shot between the pipes.

Tampa Bay had tied the game. Parnillo clenched both fists and banged on the roof of the sedan.

"Yes, yes, yes!" he said, though he felt slightly embarrassed over his sophomoric behavior.

Parnillo had no idea that a dark figure was watching him from behind a large azalea shrub.

The security guard was still watching the replay of the game-tying goal when a dart struck him in the neck.

Parnillo felt a terrible pain in his neck.

"St. Christopher, protect me!" he said.

A second dart struck him in the left shoulder.

Parnillo slumped forward onto the steering wheel. He was motionless. The tablet's glow illuminated his serene looking face.

Chapter Twenty Seven

Father Claude was tired and slightly drunk. It was approaching ten-thirty, and he wanted to go to bed. First, though, he wanted to make certain that the security guard was staying alert.

No telling what that idiot is up to, he thought.

The retired priest did not place much value in this additional security, but he intended to be sure the man sitting in the white Impala outside was doing his job.

Father Claude lived on the third floor of the apartment building, which actually was a converted mansion built in 1895.

The seventy-nine year old French Canadian priest loved this old structure. He especially prized having the top floor master bedroom, which afforded him a glimpse of Tampa Bay. Seniority has its perks, Father Claude said to any of the other retired priests who pretended to listen to him.

The four murdered priests had made Father Claude extremely edgy.

He drank more wine than he should.

He rarely left his apartment.

And he gave up his daily morning walks on the Bayshore Boulevard sidewalk, its seven miles comprising the longest continuous walkway in the world.

No more gorgeous little boys walking astride their insufferable and overprotective mothers, he thought.

Now he had the added anxiety of keeping an eye on this security guard.

Father Claude opened his curtains about six inches and peeked out the front window.

Well, look at that, Father Claude thought. That cretin is sleeping in his car! That's it. I'm calling his supervisor.

He closed the curtains and picked up his landline phone, which he kept on a nightstand next to his unmade bed.

The last couple days, he had called Secure Tampa Bay enough times to complain that he had memorized the phone number.

But before dialling the phone number, he reached across the bed and closed his laptop. He was streaming a voyeur website that featured a hidden camera filming a high school wrestling team showering together in a locker room. The website was called Husky Sandusky and was quite expensive. Father Claude suspected the shower scene was a porno set up, but he didn't care — the boys lathering up each other appeared young enough to be illegal.

And he certainly did not want their giggles and moans to be heard when he called Secure Tampa Bay.

The line rang only once, then an operator came on.

"Father Claude, what a surprise. And what can we do for you tonight?" the operator said.

"Don't be sarcastic with me, young man," Father Claude said. "I'm calling to inform you that Parcheesi or Palermo or something or other is sound asleep in his vehicle!"

"That's of great concern to us, Father Claude," the operation said. "Are you certain the security officer is asleep in his cruiser?"

"I am most certainly certain that he's asleep. He's not moving and is hunched over with his head on the steering wheel," the priest said, incredulous that this voice over the telephone would challenge his authority.

There was silence for about ten seconds.

"Hello?" Father Claude said.

"Yes, I'm still on the line, Father Claude," the operation said. "That's Officer Parnillo on duty. It's not like him to be sleeping on the job. However, we will contact him immediately. Meanwhile, stay inside, lock your doors, and stay away from windows. We'll call you as soon as this situation is resolved, okay?"

There was no answer from Father Claude.

The operator could hear only laughter and what seemed to be moaning.

"Father Claude, are you still on the line?" the operator asked.

The old priest could not answer because an arrow had pierced his forehead. The arrowhead protruded from the back of his head.

Father Claude was slumped over in his bed.

His laptop had been re-opened.

The boys in the Husky Sandusky video stream were lathering, rinsing, and repeating.

Stealthily leaving the dead priest's bedroom, the lone figure clad in black whispered, "Pederest in peace."

Chapter Twenty Eight

It was Saturday night at Namaste, and the night club was packed, mostly by well-dressed couples with a few tables occupied by single men and women.

As he did most every week, Jake had arranged for twenty couples from all over the United States, Europe, and the Middle East to fly in for an all-inclusive weekend in Tampa Bay.

Jake always put up these couples in luxurious suites at the Renaissance Hotel at International Plaza. He reserved the best tables for them either at Kennedy's, Bern's, or the Capital Grille for a late Friday night supper. After sleeping in until noon on Saturday, the couples would be driven to the Columbia in Ybor City for lunch, then go shopping at International Plaza, Westshore, or Wiregrass. Occasionally, Jake would arrange for the couples to travel south for lunch and shopping at St. Armand's Circle in Sarasota. He always was surprised when couples wanted to hunt for bargains at nearby outlet malls.

On Saturday evening, the couples would dress elegantly and spend the entire evening at Namaste, having dinner and drinks while enjoying the cabaret performances.

On Sunday morning, the couples were driven to the Safety Harbor Spa and Resort. They played tennis, swam, worked out in the fitness center, and got a variety of spa treatments.

By six p.m. Sunday evening, these couples would have boarded commercial flights or their own private jets at Tampa International Airport.

Jake charged each couple twenty-five thousand dollars for this weekend in Tampa Bay. Many couples reserved a weekend three or four times a year.

So Saturday nights always were extremely profitable for the performers, who often made upwards of three or four thousand dollars in gratuities for each performer on a Saturday night. Even Jake received a few hundred dollars for his piano playing. He called these tips "love offerings" and donated them to the Centre for Women in Tampa.

At Reed's insistence, Jake did not factor in seniority or skill level when selecting the Saturday night line-up. He simply alphabetized the performer's stage names and went down the alphabet in filling out the ten performer line-up for a particular Saturday night. No trading on the performer's part. No special requests allowed by guests. No politics, no dissension. No fuss, no muss. Such a simple, clever plan on Reed's part — every time Jake filled out the rotation, he was reminded that Reed was as brilliant as she was beautiful.

Usually, Saturday nights went smoothly at Namaste. The guests almost always showed good manners and proper decorum. The performers basked in their adoration while receiving generous gratuities from them. Jake could concentrate on his piano playing, since Andre and his security staff kept a benevolent and professional watch.

However, this particular night at Namaste was going to be a genuine challenge, since Petrov knew just how important Saturday nights were to the cabaret nightclub.

Chapter Twenty Nine

At precisely eleven p.m., Petrov and his two bodyguards entered Namaste.

Petrov wore a dark blue suit with a white dress shirt and a light blue silk tie.

The bodyguards wore black trench coats over charcoal suits. Oddly, the two men wore matching ostrich boots.

Andre was standing by the front desk when Petrov walked in. It was no happenstance; Andre saw on the exterior security camera Petrov's white Audi A8 pull into Namaste's parking lot.

"Good evening, Mr. Petrov," Andre said. "How are you on this chilly Florida night?"

"I am good, Andre, my brother from another mother," Petrov said. His bodyguards said nothing. They simply stared at Andre with a doll's dead eyes.

"Are we going to play nice tonight, Mr. Petrov?" Andre asked.

"Sure, why not? All I want to do is have a few Johnny Blue's and see some nice tits," Petrov said.

Andre frowned at Petrov.

"Okay, okay, sorry," Petrov said. "Drinks and a show, is all, okee, dokee?"

"Very well, Mr. Petrov. Now, would your colleagues like to check their coats?" Andre asked.

"'Colleagues,' Hah! That's a good one. 'Colleagues,'" Petrov said.

Petrov laughed too loudly. "Okay, this colleague will check his coat," Petrov said, pointing to the shorter of the two bodyguards. "And the other colleague wants to keep his coat on. He's not feeling good. Cold or something."

Petrov spoke in Russian to the shorter bodyguard, who then checked his overcoat.

The second bodyguard didn't move.

"I'll need to wand this gentleman if he insists on wearing his coat." Andre said.

Petrov smiled.

"Sure, no problem," he said.

Petrov spoke in Russian to the bodyguard still wearing his coat.

"Mr. Petrov, I happen to speak Russian," Andre said. "If you refer to me as an asshole again, in any language, then you and I will step outside and take it to a level that you'll regret for a very long time. And I mean regret deeply."

"Well, kiss my mother goodbye and put her on a gulag train," Petrov said. "You speak Russian, huh? Please forgive me, Andre. Go ahead, do the wand thing on my sick colleague."

Petrov chuckled menacingly.

Andre spoke Russian to the bodyguard, who raised his arms slightly. Andre ran the metal detector up and down the bodyguard's body, front and back, between his legs.

No alarm sounded.

Not bothering to ask permission, Andre also wanded Petrov and the other bodyguard.

Again, no alarm sounded.

"Have an enjoyable time at Namaste, but behave yourselves," Andre said. "*Spasido, gospoda.*"

The three Russians entered the nightclub's main room while Andre held the door for them.

Contessa was performing her final dance before a receptive audience for over two hundred guests. Wearing only bright red yoga pants, she moved with grace and confidence and sensuality. She swayed with the beat of a Hans Zimmer composition playing over the sound system. Her petite bare breasts, which each would fill no more than a champagne glass, glistened with perspiration.

Jake sat at the piano, riffing with the Zimmer composition.

A collective gasp filled the room as Contessa finished with a full straddle split.

And yet Petrov paid no attention to Contessa's performance. He was occupied with looking for an empty table near the exit.

Guests were still standing and applauding for Contessa as Petrov and his bodyguards hurriedly sat down at an unoccupied table.

Petrov ordered two Johnny Walker Blue scotches for himself and two bottles of Fiji water for each bodyguard. When the server brought the tray of drinks to his table, Petrov paid in cash, giving her an overly generous tip.

Later in the night, the server would tell Andre that Petrov seemed to be in one bloody rush.

Chapter Thirty

Sierra walked out to center stage for her first performance. At six feet, two inches, she was the tallest of Namaste's performers. She wore her hair in long blonde curls that extended down her back.

Tonight she was wearing a sports bra, a tee shirt, and yoga pants, all in white. Her best physical features were her long, shapely legs and her rounded, muscular buttocks. She also had a confident and joyful smile, a trademark of hers.

Petrov stared at Sierra as she began her first dance.

"Not bad," Petrov said to no one in particular. "Nice body, big tits, and fuck, what an ass!"

Petrov tossed back the remainder of his first Johnny Walker Blue, then wiped his mouth with the sleeve of his suitcoat.

The bodyguards sat silently, drinking large gulps of Fiji water directly from the bottle.

The bodyguard in the trench coat kept trying to make eye contact with Petrov.

Petrov looked at him and said in Russian, "Not yet, relax. Soon, soon come."

Sierra finished her opening dance number to hearty applause. Several couples walked to the center stage and gave her generous tips.

Before starting her second performance, Sierra slowly took off her white tee shirt. She tossed the shirt to a young woman sitting with two other women at a table near the stage. The woman held the tee shirt and blew a kiss to Sierra, who retuned the gesture.

Bunch of fucking lesbos, Petrov thought.

Sierra then began dancing as if she were performing a gymnastics floor routine. At one point, she even did a slow back hand spring. She finished the performance to enthusiastic applause, rewarding the audience with her world-conquering smile.

"Not too bad," Petrov said. "Like to see her on the pole, though."

Jake walked back out to his piano. He began playing his own composition.

Sierra started her final performance by doffing her white sports bra, revealing her pendulous breasts.

The audience got silent. There was a tangible erotic vibe in the air.

Sierra put the audience under her spell with her lithe, sensual dance moves.

Petrov finished his second Johnny Walker Blue. He then nodded to the bodyguard wearing the trench coat.

The body guard nodded back to Petrov, then he reached into his coat and pulled out a long, wide object that appeared to be wiggling.

He leaned forward and placed the object on the floor. The body guard removed a piece of black tape from one end of the object. He released the object, which immediately began crawling underneath the tables, heading in a roundabout manner to the dance stage.

It was an alligator.

Only about three-feet long and maybe twenty-five pounds, it was an alligator, nonetheless.

The first person to spot the gator was an older man sipping Wild Turkey and Coke from a Waterford crystal tumbler. When the gator slithered across his croc loafers, the man looked down and emitted a high-pitch scream. He dropped his tumbler, jumped out of his chair, and backed away from the gator.

"Holy mother of God," he exclaimed.

Other guests saw the alligator and began yelling and screaming.

Petrov and his body guards rose from their table. They gingerly made their way to the front exit.

Our work is done here, Petrov thought, so let the fun begin.

Sierra noticed the commotion, couldn't detect its source, and continued to dance.

Jake had his back to the audience and kept playing his piano.

Andre, though, moved deliberately toward the dance stage.

Meanwhile, three women rose from their table. One of the women clutched Sierra's white tee shirt. They didn't appear alarmed, but they deftly moved away from the growing chaos.

Petrov paused to study these three women.

He said in Russian to his body guards, "Look, look — it's those bitches that were at El Castillo the night priesty boy got murdered."

The body guards nodded in agreement.

The three women were still a good twenty feet from Petrov.

He faced a dilemma: he needed to leave Namaste, but then he'd miss the chance to confront these women. After all, he figured, if they knew something about the murder at El Castillo, or, better yet, had a hand in the murder, then he could blackmail them into being his submissives in a torture chamber session.

No, Petrov thought, time to get the fuck outta here.

The three Russians left Namaste just as Andre was able to grab the gator by its tail and snout.

Though Andre did not want to injure the gator, he knew he had to get it out of the night club before it bit someone.

Then he heard Sierra call out to him.

"Andre, Andre! Bring me my buddy." Sierra said. "I was wondering where he'd gotten to. Lift him up so everyone can see."

Andre paused briefly, then smiled at Sierra.

The gator had stopped squirming. It appeared as if it didn't mind Andre's firm yet gentle grasp.

Andre dutifully held the alligator over his head. The audience gave out a collective sigh of relief. The guests were all standing. Those few who had attempted to leave Namaste were returning now to the front of the stage.

Jake was fully aware of the situation, yet he didn't miss a beat in his piano playing.

Still holding the gator above his head, Andre wound his way through the crowd and headed toward Sierra on stage.

"That's right, Andre, bring me my beautiful baby," Sierra said.

With her arms stretched out in front of her, Sierra knelt on her right knee.

The audience happily parted so Andre and the alligator could reach the front stage.

Andre gently handed the gator to Sierra, who grasped the gator by its nose and tail.

Sierra gave the gator a kiss, then lifted it above her head and began dancing slowly with it.

The audience didn't want to frighten the gator, so the cheers and clapping were somewhat muted. But everyone clearly was excited over this extraordinary scene.

Several guests showered the stage with one-hundred dollar bills. Sierra and her alligator were a smash hit at Namaste.

Jake had finished playing his composition and sat on the piano bench while watching Sierra and the gator walk off the stage.

He knew he needed to call the Florida wildlife folks, but for now he wanted to relish this amazing moment.

We always should be prepared to act extemporaneously, he thought.

Out came Jake's very own Mona Lisa smile, for he appreciated that Sierra's quick thinking saved Namaste from an embarrassing story that would have made it in virtually every international and national news outlet.

I can just see the headline, he thought, "Florida Being Florida Again." Man, God bless that beautiful Swede.

Chapter Thirty One

Reed and Jake relaxed on the king-size bed in their master bedroom. Their naked and perspiring bodies were intertwined.

The couple had awakened at dawn and made love with passionate fierceness.

They got an early start to lovemaking because they understood that this Sunday would require their focusing on how to deal with Petrov and how they would go about finding the priest killer.

Jake cupped one of Reed's breasts. She responded by snuggling closer to him and nibbling on his ear lobe.

Then she paused.

"My handsome husband, nothing would delight me more than to make love with you again," Reed said. "But we have to talk."

Jake chuckled.

"That sounds ominous," he said.

Reed bit a little harder on Jake's ear lobe.

"You know what I mean, wise guy," she said. "We've got to figure out what to do with Petrov. And then we need a game plan for tracking down this priest assassin."

"Sort of like standing on Sugar Beach between the two Pitons in St. Lucia, isn't it?" Jake said. "Trying to decide which one to tackle first."

Reed enjoyed how Jake framed a tough situation with images of better times and places.

"Hmm, let's deal with Petrov first," Reed said. "Besides, Ravel's coming over later this morning to help us with these very bad, yet very imperiled, priests."

Jake sat up in bed and adroitly placed a white king-size pillow across his lap.

Reed studied Jake's handsome face and muscular body. At over six-feet tall and just under two hundred pounds, Jake maintained the physique of an NBA point guard through vigorous exercise and eating healthy, nutritious food. She marveled at how he never took off a day from his demanding regimen.

And Reed appreciated her husband taking such good care of himself. In fact, she tried to appreciate him as often as possible.

"Thanks for the proper placement of the pillow, since I don't want to be distracted from the matter at hand," Reed said. "But I must say, you are looking fine."

"*Merci beaucoup, mon petite fleur,*" Jake said. "Now, what to do about Petrov?"

Reed got out of bed, walked over to her dresser, and pulled out a Utah Jazz tee shirt.

After putting on the tee shirt, which came from her prized collection of every team shirt in the NBA, she turned around and faced Jake, who was still sitting on the bed.

She, too, had a lithe, muscular body, and enjoyed exceptionally defined biceps and triceps. And like Jake, she exercised constantly, including yoga and tae kwon do forms. And she especially enjoyed Jake's tasty, sensible cooking.

"You said you were almost positive about Petrov and the alligator," Reed said.

She hopped back on to the bed. Jake couldn't help noticing that she still wasn't wearing panties.

Devil, get thee behind me, Jake thought.

"Well, we have videotape of Petrov and his goons sitting at a table near an exit," Jake said. "I suspect that the body guard wearing the overcoat was the one who released the gator. But he was pretty sneaky about it — we can't see him clearly enough taking the gator out of his coat."

Reed rested her chin on her hands.

"So it's safe to assume that Petrov did it," she said.

"Very safe, Reed," Jake said. "He's the only person there that would cause a commotion like that."

Reed nodded at Jake, then placed her hand on his knee.

"And how is Andre handling this?" she said.

"Not well. At closing last night, he gave me a hand-written letter of resignation. He believes he let us down by not catching on to Petrov's little prank," Jake said.

"Andre resigned? That's ridiculous. How could he possibly anticipate a Russian toting an alligator in his trench coat? What'd you tell him?" Reed asked.

Jake smiled warmly at Reed.

"I gave him back his letter of resignation. Told him it was an honorable gesture, that I knew he was serious about resigning, but I needed him to keep providing security at Namaste."

"Good job, Jake. Something tells me, though, Andre demanded some form of punishment for the gator security breach."

"Yes, he has to put in fifty hours of volunteer work at Clearwater Marine Aquarium, where he dropped off the alligator, which is doing just fine, by the way," Jake said.

"Good. And that was so clever of Sierra to include the gator in her performance," Reed said.

"Yes, and even better news is that no humans or reptiles were injured in the making of this imbroglio," Jake said with puckish whimsy.

"Excellent. Now, why do you think Petrov pulled this stunt in the first place?" Reed asked.

Chapter Thirty Two

"Petrov is trying to intimidate us into selling Namaste to him," Jake said. "Please don't think for one second that he wants to partner with us. He wants to push us out and grab the entire nightclub."

"Well, it didn't work, did it," Reed said. "He'll need to do more than unleash a baby gator on us."

"Yes, although that was Petrov's opening salvo — Conway bracing you in your office and Petrov's goons setting loose a gator in Namaste. He knows he's banned now from Namaste. And Conway doesn't dare come back to your office, especially after the ass kickin' you gave him."

Reed grinned in a very satisfying manner.

"So what's his next move?" she said.

"I wouldn't put it above Petrov to arrange for health inspectors and the fire marshall to make surprise inspections at Namaste," Jake said.

Reed became very serious.

"I know you run a clean and safe operation, so let's not worry too much about inspectors descending on Namaste like a bunch of flying monkeys," she said.

"Nice *Wizard of Oz* reference," Jake said. "But I'm still going to have the club re-cleaned from top to bottom, front to back. I'll also double-check our sprinkler system and get new fire extinguishers. Wouldn't hurt to have our electrical system looked at, and plumbing, too."

Reed nodded her approval.

The man has amazing foresight, she thought.

"Jake, are Namaste's performers in any danger?" she said.

"I think it's likely," Jake said. "Petrov is a first-class thug. Violence is his preferred method of intimidation. And he especially likes to rough up women. Some of my sources say Petrov could be involved with two missing women in Tampa Bay. So, yes, our performers are at risk until we neutralize Petrov."

Reed got out of bed and walked over to the floor-length windows. She grabbed the tiny remote that controlled the window drapes.

She pressed a button on the remote. With a gentle whir, the drapes closed electronically, darkening the master bedroom.

"We're at risk, too, aren't we Jake," she said.

Jake sprung out of bed and walked to Reed. He held her in arms.

"Yes, my love, we are at risk," Jake said. "But you know what, with or without Petrov, it's still a red-ass world out there. We know how to take care of ourselves. We know how to survive and thrive. And we'll keep watching each other's back, all right?"

Reed and Jake kissed deeply and lovingly.

He held her beautiful small face in his large hands.

"And the best way to deal with Petrov, my sweet wife, is to take the fight to him, make him regret he started this war," Jake said. "We'll build a momentum to battle."

"How are we going to do that?" Reed asked.

Jake smiled slyly.

"If it's okay with you, I'll spare you the details," he said. "But I've already got a little sumpin' sumpin' planned for Petrov. I just need Andre and Ravel's assistance."

"Ravel? No wonder you perked up when I told you she was coming over. So is this special plan illegal? Is that why you want to spare me the details, because I wouldn't approve?" Reed asked.

"What I've got in mind isn't so much illegal as it is extra-legal," Jake said. "Still, you probably wouldn't approve."

"Extra-legal? Okay, fine, spare me the details this time. Except, tell me this: will it piss off Petrov?"

Jake laughed.

"Frankly, my dear, it will drive him crazy."

Extra-legal, Reed thought, now just what does my Jake have going on?

Chapter Thirty Three

Jake and Reed were getting dressed in their bedroom when the doorbell rang three times. Ravel, as usual, was right on time.

Reed hurriedly put on jeans to go with her Utah Jazz tee shirt. She remained barefoot. Two swipes with the hairbrush and her golden hair was perfect.

Jake donned a white linen Caribbean shirt with matching linen slacks. Even in a casual setting, Jake never wore jeans, shorts, or tee shirts. He put on a pair of tan Mephisto sandals. He preferred leaving slovenly dressing to the kiddies.

The doorbell rang again. Three times. Again.

"Uh oh, we've pissed off Swiss Miss," Jake said.

"Jake, don't start calling her that again," Reed said. "And for god's sake, don't start cracking that Gruyere is no Gouda," she said with an impish smile.

"I promise to behave, Beautiful. How about I make coffee and you answer the door? And check the video monitor before you open the door."

"Yes, sir!" Reed said with a faux military tone.

To the left of the large, heavy oak front door was a small video monitor attached to the wall.

Reed looked at the monitor and there was Ravel standing at the front door. A black knapsack hung over her shoulder. Her right hand rested on her right hip. Her right foot was tapping.

Ravel looked up and spotted the tiny red light on top of the miniature camera above the doorway.

"What the hell, Reed, let me the fuck in," she said into the camera.

Reed chuckled. Since she and Jake had the top floor of the apartment building all to themselves, she didn't have to worry that Ravel's yelling would bother neighbors.

"Reed, I know that's you. If you don't let me in, I'll tag your hallway," Ravel said.

Ravel reached into her knapsack and pulled out a can of neon green spray paint.

She'll do it, too, thought Reed.

She pressed a button on the console and the front door clicked open.

Ravel walked into the penthouse condominium as if she were invading the Sudetenland.

Reed was standing in the foyer.

"Sorry to keep you waiting, Ravel," Reed said insincerely.

The two women hugged. The hug lingered.

Ravel gently pressed her hips against Reed, who pulled back.

"Now, now, Ravel, we have work to do," Reed said. "Besides, I'm a happily married woman."

Ravel smiled in resignation.

"That's right, just throw Jake in my face," she said. "Well, really, don't do that."

Both women laughed.

Ravel was twenty-five years old. She stood just under five feet and weighed about ninety five pounds. She kept her black hair short. Her large eyes were a sparkling violet, and she had a tiny ski slope of a nose. Her cheekbones were high and prominent, and she had an angular jaw. She was a veritable portrait of Swiss Alpine beauty.

She kept herself fit, and was more sinewy than muscular. She had a narrow waist and short, shapely legs. Though a tiny, athletic woman, she had exceptionally large breasts.

In a word, Ravel was stunning.

And she was gay. And she was in love with Reed O'Hara. Completely in love.

Reed was aware of Ravel's passion for her. Ravel was not the first woman to make overtures to her. But Reed was in love with Jake and committed totally to their marriage.

Privately, Reed admitted to herself that Ravel was very attractive. Yet what she most loved about Ravel was her pugnacious and fearless personality.

As people often said of her, Reed found that Ravel was like no one else.

Chapter Thirty Four

About three years earlier, Ravel marched into Namaste and demanded a job.

Though technically not homeless, Ravel was an urban nomad, spending a night or two at friends' apartments, the occasional night at Salvation Army in downtown Tampa, sometimes even a night at Lowry Park Zoo, if she could sneak inside the shelter that housed the river otters.

Ravel appeared haggard and unkept when Andre walked her over to Reed's private table. Reed sat alone, sipping Acqua di Nepi mineral water and eating a garden salad. Jake was playing piano as he accompanied Contessa dancing sensually across the stage.

"Miss Reed, this young lady is Ravel," Andre said. "She'd like to speak with you about employment at Namaste. Would you prefer she make an appointment to meet with you at a more convenient time?"

Reed looked at Ravel, who wasn't smiling and appeared tired.

If I put her off, she'd probably never come back, Reed thought.

"No, Andre, it's okay," Reed said. "I'll make an exception. I'll talk with her now — quietly, of course."

Andre held the chair for Ravel, who paused disdainfully. She remained motionless and stared down at her scuffed boots.

"Andre's extending a civil courtesy to you," Reed said. "Please don't embarrass him and yourself by rejecting his gesture."

Reed understood that a man holding a chair for a woman could be viewed as old-time sexism. However, she balanced this point of view against the notion that, in this increasingly ugly world, civility was one of the few remaining ways of staving off the barbarians at the gate — civility and a fully loaded nine-millimeter Browning semi-automatic with one in the chamber.

Ravel shrugged her shoulders.

"Fine. Whatever," she said. "He can hold the chair for me."

Andre slid in her chair as she sat down.

"Thank you, Andre," Ravel said. "I'm just not accustomed to people being civil toward me."

"I understand, *molodaya ledi*," Andre said.

"Son of a bitch, you speak Russian," Ravel said. "*Blagodaryu vas za to, chto gospodein.*"

Andre smiled.

"*Privetstvennyye, molodaya ledi*," he said.

Reed was studying this exchange.

"Sorry to be nosy, Andre," Reed said. "But what did you just say?"

"Ravel thanked me for being a gentleman, and I simply told her she was welcome."

Andre bowed slightly, then strode away from the two women.

Contessa had finished her final performance.

There would be twenty minutes before Sierra would take the stage, allowing ample time for Reed to interview Ravel.

"So, Ravel," Reed said, pushing aside her salad. "That's a beautiful name. Did you parents name you after the French composer Maurice Ravel?"

See, I do listen to Jake when he goes on about classical music, Reed thought.

"Yes," Ravel said. "My parents are French Swiss. In fact, I was born in Montreux on Lake Geneva. My parents are proud to be Swiss, but they treasure their French heritage. They love Maurice Ravel, particularly his operas, not just because he was French — he created his compositions with Swiss-like precision, and my parents love that quality about him."

God, she sounds just like Jake, Reed thought.

She nodded at Ravel.

Only, Ravel seemed animated by more than Maurice Ravel and classical music. Reed hoped that Ravel wasn't tweaking, a sure sign of methamphetamine abuse.

"And besides, Ravel is a pretty cool name, isn't it," Reed said.

Ravel looked straight into Reed's icy blue eyes.

"Not as cool as Reed," she said.

Jesus, is this *chica* hitting on me, Reed thought.

"Yes, well, let's talk about why you want to work at Namaste," Reed said.

Artful transition be damned, she thought, time to change subjects.

Ravel smiled. She realized she had unsettled Reed.

Well, I'll be, Reed thought, that's a Mona Lisa smile. I knew I should have trademarked it.

"I've heard good things about Namaste, that you help women improve their lives," Ravel said.

"Yes, and that includes prohibiting illegal drug use," Reed said.

"What the hell does that mean?" Ravel asked.

"It means, Ravel, that before we hire you, you'll have to quit using meth," Reed said.

Ravel looked down at her lap.

"Is it that obvious?" she asked.

"The pale, blotchy complexion? Smiling while hiding your teeth? Your jittery temperament. Your readily apparent weight loss? Yes, Ravel, it's that obvious," Reed said.

A large tear rolled down Ravel's cheek.

"Fine, Reed, how about I just get the fuck out of here," Ravel said.

Reed had heard petulant responses like that more times than she could count.

Ravel, she thought, you're not getting off that easily.

Chapter Thirty Five

Ravel started to get up from the table.

Reed put her hand on Ravel's forearm.

"Don't be so peevish, Ravel. You've more or less admitted to meth abuse. A big first step. Now, the even bigger second step," Reed said.

Ravel reached out and held Reed's hand.

"What's the next step?" she said.

Reed let go of Ravel's hand and wiped the tear from Ravel's face.

"The next step is a two-parter," Reed said. "First, stop crying — that's just feminine manipulation. Second, we'll get you into a treatment program at Tampa General Hospital. It's an excellent program that gets great results. I'll pay for it. And I want you to enter the program even if we don't hire you."

Ravel pulled back.

"What's your angle, Reed?" she asked.

Reed leaned in closer to Ravel.

"My angle? It's simple: I have the means, motive, and opportunity to help women in trouble. And *you* are in a lot of trouble," Reed said.

As she said this to Ravel, Reed tapped the tabletop with a fingernail. Tap, tap, tap.

Reed glared at Ravel, who glared right back at Reed.

Ravel blinked first.

"Okay, if I agree to get treatment, will you hire me and also stop that *fucking* tapping?" Ravel asked.

Reed showed Ravel one of her better Mona Lisa smiles.

"Don't make me regret this, Ravel," Reed said. "Yes, I'll hire you, but you have to start treatment today. I have a friend, Judi Ploszek, who's an executive at Tampa General. I'll ask Judi to make arrangements for your admittance."

Ravel sat straight up, her shoulders squared.

"All right, I'll do it," she said. "I don't want to live like this anymore."

"I'm glad to hear that. I'll call Judi and get you registered at TGH. I suspect you'll be able to enter the program later tonight."

"How long will I be in?"

"Most likely at least a month, perhaps longer," Reed said.

"And I'll have a job waiting for me when I get out?" Ravel asked.

"Yes, you will," Reed said. "I hope that you have a background in dance or yoga or gymnastics."

Ravel appeared puzzled.

"I trained in ballet in Switzerland for twelve years, then I blew out a knee and never fully recovered. I can't dance anymore," Ravel said.

"That's going to be a problem if you want to be a Namaste performer," Reed said.

"I never said I wanted to dance here," Ravel said.

"Then what do you want to do? Serve tables? Tend bar?"

"Nope," Ravel said.

"What then?"

"I want to be your office manager," Ravel said.

The balls on this woman, Reed thought.

"Sorry, but my husband, Jake Dupree, who's over on the piano there, manages Namaste," Reed said. "Jake is co-owner and runs day-to-day operations here."

"And he does a pretty shitty job," Ravel said.

"How so?" Reed said. "Wait a minute. How would you know what kind of job that Jake is doing?"

Revel smiled the smile — the one she apparently had stolen from Reed.

"Let's just say I'm computer savvy," she said.

"Have you hacked into our computer system?" Reed said.

Ravel nodded affirmatively.

"Yup," she said. "Thought I'd do some digital mining before this interview. And there's a clear need for more efficient accounting, particularly when it comes to tax liability."

"I don't know whether to listen to you or to kick your little ass out of here," Reed said. She pushed aside her salad and leaned in at Ravel.

"Do what you like, Reed, but it's in your best interest to hear me out," Ravel said.

Both women now sat with their arms folded.

Both women now sat in complete silence.

This time, Reed blinked.

"Here's the deal, Ravel. I'll give you one shot, so choose your strongest recommendation. If I'm impressed, we'll take you on as Jake's assistant. If I'm not impressed, you hit the bricks. Either way, you still have to enter the TGH treatment program."

Ravel didn't respond. Instead, she stared at Sierra, who was walking toward center stage to begin her performance. Sierra gave Ravel a sly wink.

"Ravel, please stay focused," Reed said. "Do we have a deal?"

Ravel looked at Reed and again nodded affirmatively. She couldn't remember the last time she had been so agreeable.

"You have a deal, Reed. I think I can trust you to make the right decision. But whatever your decision, I'll honor it, okay?"

"All right, let's hear your pitch then," Reed said.

"I've gone over all of Namaste's books, your spread sheets, your billings, all of your federal tax records, and . . ."

"What the hell, Ravel!" Reed exclaimed. Several people, including Jake, looked over at her table.

Chapter Thirty Six

"Relax, Reed, I consider myself a black hat hacker nonpareil, I'm the best, and that's just a fucking fact," Ravel said. "You have a decent security system — most hackers would have to work hard enough that they'd eventually think it wasn't worth the time or effort. After all, you're not the NSA or Interpol or the London Stock Exchange. You're not worth the sweat equity for these lesser souls. I mined into Namaste because I wanted to know a lot about you before we met."

Jesus, the meth's really kicking in, Reed thought. Ravel is tweaking like mad dogs and Englishmen.

"All right, Ravel, let's get a grip here, okay? I'm sure you're a very good hacker, but that doesn't excuse your invading my privacy, your helping yourself to proprietary information," Reed said.

"I live by my own rules," Ravel said. "Do you want to hear my recommendation or not?"

Though exasperated with Ravel, Reed truly wanted to hear out the woman.

"Go on, Ravel," Reed said. "What's your best pitch?"

"Here goes. As tempted as I am to discuss Namaste's day-to-day business operations — where I could improve your profit margin by twenty percent — my very best proposal involves federal taxes," Ravel said.

"Whoa, hold on. I'm not going off shore or get involved in some cockeyed tax scheme that defrauds the IRS and sends me to federal prison," Reed said.

"Please," Ravel said. "Give me a little credit. What I recommend is legal — totally above board — and taken right from the federal tax code, which, by the way, is some seriously sexy reading."

You know, she sounds sincere about liking to read the tax code, Reed thought, which is kind of hinky and nerdy.

"What have you got in mind?" Reed said.

"It's simple, it's beautiful, and it's save you a lot of money," Ravel said. "You're aware, of course, that Namaste is an LLC, a limited liability company, right?"

"Yes," Reed said in a condescending tone.

"Well, even though you're an LLC, you're being taxed as a corporation. Why not elect to be treated as a disregarded entity and save about a quarter-mil in corporate income taxes?" Ravel said.

"And it's all legal?" Reed asked.

"Absolutely," Ravel answered.

"And this is from the tax code?"

"Absolutely."

"Show me," Reed demanded.

"No problem, *chica bonita*," Ravel said.

Ravel took out a laptop from her knapsack and set it on the table. She tapped on her keyboard and, in less than thirty seconds, called up the federal tax code. She went straight to the section on disregarded entities.

"Here it is," Ravel said proudly.

She turned around her laptop so Reed could read the pertinent tax code section.

"Well, I'll be damned," Reed said. "You're right, Ravel. How did you find this?"

Out came Ravel's Mona Lisa smile.

"I love reading the U.S. tax code," Ravel said. "I discover over and over again that angels and demons are hiding in the code."

Did she mean tax code or computer code, Reed thought, probably both, I'd guess.

"Congratulations, Ravel. You sold me. Once you've finished the treatment program at TGH, you'll have a job waiting for you at Namaste. As the new assistant to the office manager," Reed said.

Ravel smiled broadly at Reed, then saluted smartly to her new employer. She asked politely for a large glass of cranberry juice with crushed ice, as well as one of the same salads Reed was eating.

Reed happily agreed to Ravel's request.

Chapter Thirty Seven

And that's how Ravel became Reed's left-hand woman — with Jake being her right-hand man.

On this particular Sunday in late February in Reed and Jake's penthouse, Ravel was ready to report on her research into the priest murders.

She had set up her beloved laptop on the leather coffee table in the large living room.

Jake carried a tray with a large pot of coffee, cups and saucers, and cream and sugar cubes into the living room. He set the tray on the coffee table, then sat down in one of the comfortable leather chairs. He immediately pushed down the plunger on the Bodum.

Reed and Ravel sat together on the matching leather sofa.

Ravel poured coffee for Reed and Jake as well as for herself.

"All right, you two, I've put in nearly sixty hours of researching, planning, and strategizing," Ravel said. "I'm not trying to impress you, I simply want you to understand that everything has been data mined thoroughly and my plan of action is meticulously thought out."

Reed was impressed with Ravel's clear-headed remarks. Indeed, Ravel had come a long way since overcoming addictions to tobacco, alcohol, and methamphetamine.

Jake finished his first cup of coffee.

"Thanks, Ravel," he said. "Your Swiss nature is showing through, and we appreciate it."

Ravel only nodded at Jake. It was her reserved, cautious way of saying thank you. After all, she was Swiss, making her genetically wired to be leery of praise and compliments. She was raised to believe that if you weren't Swiss, then you're a suspicious outsider.

"You know what else is showing through?" Ravel said.

She looked directly at Reed.

"Your boobs," Ravel said. "Think you could put on a bra so I won't be so fucking distracted during my presentation?"

Ravel smiled lasciviously at Reed, who had not crossed her arms to cover her breasts.

Both Reed and Jake burst out laughing.

Ravel remained deeply in love with Reed, but it was unrequited — Reed and Jake were too much in love to allow in an outsider.

So Ravel was left with simply being playful with Reed.

And Jake and Reed viewed Ravel's overtures as harmless, even charming.

"No, Ravel," Reed said. "I won't put on a bra. You'll simply have to focus on your report. Now let's hear it before another priest is murdered."

Ravel poured herself more coffee, then stared at her laptop.

"All right, I'll report on the murdered priests first," Ravel said. "Then I'll fill you in on the police special task force. Finally, I'll lay out a game plan for us."

"Let's do it," Reed said impatiently.

"Chill, *chica*, this train's on time and on the track," Ravel said. "Now, the murdered priests so far: Robert Cosgrove, Jules Lidre, David Kerry, Andrew Morrison, and Claude Blatt — who's the most recent victim, if that's what you'd call him."

"Don't disagree with you, Ravel," Jake said. "But editorializing so soon in your report?"

"Spare me, Jake," Ravel said. "These perverts were all part of the Vatican's Exodus program. Using Father Angel as its ramrod, the Catholic Church cattle drove three hundred and fifty of its worst offenders and corralled them in Tampa Bay, so these men could be watched over by the Church. We're talking about the worst of the worst — hardcore, serial child molesters. From my vantage point, these five dead pervs deserved what they got."

Reed was thankful that a cooler, calmer head such as herself was in charge here.

"How'd you find out about Exodus, Ravel?" Reed said, clearly attempting to keep her team on point.

"Simple, I hacked into the Vatican's computer mainframe," Ravel said. "It took a while. The Vatican has some seriously bitching security. Father Angel's Special Security office was almost unbreachable. And getting out without being noticed was almost fucking impossible."

Reed understood how confident Ravel was in her hacking skills. So for Ravel to admit a security system was "almost unbreachable" meant Father Angel felt protected enough to be open and candid online. Therefore, the data that Ravel was mining must be entirely reliable and accurate.

Reed nodded to Ravel, encouraging her to proceed with the report.

"But eventually I got into the system, and I learned that the Vatican has been dealing with almost twenty-five thousand problem priests since 1950," Ravel said. "We're talking about thousands of perverts from all over the world having their way with children for nearly seven decades. And really, who knows how far back this horror goes."

Ravel caught her breath.

"Then there are the enablers," she said. "Hundreds of cardinals, bishops, and monsignors busy covering up, moving the pervs to different parishes that amount to fresh hunting grounds, and, of course, quieting victims and their families by paying them off and making them sign non-disclosure agreements."

"It's goddamn sick, is what it is," Jake said. "And how long has Exodus been up and running?"

"Almost two years," Ravel said. "Father Angel was pleased with Exodus' progress, before the murders, of course. In fact, he was using

Exodus as a template: multiple programs would be set up throughout Florida and the rest of the Deep South, all modeled after Exodus. Father Angel calls it the March of Tens — in ten years, ten thousand perv priests would be bivouacked in one hundred Exodus programs in ten southern states."

"Holy shit," Reed said.

"Holy shit, indeed, *chica guapa*," Ravel said. "The whole intent of Exodus is to put the pedophiles under wraps, keeping them off the police and media radar. It's a cover-up of biblical proportions."

Reed and Jake sat in shocked silence. Jake reached out and held Reed's hand. The couple lowered their heads — not in prayer, but in mutual acknowledgement that they had willfully entered a darkly dangerous underworld.

Chapter Thirty Eight

Reed gathered her thoughts.

"Ravel, why did Father Angel hire us to find the killer?" she said.

Ravel chuckled quietly.

"Two reasons, Reed," Ravel said. "He wants the killer found quietly and before the police find him, so that Exodus doesn't get exposed — pardon the pun. And he needed the services of the most talented and determined investigator in Tampa Bay. That's you, of course. I also suspect he thinks he can control you because you're a woman."

Reed and Jake looked at each other, then Jake spoke.

"What's his end game, Ravel?" he said. "Can you tell from your research if he actually will turn over the killer to law enforcement?"

Ravel finished her second cup of coffee, then poured herself a third cup.

"No fucking way, Jakester," Ravel said. "When we find the killer, Father Angel will dispose of him without police involvement."

"I'm not going to let that happen," Reed said. "We'll find the killer, perhaps let Father Angel speak briefly with him, then we'll sure as hell turn him over to the police."

"Speaking of police, I now want to let you know where the task force is in its investigation of the murders," Ravel said.

Reed got up from the sofa, picked up the coffee pot, walked over to Jake, and re-filled his coffee cup. She then re-filled her own coffee cup

"What's going on with the task force, Ravel?" Reed asked.

"Let me retrieve the files," Ravel said.

She tapped her keyboard and the task force's secured website came up. She studied the screen for about five minutes, then closed her laptop.

"The task force knows a lot about the homicides, but isn't even close to identifying any suspects," Ravel said.

"What kind of evidence has the task force gathered?" Jake said.

Ravel smiled impishly.

"I'm sure you know the priests were murdered with a bow and arrow," Ravel said. "What I'm sure you don't know is that a crossbow was used."

"Come on, a crossbow?" Jake said.

"Yes, a crossbow," Ravel said.

Reed interjected. She was kicking herself for not mentioning the crossbow to Jake earlier.

"It makes perfect sense, Jake," Reed said. "A crossbow is quiet, compact, and lethal."

Ravel nodded eagerly at Reed. "You're right, Reed. According to the police investigations, a crossbow is extremely powerful, more so than your traditional bow. In the right hands, crossbows are very accurate."

Jake absentmindedly raised his hand, as if he were asking permission to speak.

"Jake, do you have something to share with the class, or do you have to go potty?" Ravel said.

"No, smartass. I wanted to know if the task force is developing a profile on this serial killer — maybe there's something there that we can use to find this guy," Jake said.

Out came Ravel's wan smile.

"Well, Jakester, that's an excellent thought," Ravel said. "You get a virtual cannoli. In all five homicides, crossbow arrows punctured the victims' heads, chests, and crotches. These are acts of revenge or vigilantism. The killer has no faith in the judicial system. Somehow, he knows these pedophiles are resting safely in the ample bosom of the Catholic Church and the secular authorities can't touch them — again, pardon the pun."

"So the killer is the unholy trinity of judge, jury, and executioner," Reed said.

"Nice touch extending the metaphor," Ravel said. "and there's one more detail about the fifth murder you'll find interesting."

"What's that?" Jake asked.

"Before the killer entered Blatt's apartment, he used a blow dart — stop laughing, you two! — to render the security guard unconscious" Ravel said. "This is a killer with something of a conscience. Why not just kill the security guard? Then there'd be no chance of interference or identification, right? Because this isn't some fucked up sociopath who murders indiscriminately. This killer is focused entirely on one thing: making these perv priests pay for their sicko acts. And a curious little detail: the security guard is a devout Catholic."

Chapter Thirty Nine

Jake left Reed and Ravel in the living room to make another pot of coffee. He busied himself in the galley kitchen, grinding the coffee beans, putting the kettle on the range, and preparing the French press.

Reed and Ravel remained sitting next to each other on the leather sofa.

Ravel studied Reed, who was gazing out the picture window. Though Reed's eyes, long neck, and exquisite body got Ravel all flustered, it was Reed's golden, straight hair that most entranced her.

God, she's beautiful, Ravel thought, I wish I could reach across and kiss her, run my tongue down her neck, and touch her . . . .

"I know what you're thinking, Ravel," Reed said, turning her ice blue gaze on Ravel. "It's not going to happen, *chica*. I'm committed to my man. So let's get back to work, all right?"

Ravel nodded in the affirmative.

Look at that, Reed thought, I actually made Ravel blush.

"Fresh coffee anyone?" Jake said.

He carried into the living room a tray with a pot of coffee and a plate of croissants on it. Jake wasn't surprised to feel sexual tension in the air, though he preferred to be a gentleman by not mentioning it to the women.

"Thank you, sweetheart," Reed said. "We'd love more of your delicious coffee, and let's devour those croissants — from Alessi's, I hope?"

"Better believe it, baby," Jake said.

The trio drank coffee and ate the croissants. No one spoke for several minutes.

Reed finally broke the silence.

"Okay, my lovely co-conspirators, time to formulate a plan," she said. "Ravel, I'll bet the common thread that intertwines the five dead priests is that they all committed especially egregious acts of sexual depravity on children."

Ravel sat straight up, opened her laptop, and called up the Vatican's files on the murdered priests. She studied these files for several minutes.

"You're right, Reed," Ravel said. "These guys were absolute monsters. God, I didn't read their profiles carefully enough the first time, maybe because their depravity is overwhelming."

Ravel bowed her head, put her face in her hands, and sobbed quietly.

Reed put a hand on Ravel's shoulder.

"Ravel, take a break and let me read the files," Reed said. "I need to know what's in them."

Ravel slid her laptop over to Reed, who began clicking through files.

"You've been warned," Ravel said to Reed.

Jake came over and sat next to Reed. He read the files along with Reed.

"Jesus Christ," Jake said.

Only Jesus had nothing to do with this perverse pathology.

Going over the Vatican files, which were Gestapo like in their unflinching, exhaustive detail, Jake and Reed learned that these five dead priests had sodomized children, beaten them, forced them to perform oral sex, filmed them performing sex acts, and, most horrifically, probably murdered three of the children. The matter-of-fact tone in these files was especially galling.

All of these crimes were committed in the United States. Over two hundred children were abused. Those victims who eventually came forward were adults. So much time had passed that there was little that law enforcement could do — statute of limitations kicked in, there was little evidence to support the allegations, the Catholic church refused to cooperate, payoffs were made in exchange for silence.

Of course, there were civil lawsuits filed against the priests and the Catholic church. All of the lawsuits connected to the five murdered priests were settled quietly, with no admission of guilt. In exchange for almost one-hundred million dollars, the victims and their families agreed not to speak publicly about the five priests' crimes.

Initially, the news media focused intently on these allegations of extreme child abuse, primarily because of the multitude of salacious details.

Naturally, the Catholic church unleashed a public relations campaign that amounted to equivocation and even outright denial. The Spanish Armada of attorneys, public relations experts, and Church spokesmen executed a well-coordinated counter offensive, essentially dismissing the victims' claims as gross exaggerations, even salacious lies, designed to gain attention in this prurient pop culture and thereby extort money from the Church. The coordinated effort was to deny, obfuscate, belittle, lie.

Almost all of the victims who accepted settlements remained silent and out of the public spotlight.

Tragically, four of the victims committed suicide. These poor souls probably concluded that they wouldn't receive any justice, that these priests, these men of God, had gotten away with their crimes and were free to find new victims.

And the three children who disappeared? The Vatican investigation concluded that Father Cosgrove indeed had strangled these children, ages twelve, thirteen, and fifteen, two boys and a girl. He murdered the children to silence them. And law enforcement never could prove his crimes, primarily because Father Cosgrove had disposed of the bodies quite thoroughly.

The Church did not punish these five priests. After they confessed their sins and performed their penance, the priests were moved to other parishes. The new parishes had no idea what they were getting in these re-assigned priests.

According to the Vatican files, the five murdered priests had not yet committed any pedophilic crimes upon entering the Exodus program, making the Vatican suspect Exodus might actually work.

Exodus is a Greek word meaning departure, Reed thought, only I seriously doubt these five assholes ever departed from their perverted behavior, at least not before those arrows pierced their hearts.

Chapter Forty

Reed paused from reading the Vatican files.

She looked over at Ravel, who was curled up in a corner of the leather sofa.

"Ravel, are you okay?" Reed said.

Ravel nodded affirmatively, though a tear rolled down her check.

Got to be the most emotional Swiss I've ever met, Reed thought.

"We have to be strong, Ravel," Reed said. "Your research was brilliant. And your reaction to this papal cesspool is understandable. Jake and I are nauseous as well. But this is the price we pay for getting so close to pure, unrestrained evil."

Jake nodded solemnly, as he put his arm around Reed's shoulders.

"Why do you call it that?" Ravel said.

"What do you mean?" Reed said, genuinely puzzled by Ravel's apparent non sequitur.

"'Research,'" Ravel said. "You know fucking well that it's hacking, beautiful black hacking, exquisitely illegal, mighty and darkly righteous. The lawyer in you prevents you from acknowledging my black art. But you sure as shit don't mind using me to find these dirty secrets, do you?"

Jake spoke up before Reed could respond.

"Ravel's right, Reed," he said. "You can't always have it both ways. Go the legal route and we'll probably never find the killer. I think you need to hop off that cross of yours and give Ravel her due — she's casting light on this evil underworld, and you damn well better realize we're all breaking the rules here."

Reed propped an elbow on her knee and rested her chin in her hand. She was silent for a full minute.

Her beautiful blonde hair fell forward slightly over her face.

Then she spoke.

"You're both right," she said. "We wouldn't be where we are now without Ravel's *hacking*."

"No air quotes?" Ravel said.

"No air quotes, *chica*," Reed said.

Both Ravel and Jake smiled.

"Now let's get back to the matter at hand, shall we," Reed said. "I suspect strongly that the killer somehow had access to these same Vatican files. He may have reviewed all three-hundred fifty retired priests in the Exodus program. Notice how horrible these five priests were? Maybe they were the first to be killed because they were the absolute worst of the lot. Isn't it safe to assume, then, that the killer has categorized all of the Exodus priests into a kind of hierarchy of evil?"

"I think you're spot on," Jake said. "So why don't we study all of these Vatican files and attempt to duplicate the killer's priest hierarchy? We could end up with the killer's very blueprint for assassination."

Ravel came out of her fetal curl on the sofa.

"Because, dumbass, we don't have to do a complete hierarchy," Ravel said. "Just determine the next five worst of these fuckers, stake them out, and wait for the killer to come to us."

Sitting between Ravel and Jake, Reed placed a beautifully manicured hand on each of their shoulders.

"You're both just so brilliant," Reed said. "That's exactly what we're going to do. Ravel, transfer the Vatican files to my laptop and then to Jake's."

"Will do," Ravel said. "I recently amped up your memory capacity on both laptops, so you guys can handle the huge download."

The little shit's been in our computers again, Reed thought.

"Thanks, I think" she said.

"You're welcome, I think, "Ravel said.

"As long as we can stomach it, each of us will study the three-hundred forty-five remaining priest files. Each of us will comprise a list of the next five priests most likely to be assassinated. We'll collate these individual hit lists into a master list, and go from there."

Ravel and Jake nodded their approval.

Chapter Forty One

Four hours later, the trio finished compiling their individual lists of the next five pedophilic priests most likely to be crucified by crossbow arrows.

Reed, Jake, and Ravel had been sitting at the large mahogany dinner table in the dining room.

Jake had set a pitcher of Evian water with three Waterford goblets on the table. He twice re-filled the water pitcher. Jake also had placed a box of facial tissues on the table. The trio's resolve was such that the tissues never were used.

Reed gathered the lists from Jake and Ravel. Her task was to compile a master list of candidates most likely — most deservingly, actually — to be executed vigilante style.

She discovered that the individual lists differed only slightly: Reed's and Jake's were identical; Ravel had one priest not on their lists, a Father Bertrand Bertolli from Cleveland, Ohio.

Reed used her laptop to review the relevant Vatican files, including Ravel's selection of Bertolli.

Jake sat at the table and sipped Evian. He plucked a lemon slice from the water goblet and began chewing on the sour fruit.

Ravel had both elbows on the table. Her right foot tapped nervously.

Neither Ravel nor Jake spoke while Reed completed her master list. Reed closed the laptop.

"Ravel, you were smart to include Bertolli," Reed said. "He nudges out our fifth choice."

Ravel beamed as if Reed had awarded her a gold star.

"Yeah, Bertolli is a first-class shit, isn't he," Ravel said. "He's got a real taste for altar boys. There were forty three reported cases in his Cleveland parish, so you can just imagine how many boys he actually assaulted."

Jake spoke up.

"It's as if we're participating in a *noir* fantasy league," he said. "We choose our perv teams, then Commissioner O'Hara assembles the all-star team."

"True that, Jake, true that," Ravel said.

"All right, we have our master list," Reed said. "The line-up is Andrew Jones, Calvin Calhoun, Isaac Ludlow, Paco Hernandez, and Bertrand Bertolli."

"The fact that our individual lists were nearly identical suggests that the killer probably came up with a similar hit list," Jake said.

"Sometimes, Jake, you actually show signs of alien lifeform intelligence," Ravel said, with an almost coquetish smile.

"Why, thank you, Ravel," Jake said.

"Not to break up your little love fest, but we need to set up the five stake outs," Reed said.

"How many people per stakeout?" Jake said.

"Two each, for a total of ten," Reed said.

"'For a total of ten?'" Ravel said. "Thanks for working that out for us. Impressive, and you didn't use a calculator."

Reed paused, then laughed.

"Whatever, Swiss Bliss," Reed said. "Jake and I will take Jones; Andre and Tatiana will stake out Calhoun; Sierra and my bud Ronda get Ludlow; Elena and Roman will take Hernandez; Contessa and her husband Malio will be on Bertolli."

Ravel slapped her hand on the mahogany table.

"That's fucking unfair," she said. "Why aren't you using me? Why don't I get Bertolli?"

"Ravel, you're going to manage Namaste," Reed said. "You'll be in complete charge. Only don't even think about having fondue night again."

Ravel giggled.

"That's right, just throw my fondue idea in my face," she said. "I swear to god, while you and Jake are gone, fondue night will be every night, and I'm going to change the club's name to Matterhorny's."

Reed couldn't restrain her own giggle.

"No, no you're not, Ravel," she said. "You're going to operate Namaste in a responsible manner. You're fully capable of overseeing Namaste. We need you, and we believe in you."

"But you're taking four of our best performers," Ravel said. "And Andre can't do a stake out and provide security at Namaste."

Jake spoke up.

"Benecio will do a fine job keeping Namaste safe," he said.

"You'll still have plenty of beautiful and talented performers," Reed said. "Simply adjust the schedule and notify the performers."

"All right, okay," Ravel said. "I'm just pissed I can't go on a stakeout."

"It's going to be more tedious than exciting, Ravel," Reed said.

Besides, Reed thought, I refuse to put my precious Swiss genius in harm's way.

"All right, ladies, before we wrap up here and go to Kennedy's for dinner, I have a special request for Ravel," Jake said.

"Do I need to leave the room?" Reed said.

"Probably," Jake said. "Andre and I have a surprise planned for Victor Petrov — it's payback for the alligator stunt at Namaste."

"Jesus, I've forgotten about that jerk," Reed said. "Fine, I'll go change for dinner."

Reed rose from the dining table and headed to the master bedroom.

"And please put on a bra," Ravel said.

Reed patted her right buttock at Ravel.

"So, Jake, what do you have on your mind besides a nice head of hair?" Ravel said.

"Why, Ravel, I didn't think you noticed my gorgeous French wave," Jake said.

"Whatever," Ravel said. "What are you up to?"

Jake explained his plan to Ravel.

"So at exactly two a.m. tonight, I need you to knock out the exterior lighting in the VIP parking lot across the street from the Don Cesar Hotel on St. Pete Beach," Jake said. "No more than for thirty minutes, okay?"

"Will that be long enough for you and Andre to do your dirty voodoo?" Ravel said.

"Yes," Jake said.

"Then of course I can do it," Ravel said.

"*Merci*, Ravel. Now let's go to Kennedy's. I'm starving," Jake said.

Reed emerged from the bedroom. She wore a white blouse, black slacks, heels, and a black leather jacket.

Ravel studied Reed.

Fuck sakes, she's hot, Ravel thought.

The trio left the penthouse.

Chapter Forty Two

It was almost eight a.m., and Victor Petrov needed to leave his suite at the Don Cesar Hotel as soon as possible. He had to drive to the Orlando International Airport and meet his superiors, who were flying in from Moscow.

His superiors' stated purpose of the visit was to look at a strip club, a massage parlor, and two escort services in Orlando. However, Petrov understood that they actually wanted to grill him in person for not closing the Namaste deal. He knew face-to-face encounters rarely turned out well in the Russian underworld.

The flight from Moscow wasn't arriving in Orlando until noon. Petrov was nervous about this visit, so he planned on getting to the airport well ahead of the plane touching down.

Even with the heavy morning traffic on Interstate 4, Petrov figured it would take him less than three hours to get to the airport. If he were early, he could have a couple cocktails in an airport lounge before his bosses arrived.

And he knew he would make excellent time in his prized Audi A8 sports sedan.

Take my Audi over a woman any time, Petrov thought, 'cause it's bitchin' and never bitches.

Indeed, the Audi A8 was an admirable feat of German engineering. The flagship sedan was fast, well appointed, and filled with advanced technology.

Petrov opted for the twelve-cylinder engine that boasted five-hundred horsepower and sprinted to sixty miles an hour in slightly less than four seconds.

And the car was expensive — Petrov spent over $150,000 on his A8.

Of course, Petrov loved his A8. The car was a tangible measure of how far he had come from growing up in a brutal, hard scrabble Moscow slum, where he was always hungry and dirty and unloved.

Understandably, then, Petrov was shocked when he spotted his car parked in in its usual VIP parking space.

"Motherfucker!" he exclaimed. His knees buckled.

Petrov's obscenity echoed throughout the covered parking lot.

One man, about fifty feet from Petrov, paused before getting into his Jaguar. He looked at the Audi, then at Petrov. Wisely, he got into his car and sped off. Quickly.

Petrov stumbled toward his Audi, his arms outstretched, as if pleading for the scene before him to be a nightmarish dreamscape.

Only the scene was not a dream, Petrov realized. His Audi A8 had both its hood and trunk open. The driver's side windows were down.

There was a static pool of gray sludge peeking out from underneath the engine block.

As Petrov got to within a meter of his car, he realized the extent of damage — no, the extent of violation — his automobile had endured.

The Audi engine, among the finest in the world, was covered in quick-setting concrete.

Petrov looked inside the Audi's substantial trunk. It was half-way filled with the same concrete. Petrov had left his golf bag in the trunk. Some of the club heads stuck out above the set concrete; they resembled a flock of ducks sitting on a gray pond.

Petrov then noticed a wide-mouthed funnel protruding from the opening to the gas tank. The interior of the funnel was lined with dried concrete.

Finally, Petrov brought himself to examine the A8's cabin.

The floorboards were covered with hardened concrete.

Scribbled in red sharpie on the driver's leather seat was a happy face and the message, "Gator done."

One might assume that Petrov would become an exploding nesting doll, screaming more obscenities and jumping about crazily, that he would spin out of control and wildly crash and burn.

One also would be wrong.

Petrov merely pulled out his mobile phone and called his bodyguards, who were enjoying a day off at the hotel's poolside that looked out over the Gulf of Mexico.

"Yeah, it's me," Petrov said in Russian. "Dupree fucked up my Audi. What? Filled it with concrete. Don't you fucking laugh! Call the police and my insurance company. And call Conway — we're going to sue this fucking hotel. Then get me a rental. No, not an Audi. A Jag or a Benz. And hurry up, I gotta get to Orlando to meet the flight. What? Fuck yeah, I'm pissed. Don't worry, we're going to take care of Dupree and O'Hara. Just not now. Believe me, they're gonna be in a world of hurt."

Petrov knew his moment had arrived. He would get even with Reed and Jake, and gain control of Namaste at the same time.

I know those fuckers' soft spot, he thought.

Chapter Forty Three

That same Monday morning, Reed and Jake stood on the Bayshore Boulevard walkway directly across the street from their condominium building.

The pair had agreed to meet Father Angel on Bayshore. This way, they could get in a fine walk while informing Father Angel of their plan to apprehend the priest killer in a comprehensive dragnet.

Reed insisted that Jake not refer to the assassin by the nickname PPK — the Perv Priest Killer — in Father Angel's presence.

Jake accepted Reed's admonishment, though there was a playful element in his demeanor, a quality Reed almost found attractive in her husband.

"I can trust you, right, not to annoy Father Angel?" Reed said.

"Sure, of course, baby," Jake said. He wouldn't make eye contact with Reed.

"Then why do you have that sly little grin? You look like a satisfied Parisian pickpocket," Reed said.

"Oh, that," Jake said. "Let's just say that Victor Petrov isn't having a happy Monday morning, though I shouldn't go into concrete detail."

"Jake, what have you done?" Reed said. "Wait, check that. Spare me the specifics. I have enough to worry about right now."

Jake held Reed's hands.

"No worries, my love," Jake said. "I'm certain Petrov knows better now than to mess with us again."

"I hope so, Jake."

Father Angel was ten minutes late, but finally he appeared.

"I am so sorry, Ms. O'Hara and Mr. Dupree, but I'm afraid I am locked eternally into Italian time — better late than never, I suppose," Father Angel said.

Father Angel shook hands first with Reed, then with Jake.

Better to acknowledge the alpha first, Father Angel thought.

"Shall we walk?" Reed said.

Father Angel nodded his approval.

"Of course, and what a treat for me to walk on Bayshore Boulevard. The bay is so beautiful, and the grand mansions along this boulevard are quite impressive," the priest said.

"How do you like Tampa so far, Father?" Jake said, striking a friendly and inviting tone.

"Ah, Mr. Dupree, Tampa is delightfully different from Rome," Father Angel said. "Tampa is a thriving port city that has a rich international flavor. The food alone is marvelous — Cuban, Mexican, Jamaican, Indian, Vietnamese, Thai. I especially enjoy the paella and ropa viejas and black beans with rice at the Columbia Restaurant."

"Father Angel, have you had breakfast yet?" Reed said.

"Is it that obvious?" Father Angel said.

All three laughed politely.

"No, I haven't yet had breakfast, but I intend to go to La Teresita in West Tampa and enjoy toasted Cuban bread with a *café con leche*," Father Angel said.

"When you get a chance, Father, please visit Alessi's Bakery on Cypress Avenue," Reed said. "There's both Italian and Hispanic cuisine, and probably the best croissants and cannoli in Tampa Bay."

"Alessi's Bakery. Thank you for the recommendation, Ms. O'Hara," Father Angel said. "I shall try to visit the baker tomorrow morning."

Father Angel thought of the empty Alessi's pastry box in his motel room.

Phil Alessi's cannoli aren't too bad, he thought.

The trio then walked the Bayshore walkway in silence.

Runners, in-line skaters, cyclists, and fellow walkers were in great numbers on the wide sidewalk.

Jake caught Father Angel ogling an attractive woman running while pushing a double sports stroller.

"Have you made progress, Ms. O'Hara?" Father Angel said, trying not to think of the Madonna in running shorts who just passed him.

"Yes, we've made some progress, at least in our understanding of what we're dealing with," Reed said. "With this enhanced understanding, we've set up a trap to capture the killer."

The trio paused on the walkway to watch a pair of dolphins surface, dive, and re-surface in Tampa Bay.

"I have become aware, Ms. O'Hara, that you have been — how shall I phrase this — exploring the Vatican files on our brothers in crisis," Father Angel said. "I hope the avalanche of disgusting accusations, vitriolic lies, and gross hyperbole didn't overwhelm your feminine sensibilities."

Reed folded her arms across her chest.

"My feminine sensibilities, Father?" Reed said. "You're taking a patrician attitude toward me. To clarify, it was my *feminist* sensibilities that were deeply offended by your colleagues' aberrant behavior."

Humph, let her avoid addressing the hacking, Father Angel thought. Won't let that happen again. Clever little shit, she is. Besides, she knows now I'm keeping an eye on her.

Reed glared at Father Angel.

"Please forgive me, Ms. O'Hara," Father Angel said. "I'm afraid I've become accustomed to the old ways of thinking."

Such as a woman should stay the fuck out of the Vatican's main frame, he thought.

"Truly, I'm an old fool too set in his ways to manage in this new world," Father Angel added.

"Spare me the pathos," Reed said. "You're provoking us into tipping our cards about what we know about the Exodus program."

Just tipped your cards right there, dearest, Father Angel thought. Shouldn't let anger override reticence.

"Ms. O'Hara, I must protest," Father Angel said.

"Protest away, Father Angel," Reed said. "But you're only sidetracking us. Let's get back on track by having us explain our plan for finding this killer."

"Absolutely, Ms. O'Hara," Father Angel said.

The trio resumed their walk along the Bayshore.

"We estimate the five murdered priests were the worst of this miserable lot," Jake said. "We've come up with the next five worst: Bertolli, Jones, Calhoun, Ludlow, and Hernandez."

Father Angel began to speak, then wisely fell silent.

How in the name of God and the Holy Father did these cretins get into our system, Father Angel wondered.

"We're going to stake out these five priests starting tonight. Please make sure they're home, and call off private security on these men," Jake said.

Well, look at that, Father Angel thought, the big oaf is trying to show me that he has some balls.

Chapter Forty Four

Though it was mid-winter in Florida, the morning was getting warmer, almost hot.

Father Angel struggled to keep up with Reed and Jake's pace.

Jake noticed that Father Angel was perspiring and breathing heavily.

"Sorry, Father," Jake said. "Reed doesn't understand the concept of a casual stroll — I'm afraid it's lead, follow, or get out of the way for her."

Reed slowed her pace, though she was none too happy about it. She knew full well that the priest was in excellent shape — he only was being manipulative.

"Thank you for slowing down, Ms. O'Hara," Father Angel said. "Do you believe you have adequate support for a stakeout of this size?"

Reed gave Father Angel an ice-blue stare.

"Don't worry, we've got this covered," she said. Reed didn't care that Father Angel was aware that she didn't like him.

"I could have two members of my Vatican staff here by tomorrow morning, if you believe they could be of assistance," Father Angel said.

"Unnecessary, but thank you," Reed said. "Besides, something tells me that Antonio and Bumandi are already on their way to Tampa."

Now how in the hell does she know their names, Father Angel wondered silently.

"Well, yes, they are en route, but only because they are my personal assistants, and I need help coordinating private security for the Exodus brothers," Father Angel said. "May I continue to assume that, when you apprehend this killer, you then will allow me an audience with him?"

Reed walked to the walkway's cement balustrade. She was surprised pleasantly to notice that the pair of dolphins actually was a mother and her baby. The baby kept just a few inches from its mother's side. The pair arched out of the water in perfect sync.

"Yes, Father Angel, you'll have your audience, assuming, of course, we can take this person alive," Reed said. "After your audience, we will turn him over promptly to law enforcement."

"Of course," Father Angel said.

Reed remained doubtful of Father Angel's sincerity.

The trio resumed walking, then paused again at the intersection of Bayshore Boulevard and Bay-to-Bay Avenue.

"Father Angel, we're going to cross here and have breakfast at a nearby French bistro," Jake said. "Would you like to join us?"

Ah, he's O'Hara's little factotum, Father Angel thought. Jesus Christ, this man needs to find his balls. Probably discover them bouncing around in O'Hara's pocket.

"No thank you, Mr. Dupree, I must return to my makeshift office at the motel," Father Angel replied.

With that, Reed and Jake crossed the boulevard, leaving Father Angel to admire the dolphins.

Father Angel stood alone for several minutes. He found the dolphins mesmerizing.

"Nice fish," he said aloud to no one in particular.

Father Angel noticed that Lady Madonna and her sports stroller filled with strawberry blonde twins had turned around at Ballast Point and were heading straight toward him.

Talk about nice fish, Father Angel thought.

Chapter Forty Five

At roughly the same time Jake and Reed were having breakfast at the French bistro, Ravel was working out with Sierra at their athletic club.

For a Monday morning, the fitness center was surprisingly busy. That was because a squadron of soccer moms had landed in their Escalades and Range Rovers and Navigators. There wasn't a single mini-van in the lot.

Ravel was put out that she could just barely squeeze her Porsche Boxster between two behemoth SUVs.

Like these other mothers, Sierra had dropped off her four-year-old daughter at the club's daycare center, which already had twenty children playing at art centers, computer stations, and climbing mazes. The play area resembled an ant hill gone Godzilla.

Most of the mothers went off to yoga sessions, spin classes, and private workouts with personal trainers. Sierra, though, preferred exercising alone on the club's expansive fitness floor.

Today, however, was a bonus for her: Sierra got to work out with Ravel, who normally avoided the soccer mom invasion. She admittedly had a harder time avoiding the company of Sierra.

Sierra and Ravel had made love on a few occasions. Sierra was so taken with Ravel that she suggested the two women move in together. Ravel prevaricated — she preferred a friends-with-benefits arrangement, since her greatest passion, though not reciprocated, was for Reed O'Hara. Sierra appeared satisfied with this arrangement.

Walking briskly on side-by-side treadmills, the pair of women was a study in contrasts. Ravel was thin, short, and a Swiss brunette. Sierra was muscular, tall, and a Swedish blonde.

Ravel wore a long-sleeve tee shirt and yoga pants. She insisted on wearing off-brand running shoes until they completely fell apart. Ravel bristled at anyone who called her cheap; she preferred "fiscally conservative."

Sierra, however, was resplendent in a floral pattern sports bra and bright green running shorts. She preferred ASICS running shoes, which she changed every two months.

Sierra didn't mind Ravel stealing a glance at her breasts, which bounced slightly with each step.

"Magnificent, aren't they?" Sierra said. "Remind you of the Swiss Alps?"

"Whatever, Sierra, I'm just browsing," Ravel said. "So you're on stakeout tonight?"

Sierra grinned at Ravel.

"Changing the subject quickly, I see," Sierra said. "And yes, I'm on stakeout this evening."

"When do you have to be there?" Ravel asked.

"At nine, and not a minute later," Sierra said.

Sierra took a drink from a water bottle.

"I know it's only the first night, but I have a feeling that this plan will work," Sierra said.

She didn't care for people describing her as a visionary or a psychic, but when Sierra had a feeling about a situation, it usually came true. One of the many reasons that Ravel and Sierra bonded was that they both possessed this near-psychic ability. The pair practically had entire conversations without uttering a word.

"You sense that you all will catch the killer tonight?" Ravel said, who obviously was intrigued.

"I do," Sierra said. "As crazy as it sounds, I sense this killer knows exactly what we're up to, and that he's up for the challenge."

"Well, good luck, babe, 'cause I know you'd rather perform than sit around watching over some dirty old priest," Ravel said.

"Sure, I'd rather perform, but I'd do whatever Reed asks," Sierra said. "Kind of difficult turning down the woman who saved my life."

Sierra's thoughts drifted off to when she first encountered Reed O'Hara.

Chapter Forty Six

And that wasn't an exaggeration about Reed saving her life, for Sierra had been dying steadily from heroin addiction, until Reed intervened.

Sierra had been a prostitute working primarily on Florida Avenue in the Seminole Heights neighborhood, which had retained its bungalow charm despite the influx of homeless people, prostitutes, and drug dealers.

Sierra had been spotted on Hillsborough Avenue by Nat Doliner, a corporate attorney who lived in Carrollwood, yet watched over several neighborhood watch groups that included Seminole Heights. By day, Doliner was a dedicated, scrupulous dealmaker in the corporate world. By night, he drove through various neighborhoods in his pearl white Lexus sedan, conferring with neighborhood watch captains, oftentimes doing the tiring legwork of looking out for burglars and muggers, drug dealers and users, pimps and prostitutes.

When Doliner saw Sierra, he knew right off that she was a drug-addled prostitute. As he approached Sierra, she thought she had a potential customer. Doliner quickly dissuaded her of that notion. Instead, he told her to leave Seminole Heights or he would call the Tampa Police Department. But just before she shambled off, Doliner gave Reed's business card to Sierra.

"Call Reed O'Hara," Doliner said. "She might be able to help you."

Sierra did, in fact, call Reed the next morning.

The two women met at an independent coffee shop on Florida Avenue.

It was eight in the morning, and Sierra clearly had been awake all night.

Sierra was a hot mess. Her arms bore bruises and track marks. Her long blonde hair was disheveled. She was thin and haggard. It would not be long before she was yet another victim of the revived heroin epidemic.

Reed bought a latte for Sierra, who put ten packets of sugar in her coffee. She was perfectly comfortable having empty sugar packets fall in her lap.

"Sierra, you're in rough shape, so I'll be firm, but kind," Reed said. "You need to stop using, and you need to stop selling your body. I can get you into a treatment program this morning. If all goes well, and you recover and get healthy again, I'll consider you for employment at my cabaret club."

Sierra began sobbing almost uncontrollably.

"Please, I need your help," she said. "My pimp is holding my little girl and he has my Swedish passport."

"No worries, Sierra," Reed said. "I'll have my husband Jake Dupree speak with your pimp. Jake can be a very persuasive fellow. Believe me, he will get your daughter and your passport.

Immense tears now were falling into Sierra's latte.

"I am so bad off, I'm going to have to trust you," Sierra said.

In the span of three months, Sierra overcame her heroin addiction, threw herself into an aggressive exercise and yoga regimen, and studied ballet.

After six months at Namaste, Sierra became one of the club's premier performers. She had become a portrait of health and vibrancy.

The only bad news from Sierra's renaissance was that Jake broke his right hand while persuading Sierra's pimp to release her from sexual slavery and to give back her daughter and passport. Jake didn't mind, as it was the third or fourth time he had broken his hand while trying to make a new friend.

Chapter Forty Seven

Sierra also became something of a lethal weapon.

She earned a first-degree black belt in tae kwon do at the same dojang where Reed studied the Korean martial art.

Sierra also achieved marksman status in semi-automatic rifles and pistols.

In fact, she planned on bringing her nine-millimeter Sig Sauer, along with her concealed weapons permit, to the stakeout.

Sierra and Ravel finished their workout at their athletic club. As they walked to the women's locker room, an attractive woman in her late twenties walked by them.

Ravel stared at the woman's backside for just a little too long; the woman turned her head and caught Ravel ogling her. The woman smiled at Ravel, who smiled back.

"Can you believe she's a *happily married* mother of three?" Sierra said.

"I don't know which is more unbelievable — that she's happily married or that she had three little monsters and still has a killer body," Ravel said.

Ravel and Sierra got undressed in the locker room, donned towels, and walked over to the large whirlpool. They dropped their towels and stepped naked into the hot, bubbling water. Both women let the hot, bubbly water envelop them.

Since they were alone in the whirlpool room, as the soccer moms were a good twenty minutes away from descending en masse on the locker room, Ravel and Sierra felt comfortable holding hands in the whirlpool.

"Ready to manage Namaste tonight?" Sierra asked.

"Yeah, I'm ready to rock," Ravel said. "I had to juggle the schedule and make a lot of phone calls, but it's all cool. I'll miss you, though."

Sierra squeezed Ravel's hand.

"You're up to something, though," Sierra said.

"What do you mean?" Ravel said in an archly innocent tone.

"I can feel it," Sierra said. "You've got something in the works."

"God, that's not a sixth sense you have, it's a Swedish seventh sense," Ravel said. "Yes, before I go over to Namaste, I'm going to check out a hunch of mine."

"What hunch?" Sierra said. She let go of Ravel's hand and began swirling her index finger in Ravel's navel.

"I've found five archery ranges around Tampa Bay," Ravel said. "I'm going to visit them this afternoon."

"Why?"

"I bet the PPK has been to one of the ranges, you know, to fine tune his crossbow skills," Ravel said, as she enjoyed Sierra's sensual touch.

"Does Reed know you're doing this?" Sierra asked.

"Nope, and I'm not going to tell her until later on," Ravel said. "I don't need her approval and it really pisses me off that I got excluded from the stakeout."

"Well, please be careful, my love," Sierra said. She again grasped Ravel's hand.

The two women got out of the whirlpool, showered, and got dressed.

As Ravel left the locker room, she spotted the mother of three getting dressed.

Ravel winked at her.

The mother of three dropped her towel, faced Ravel to show off her gorgeous body, and winked back at Ravel.

Chapter Forty Eight

It was almost nine p.m. before Reed and Rake had settled in their stakeout of Father Andrew Jones' bungalow in Seminole Heights.

Father Angel had pulled the private security from Seminole Heights and other targeted Tampa Bay communities. That left Jones and four other priests, albeit of slightly less ill repute than Jones, completely exposed to the priest assassin.

Over her smart phone, Reed informed Nat Doliner, the district neighborhood watch captain, that she and Jake would be in Jake's red Range Rover parked on Elm Street just fifty feet from Jones' bungalow.

"All I can tell you, Nat, is that we'll be on an investigative stakeout, probably all night," Reed said.

"No problem, Reed," Doliner said. "At least we'll know Elm Street will be watched over by the best in the business. How about I call off that street's watch team?"

"Perfect, Nat" Reed said. "Thanks so much." She ended the call.

"How about the Tampa Police?" Jake said.

"They're spread so thin, I doubt TPD will notice us," Reed said.

Reed sat in the driver's seat, even though it was Jake's Range Rover. Jake had long gotten over Reed's insistence that she preferred to drive, whether it was his auto or her black Mustang GT.

Jake understood that Reed was most powerful when she was in charge and in control.

What the hell, she's a better driver than I am, Jake thought.

Jake sat in the back of the Range Rover, behind the front passenger seat.

This seating arrangement gave the couple a near-complete view of the surroundings.

The couple brought satchels filled with gear.

Reed's leather satchel, which she bought for a thousand Euros at Galeries LaFayette in Paris, held a Browning nine-millimeter pistol, two spare clips, a retractable police baton, plastic flex cuffs, a pepper spray canister, a bottle of Fiji water, and six energy bars.

Jake's nylon satchel, which he bought for four dollars at a Ruskin flea market, held a Glock nine-millimeter pistol and two spare clips, an emergency medical kit, his tablet, a flashlight, a bottle of Voss water, a thermos of coffee, and a bag of trail mix.

Reed texted the other four teams that were staked out throughout Tampa Bay.

All four teams reported they were in position and hadn't yet spotted anything amiss.

Sierra, who was teamed with private investigator Ronda Aguilera to watch over Father Isaac Ludlow, texted Reed that Ravel was going to check out archery ranges before going to Namaste.

Reed exploded with Irish anger.

"God damn it, Jake, Ravel went rogue on us again," Reed said.

"How so, baby?" Jake said.

"According to Sierra, Ravel took it upon herself to snoop around archery ranges," Reed said. "It's a good idea, but she should have cleared it with us."

"Nothing wrong with taking a little initiative, Reed," Jake said.

"I understand that, but we've got a dangerous killer running amok, and don't forget Petrov — he's going to be looking for a payback after what you did to his Audi," Reed said.

"How'd you find out about that?" Jake asked.

"I got it out of Andre," Reed said. "And for obvious reasons, don't reimburse yourself for the concrete out of the Namaste expense account."

Jake snorted from the back seat as if he were French bulldog.

"Jake, you could try to sound more repentant," Reed said.

"All right, how's this: Father, forgive me, it has been way too fucking long since my last confession," Jake said. "I hope you've got plenty of time, because I have a ton of sins to confess, including filling Petrov's Audi with concrete."

"Are we talking of a cornucopia of sins, my son?" Reed said.

She was in the mood to play along with Jake's mock confessional. She clearly had gotten over being angry with Ravel.

"Yes, a big-ass cornucopia, oh, holy one," Jake said.

"Including marital infidelities?" Reed asked.

"Infidelities, no, lust in the heart, you betcha," Jake said.

"Lust, really. Lust for what or for whom?"

"Lust for my wife's perfect breasts," Jake said.

"That'll be enough of that, young man," Reed said. "Quietly — and I emphasize quietly — say ten Our Father's and five Hail Mary's, and you will be forgiven."

"Okee, artichokee," Jake said.

"Now please, let's get back to work," Reed said.

"*Mais bien sur, mon amour,*" Jake said.

"*I dteagmhail leis na foirne eile,*" Reed said.

"My god, Reed, your Gaelic has gotten so beautiful," Jake said. "And yes, I'll be glad to contact the other teams – only how about I wait about fifteen minutes since you just contacted them."

"Getting antsy already, aren't I," Reed said.

Chapter Forty Nine

Using his tablet, Jake sent e-mails to the other four stakeout teams, requesting they provide status reports.

Contessa and her husband Malio, observing Father Bertrand Bertolli in Dunedin in Pinellas County, reported that Bertolli was watching a hockey game on television and drinking heavily. No signs of trouble, they reported.

Andre and Tatiana responded next. They were assigned to Father Calvin Calhoun, who apparently was already in bed, his small house in Clearwater completely darkened.

Sierra and Ronda Aguilera were keeping an eye on Father Isaac Ludlow in West Tampa.

Nothing to report, Sierra responded.

Reed very purposefully paired Sierra with Ronda. They worked well together, and each woman was skilled in martial arts and firearms use. Both women liked each other, yet there was little chance of distractful sexual energy between them — while Sierra was gay, Ronda was a straight married woman and a mother of three children.

Ronda also provided a helpful perspective to this assignment: she was a devout Hispanic Catholic whose very religious foundation had been shaken, though not destroyed, by the Catholic priest scandals.

She provided Reed a useful historical perspective regarding this ugly tidal wave of child molestations.

"It's so simple and so sad, Reed," Ronda said. "The North

American Catholic Church desperately needed priests in the sixties. So the Vatican shipped its problem priests by the gross, mostly from Western Europe, to the United States."

The last team to respond was Elena and Roman, Reed's office manager. They were assigned to Father Paco Hernandez, who lived in St. Petersburg.

Elena reported that all was quiet.

Yes, all's quiet on the West Coast front, Reed thought. For now.

Reed couldn't get out of her mind Sierra's premonition that the killer would strike tonight, that the killer knew all about this stakeout, and that the killer wouldn't mind if he were caught by Reed and her cohorts.

I guess we'll see if Sierra's right, Reed thought, and she's usually spot on.

Jake had brought along a large thermos of French roast coffee. He poured them each a steaming cup.

Reed and Jake sat in silence in the red Range Rover as they sipped coffee in the darkness.

Talk about the fucking quiet before the storm, Jake thought, and man, I gotta quit cussing so much.

Chapter Fifty

It was almost three a.m. The five teams remained hard at it watching over the priests. Each team hoped it was its priest who was the most alluring bait in the trap set for the killer.

Keeping a watchful eye over Father Jones' bungalow, Reed and Jake stayed in constant contact with the other stakeout teams.

Nothing had occurred.

Unfortunately, the same could not be said at Namaste. The club had closed at 2:45 a.m.

Ravel was busy closing up.

Benecio, Andre's assistant, had watched over the departure of the performers and staff.

He smoked a cigarette in Namaste's parking lot as the caravan of sports cars, SUVs, motorcycles, and scooters left the property.

As soon as the performers and staff arrived home, they were to text Benecio that they were safe and sound.

The Namaste parking lot was empty now, except for Benecio's Ford F250 truck and Ravel's Porsche Boxster.

Benecio flicked his cigarette onto the parking lot and immediately lit another.

"Benecio, you know you're not allowed to smoke," Ravel said. She was standing only a few feet behind him.

Ravel startled Benecio.

He was aware he wasn't supposed to smoke. It was especially bad getting caught by Ravel, who was Namaste's quasi school hall monitor.

"Oh, you know, Ravel, I'm just nervous about being in charge of security tonight," Benecio said.

"Hmm, so alert are you, that I walked right up behind you without your noticing," Ravel said. "Does your smoking suggest you've compromised yourself somehow?"

Benecio took a deep drag from his cigarette. He exhaled an impressive plume of smoke that ballooned out into the chilly night air.

"Compromised? What are you talking about, Ravel?" Benecio said. He shook his head in disgust at her.

"Don't play games with me," Ravel said. "If you're in a jam, let's work together to get you out of it." Her tone had shifted from accusatory to conciliatory.

At two-hundred fifty pounds and over six feet tall, Benecio towered over the tiny Ravel. Yet his body language suggested he was intimidated by her.

Just as he was about to say something to her, a black Jaguar sedan pulled into the Namaste parking lot at a rapid pace. The Jaguar headed straight to Ravel and Benecio.

The sedan came to a screeching halt in front of Ravel.

It was too late for her to make a run for it.

Petrov's two bodyguards got out of the Jaguar. One of the bodyguards, the smaller one, opened the rear passenger door, then walked toward Ravel's Porsche Boxster. He held in his right hand a spray paint can; his other hand held a piece of paper.

The larger bodyguard walked toward Ravel.

"Benecio, what the fuck have you done?" Ravel said.

"Just looking out for myself, bitch," Benecio said. "When Petrov takes over Namaste, he's gonna make me general manager."

"Yeah, when Bavarian pigs fly," Ravel said.

She looked over at the smaller bodyguard standing in front of her Porsche Boxster. Staring at the piece of paper in his hand, he shook the can of spray paint. Then he sprayed "Lesmobile" in hot pink letters on the driver's side of the sports car.

"You fucking asshole," Ravel said to the bodyguard turned tagger.

"Let's go, you Swiss shit," the larger bodyguard said in Russian to Ravel. "Mr. Petrov wants to have a little fun with you."

Ravel smiled defiantly.

Then she took a police tactical baton from her pocket, snapped it open, and swiped at the bodyguard's knees.

Her aim was true. The bodyguard buckled to the right and yelled in pain. Ravel swatted the steel baton on the bodyguard's left shoulder, which brought him to his knees.

The other bodyguard saw what happened and sprinted toward Ravel.

Just as Ravel was about to run, Benecio struck her in the back of her head with his own tactical baton.

Ravel landed face first on the asphalt.

She was unconscious. Her small body lay in a tangled heap.

Benecio was tempted to finish off Ravel right there in the parking lot. But he restrained himself, because he knew Petrov wanted her alive. For the time being.

He called Petrov.

"Yes, we have her," Benecio said to Petrov over the phone. "I had to rough her up some, but she's alive. She hurt one of your boys, but he'll live, too."

Benecio stood over Ravel as he listened to Petrov's instructions.

Benecio nodded.

"Yes, I understand," he said to Petrov over the phone. "Just make sure you hold up your end of the deal."

The phone call ended.

Benecio looked at the two bodyguards, who were smoking while leaning against the Jaguar sedan.

"Guess you fuckers aren't going to help me," Benecio said.

No response from the bodyguards.

Benecio rolled Ravel onto her stomach. She remained unconscious.

A small amount of blood trickled from the back of her head and rolled down her neck.

Using plastic flex cuffs, Benecio handcuffed Ravel's hands behind her back. Just for sick kicks, he fondled both of her breasts.

Then he picked up Ravel and dumped her unceremoniously into the Jaguar's back seat. He used his right foot to shove Ravel's feet into the cabin. He slammed shut the car door.

Benecio took a few seconds to admire his handy work, then said to the Russians, "All right, let's do this — make it look real, but don't fucking kill me."

The smaller bodyguard flicked his cigarette, walked up to Benecio, and hit him square in the jaw.

Benecio fell unconscious to the ground. For good measure, the bodyguard kicked Benecio savagely in the ribs.

The Russians got into the Jaguar and drove away from Namaste. Ravel's tiny figure remained curled up on the back seat. She moaned slightly.

Chapter Fifty One

Everything went down too quickly at Namaste for Ravel to contact Reed. As a result, Reed and Jake sat in a darkened Range Rover in Seminole Heights, totally unaware of Ravel's kidnapping.

Besides, something was happening in Seminole Heights.

Reed became alert when a dog barked about thirty feet in the direction of Father Jones' bungalow, which was completely dark inside.

Reed noticed that the dog, which she couldn't see, began barking loudly, then suddenly stopped.

Jake spoke from the backseat.

"Reed, I know you heard that dog," he said. "Things are getting hinky out there."

"I agree," Reed said. "There doesn't appear anyone's out there, yet that dog starts barking, then stops abruptly."

Then Reed spotted a shadowy figure cross Elm Street and head directly to Father Jones' bungalow.

Even though the figure avoided the white glare of the street light, there was no way he wasn't aware of the Range Rover parked just fifty feet down the street.

It's as if he wants us to see him, Reed thought.

Reed unholstered her Browning semi-automatic pistol, flicked off the safety, and put the pistol back in its holster, which was clipped to her waistband.

She put her satchel, which still held the retractable police baton, flex cuffs, and pepper spray, over her left shoulder.

Jake pulled his black semi-automatic pistol and flashlight out of his backpack.

"Reed, should we call the police?" Jake said.

"Not just yet," she said. "We need to confirm this is the killer, take him alive, then we'll call the police."

"And will Father Angel get his audience with the killer?" Jake said.

"Yes, my love," Reed said. "A deal's a deal, after all. We capture the killer, we'll contact the police *and* Father Angel."

Reed and Jake stood in the thick darkness across the street from the priest's bungalow, which also was shrouded in darkness — the two large live oaks and the absence of a porch light made it easy for a person to approach the house undetected.

Outside of crickets chirping, there was no noise.

Reed tapped Jake's shoulder, then pointed to the house that was to the left of Father Jones' bungalow.

A large dog, perhaps a black lab, lay motionless on the house's front lawn.

"Now he's killing dogs," Jake said.

Reed raised her right index finger to her lips.

She thought she saw a figure moving to the rear of the priest's bungalow.

Both Reed and Jake clutched their pistols.

Then Reed heard a soft puffing sound followed immediately by an even softer whooshing sound.

Suddenly, Jake grabbed at the back of his neck. He yanked an object from his neck.

He and Reed stared at the object in his hand: it was a blow dart bearing black and white stripes on the shaft and a white puffball of feathers at the end.

Jake dropped the blow dart, stumbled forward, and did a face plant on the cement sidewalk.

Reed couldn't catch him in time.

"Mother of pearl!" she exclaimed.

Jake's head made an ugly thonking sound as it bounced off the cement walkway.

He began to bleed profusely, as his forehead had a gaping wound.

Reed dropped to her knees next to Jake. She took off her black leather jacket, then her black long-sleeve tee shirt. She rolled her tee shirt and wrapped the make-shift tourniquet around Jake's forehead.

"Jake! Try to stay awake," Reed said. "I'm going to get you an ambulance and get you to the hospital."

"I'm fine, don't worry about me," Jake mumbled.

The blow dart toxin and the fall on his head rendered him barely conscious.

"No, baby, you're not fine, you've got a very bad gash on your head," Reed said. "Time to pull out of this cluster fuck."

"Okay, Reed, whatever you say," Jake mumbled.

He now was barely coherent.

Reed dialed nine-one-one on her mobile phone, explained the emergency to the dispatcher, and requested both medical and police assistance.

Reed put down her phone and placed her arms around Jake. She pressed the tourniquet.

Then her phone rang. Caller ID indicated it was Ravel calling her.

Chapter Fifty Two

"What the hell, Ravel, this isn't a good time to call," Reed said into her mobile phone. "This better not be about being out of bar napkins."

Reed had pressed the speaker feature on her phone. She waited for Ravel's response as she continued to hold Jake.

Only Ravel didn't respond.

Petrov did.

"I don't give a shit if this isn't a good time to call," Petrov said. "Because if you don't cooperate, I'm going to slice this lesbian bitch into little pieces and send her back to you in a garbage bag. I'll throw in a twist tie for free."

Petrov giggled over the phone.

Reed was too stunned to speak.

"Listen, check out the text I just sent you," Petrov said. "I'll be glad to wait."

Reed switched to her texts, where she found a single photograph of Ravel: her mouth and nose were bloodied, and both of her eyes were closed by blackened hematomas.

Reed switched back to her phone line.

"Petrov, you fucking bastard, I'm going to hunt you down and end your miserable life," Reed said.

Petrov laughed hysterically.

"Stop, you're turning me on," he said. "Let's stay focused on the matter at hand — my becoming your partner at Namaste."

"Never, you bastard, never," Reed said with absolute certitude.

"In that case, I'm going to let my boys have their fun with Ravel, then I'm going to slowly put her out of her misery," Petrov responded.

"You're a sick fuck, Petrov," Reed said.

"Why thank you, O'Hara," Petrov said. "I take equal pride in my work and in my pastimes. You have forty eight hours to change your mind. I'll do my best to keep Ravel alive and my boys away from her tiny little ass."

"Petrov, call this off and send Ravel alive to me," Reed said. "Do that and maybe we can talk about Namaste."

"No deal," Petrov said. "But tell you what, as proof of life, I'll let you talk briefly with your little Swiss shit."

Petrov chuckled. Then Reed heard a muffled sound and Ravel came on the phone.

"Reed, don't deal with this asshole," Ravel said. "You can't let him get control of Namaste. And Reed, it's three women. Talk to Sierra. I love you baby."

"Oh, Ravel . . . ." Reed said.

Petrov abruptly came back on the phone.

"This lesbian lovefest is so sweet, but it's time to go," he said.

"Petrov . . ." Reed said.

"Enough talky, talky," Petrov said. "Think I'll have a chat with Ravel about these three women. I smell an opportunity or maybe it's only fucking fear I smell. But don't worry, O'Hara, I'll keep Ravel alive for forty-eight hours. We'll keep the bleeding to a minimum. The pain level, though? Well, that's another story."

Petrov laughed lasciviously.

Then there was silence.

Reed thought Petrov had hung up.

But he spoke again.

"Call me on Ravel's phone if you change your mind about Namaste. Otherwise, tick, tock, tick tock."

Then Petrov hung up.

Reed laid her phone on the sidewalk.

She refused to cry.

Instead, she held Jake close to her chest.

The sound of the sirens grew louder. The crickets in the darkness seemed almost to chide her.

Chapter Fifty Three

The two women clad in black heard the emergency sirens as well.

They had exited quietly from the rear door of Father Jones' bungalow. They stood in the complete darkness of the small backyard.

One of the women let out an impressive whippoorwill call.

A few seconds later, a return whippoorwill call, equally authentic, came from the shadows across the street and near Reed and Jake, who were huddled on the sidewalk.

Only five minutes earlier, the two women had dispatched Father Jones to the great beyond, insuring that never again would he harm a child.

While one woman, the taller of the two, stayed outside by the back door, the other woman jimmied the door, slowly opened it, and slipped inside.

The home smelled of spoiled food, dog urine, and incense.

Three empty wine bottles were lined up neatly on the small kitchen table. A twist cap was placed in the front of each empty bottle.

The kitchen sink was choked with dirty dishes. Cockroaches skittered in the sink.

A greasy frying pan and a pot half filled with tomato soup were on the stove top.

Next to the empty dog bowls on the kitchen floor was a shredded bag of dry food for large dogs.

That food must be for the sweet lab sleeping peacefully out on the lawn, the woman thought. Holy Mother, this man is such a pig.

The woman was barely five-feet tall and probably weighed less than one-hundred pounds.

She wore a black nylon head cover, exposing only her brown eyes.

She also wore a black nylon jumpsuit with matching boots that had soft rubber soles. She had on black nylon gloves with thick rubber grips in the palms.

A crossbow was slung across her back.

Around her tiny waist was a utility belt that held a large sheathed knife.

The woman walked stealthily through the kitchen, down the narrow hallway, and approached a partially closed bedroom door.

With her gloved index finger, she slowly pushed open the bedroom door. Thankfully, the door did not creak.

Father Jones was lying naked on his side on the disheveled bed.

There was an empty wine bottle on the nightstand. No glass.

Father jones was sound asleep. He was curled in fetal position with his back to the woman.

The naked priest was snoring loudly and emitting thunderous flatulence.

So gross, the woman thought, why are men such pigs?

She stood in the bedroom doorway and took the crossbow off her shoulder.

Her legs were slightly apart, her right foot a few inches forward of her left.

She aimed the crossbow at the sleeping priest, then fired an arrow into the base of his skull. There was only a slight pinging sound from the crossbow releasing the arrow.

Father Jones jerked, then moaned.

The woman fired a second arrow into the priests' back, right between his shoulder blades.

The third and last arrow entered the base of his spine. The priest twitched violently and groaned even louder.

Then it was over. In less than sixty seconds, the priest's life force and tattered soul left his body.

No more twitching and moaning. No more snoring and farting.

The woman stood over the corpse.

"See you in hell, Father Jones," she said, as she crossed herself.

The woman quietly left the bedroom, backtracked through the hallway and kitchen, and exited through the back door.

Her partner, the taller woman who was dressed similarly and had a crossbow as well, was down on one knee and scanning the backyard.

"Is it done?" she said in a tone replete with sadness and anger.

"Yes, his death was slow, painful, and much deserved," the shorter woman said.

"Preaching to the choir, my dear," the taller woman said.

The shorter woman allowed herself a slight giggle.

"Time to go," the taller woman said.

The sound of the sirens was getting louder.

The two women climbed nimbly over a side fence, went through the backyard of the bungalow next door to Father Jones', and came around to the front, not fifty feet from Reed and Jake.

Reed appeared totally focused on Jake. She held him, gently rocking him. She seemed to be speaking to him.

The two women stealthily crossed the street and quickly moved between the two bungalows fronting Father Jones' house.

Reed didn't appear to notice them; she was focused entirely on her injured husband.

The two women met up with their accomplice, also a woman dressed in identical apparel. Instead of a crossbow, this woman had a long dart gun on her back.

The trio heard the police cruiser and the fire and rescue ambulance pull up to the dead priest's bungalow.

They slipped away into the welcoming darkness.

The crickets never lost a beat.

Chapter Fifty Four

Ravel was so beaten down that it required only about thirty minutes for Petrov to learn everything he needed to know.

His bodyguards had delivered Ravel to Petrov to a large air-conditioned storage unit in Claire-Mel City, a tired, trodden community located east of the Port of Tampa. At one time a pleasant lower-middle class community, Claire-Mel City had devolved into a community of crack houses and meth labs.

Petrov's unit was in a large storage park off 78th Street. There were a few people milling about the multiple rows of storage units. Security was a tight as a prison. And no one was stupid enough to interfere with Petrov. He kept closed the sliding garage door and his bodyguards sat in lawn chairs in front of the unit.

Inside the storage unit, an overhead fluorescent light cast brutally bright light upon a grisly scene.

There were four fifty-five gallon steel drums lined up against the back wall. Three of the drums were soldered shut. The fourth drum was empty, its lid resting against the side of the drum.

The air conditioner wall unit kept the unit at seventy degrees.

Despite being shirtless, Petro was perspiring heavily. Rivulets of sweat streamed down his balding head. His body tattoos, most of which he had acquired while in Russian prisons, gave him a look of demonic menace. Each of his tattoos boasted of horrible accomplishments and deviant deeds.

Ravel was in an office chair. Her arms, waist, and legs were duct taped to the chair. Her face was bleeding badly. She sat slumped in her chair and was barely conscious.

Petrov was surprised at the toughness of this tiny woman.

He had ripped open her shirt, cut her bra, and applied pliers to her chest.

Ravel screamed in pain, yet she refused to answer Petrov's questions.

Petrov applied more pressure with the pliers.

More screams, but no answers.

One tough little bitch, Petrov thought. Humph, she hopes her screams will bring someone, but in this ghetto, no one fucking cares.

But he had to be careful with Ravel. Being so small, she could take only so much punishment. Petrov didn't want to kill her just yet. His goal was to work her over, photograph her, then contact Reed O'Hara.

So that's why Petrov struck Ravel with an open hand. And the multiple vicious slaps produced the desired effect: Ravel's nose and mouth were bleeding badly.

Before Petrov had called Reed on Ravel's phone, he was concerned that he had slapped Ravel too hard and too often. If her jaw were broken, she'd have a hard time talking to Reed.

But turns out, Ravels' jaw wasn't broken, and she was able to speak with Reed.

Now Petrov needed to find out about those three women.

Ravel resisted at first; eventually, though, she gave up everything.

After all, Ravel had no training in withstanding torture. She wasn't an operative or a field agent or a soldier. She simply was an alienated renegade who had found safe harbor in Reed O'Hara's world. Now she was trapped in Victor Petrov's steel house of horrors.

Petrov used a bamboo switch on Ravel. He swiped her repeatedly with the switch across her neck, shoulders, and chest.

She first began whimpering, then broke out into full howls.

Petrov knew he had her right in the sweet spot, where the human spirit goes to die.

"Talk, Ravel, and I'll stop hurting you," Petrov said.

Ravel nodded weakly. Petrov had won.

First, she explained to Petrov why Reed and Jake were on a stakeout in Seminole Heights, how a Father Angel from the Vatican had hired them to find the priest killer.

"That's very good, Ravel," Petrov said, as he held the bamboo over her. "Now tell me about these three women."

As Ravel spoke — mumbled, really — a bloody drool ran from her mouth. She barely could speak in complete sentences.

Petrov followed everything Ravel said, though. Much like a dentist, he had considerable experience understanding people he had just tortured.

Lead 'em right to the precipice and pull 'em back, Petrov thought. The shits will see me as their savior and tell me everything. Everything. Every time.

"The first four archery ranges . . . . didn't have anyone . . . . practicing with crossbows," Ravel said. "Owner of the fifth range — all the way out in fucking Polk County — said three women awhile back had used crossbows."

Petrov lacerated Ravel's head with the bamboo switch.

"Bitch, did I give you permission to use nasty language? No, I did not," Petrov said. "Address me in a civilized tongue."

Petrov instinctively knew he couldn't permit her to use obscene language. Ravel cussed as easily as breathing, so he couldn't let her have any sense of normalcy or equilibrium. He must keep her teetering on the edge, with himself as her only lifeline.

"I'm sorry . . .I'm sorry," Ravel said. "No more bad words . . . . I promise . . . ."

"Good, now continue, shithead," Petrov said as he tapped the bamboo switch against his leg.

Ravel nodded eagerly.

"The range owner said the three women seemed like lesbians —

way they looked at each other seemed kinda intimate like," Ravel said. "One of them even called the tall one 'sister' and the tall one told her to hush."

Holy shit, Petrov thought, this all make fucking, beautiful sense.

Ravel looked up at Petrov and saw his facial expression change from disdainful skepticism to wide-eyed recognition.

"That's right, Petrov," Ravel said. "The priest killers are three nuns, three cross-bow bearing, mother fuckin' nuns."

This time Petrov didn't strike her with the bamboo switch.

Chapter Fifty Five

Tampa homicide Detective Peter Langdon found Reed O'Hara in the waiting area of the Tampa General emergency room.

Reed was sitting with Judi Ploszek, a close friend and Chief Financial Officer at Tampa General Hospital. The two women had been close friends and confidants for over ten years.

Judi held Reed's hand as she spoke in a low voice, trying to console a distraught Reed.

After being rendered immobile by a blow dart, Jake suffered a serious gash to his forehead, and he had lost a lot of blood.

A sixth priest had been assassinated, on Reed's watch and practically right in front of her. The killer had gotten away again.

And Ravel: Petrov had kidnapped her and hurt her badly.

At this point, Reed was ready to surrender.

She just wanted Jake to make it through his injury.

She was willing to give away Namaste in order to save Ravel.

And she would return Father Angel's retainer and allow the entire deal to crater.

Reed confessed all of this to Judi, a devout Catholic, a tough Chicagoan, and a superb listener.

Judi had had enough of Reed's pity party.

"Damn it, Reed, quit feeling sorry for yourself," Judi said in a firm yet loving tone. "Now isn't the time to make important decisions. You're upset, you're exhausted, and you're not thinking clearly."

Judi gave Reed a sly smile, then she raised her eyebrows.

Reed smiled weakly at Judi, then nodded in agreement.

She was about to speak when a pudgy, rather slovenly, man approached the two women.

"Ms. O'Hara, I'm Detective Peter Langdon," the detective said. "We need to talk — alone."

Fast as a whippet, Judi turned around to the detective.

"Pete, can't you see that Reed has her hands full right now?" Judi said.

Reed looked at Judi and raised her eyebrows quizzically.

"You two know each other?" Reed said.

"Oh yes," Judi said. "Pete and I went to Notre Dame at the same time."

"So how are you, Judi?" Langdon said. "It's been awhile."

"I'm well, Peter. I see you're still carrying that piece of crap Smith and Wesson thirty-eight," Judi said.

"Hey, I got no complaints about my service revolver," Langdon said. "You still carrying that twenty-two in your right trouser sock?"

"Yes I am," Judi said.

"Gold plated?" Langdon said.

"Rose gold, actually," Judi said. "Now, do you really have to speak with Reed?"

"I sure do," Langdon said.

Reed patted Judi's arm.

"No worries, Judi," Reed said. "I really should talk with the detective."

Judi rose from her chair, glared at Langdon, and walked off without saying a word.

"Ms. O'Hara, I know my timing is lousy, but I have only a few questions," Langdon said. "Then I promise to get out of that beautiful hair of yours."

Langdon was short and about thirty pounds overweight. He wore a wrinkled University of South Florida tee shirt with jeans. His gold shield was hooked to his belt, as was his holstered Smith & Wesson .38

Special revolver. He wore Jordan 12s.

"Detective Langdon, please forgive my dear friend Judi, she tends to be over protective," Reed said.

"No problem, Ms. O'Hara," Langdon said. "I'm used to it, nobody's ever happy to see me, even my dog."

Reed chuckled.

"Detective, please call me 'Reed.'"

"Only if you call me 'Pete.'"

"You have a deal, Pete."

Chapter Fifty Six

Detective Langdon stared at Reed, at her bright blue eyes and blonde hair, at her high cheekbones and flawless skins. And her smile — so warm and inviting.

He admired her zipped up leather jacket, jeans, and tiny hiking boots, maybe the smallest hiking boots he ever had seen on a woman.

And he was impressed with how quickly Reed collected herself. As he approached her, she clearly was distraught. Yet here she was sitting in front of him, appearing calm and friendly.

The picture of poise, she is, he thought.

Langdon had heard about Reed O'Hara's mercurial Irish-American temperament, how she could switch from Old Testament wrath to New Testament charm in a flash.

Better be careful with this one, Langdon thought, but Christ, is she a babe.

"So what's on your mind, Pete?" Reed said.

Fucking in love with you, that's what's on my mind, Langdon thought.

"I, uh, need to interview you about what happened tonight," Langdon said. "May I sit down?"

"Yes, of course," Reed said. She waved her manicured hand to a chair next to hers.

The detective noted the Rolex watch on her left wrist and the impressive diamond on her left ring finger.

Langdon sat down and took a second glance at Reed's diamond ring. "So how is your husband doing?" Langdon said.

Reed, of course, knew that the detective was ogling her, and also saw him looking at her diamond ring.

Out came her Mona Lisa smile.

"I think he's going to be okay, Pete," Reed said. "He suffered a nasty concussion, and he'll need a baker's dozen of stiches to close the gash on his forehead."

"Oh, good, good," Langdon said. "I mean, not good that he needs so many stiches, but good that he's okay."

So smooth, Langdon thought, no wonder I never get laid, even by my wife.

Reed put her hand on the detective's knee.

Langdon shuddered just a bit, just enough for Reed to notice.

"I know what you meant, Pete, and thanks for inquiring about Jake," Reed said.

Lady, please don't take your hand off my knee, Langdon thought. Damn it, she did.

"I heard Jake took a blow dart to the neck," Langdon said.

Reed sat up and folded her small, delicate hands into her lap.

"Yes, it caught us totally by surprise," Reed said. "I like to be prepared for any situation that arises, but it's a bit much to anticipate a blow gun."

"The dart's toxin wasn't potentially lethal, right?" the detective said. "It just knocked out Jake, right?"

"The dart probably was meant to knock him out, but he's a large, fit man, so it incapacitated him without rendering him unconscious."

"Do you think this was the work of the priest killer?" Langdon said.

"Absolutely," Reed said. She maintained a serious expression on her face.

"So for some reason, the killer incapacitates Jake, doesn't do anything to you, then proceeds to pop Father Jones full of arrows from a freaking crossbow," Langdon said.

"That's a fairly accurate description of what occurred, at least from my vantage point," Reed said.

"Police and medical show up, killer disappears, Jake goes to Tampa General, and here you sit in the ER waiting room," Langdon said.

"Yes, that's right," Reed said.

"Why do you think the killer used a blow gun on Jake?" Langdon said. "Why not pop an arrow in him?"

"You know full well why, Detective," Reed said, her bright eyes narrowing. "The killer disabled Jake in order to disable me. Somehow, he knew I wouldn't abandon my husband."

Langdon ignored Reed's sarcastic tone.

"Get you two out of the way and Father Jones is dead meat?" Langdon said.

"Yes, but you already knew that, didn't you?" Reed said.

"Yeah, I sorta thought that was how it went down," the detective said.

Chapter Fifty Seven

"Any more questions, Pete?" Reed said.

"Only a few more," Langdon said. "I appreciate you're concerned about your husband and you're probably exhausted, so how about I get to the point."

Reed leaned forward, very purposefully showing some cleavage, as she had on only her bra underneath the leather jacket. She had been in too great a hurry to replace the tee shirt she used for Jake's tourniquet.

Langdon noticed Reed's cleavage, as well as the smears of Jake's blood on her chest.

What did the guy say to the beautiful woman in a bar, Langdon thought, oh yeah, you must be Irish, cause my cock is a Dublin.

"Yes, Pete, let's get to the point, so I can get back to focusing on my husband's well-being," Reed said.

Jesus, she's pulling me both ways, Langdon thought, and I kinda like it.

"Sure, all right," the detective said. "So you and Jake were on a stakeout, right? Why were you watching over Father Jones?"

Reed paused, then responded.

"As I'm sure you know, I am a licensed private investigator, and . . ."

"An attorney, too, right?"

"Yes, Pete, but I was at Jones' house strictly as a PI. Jones now is the sixth retired priest to be murdered in Tampa Bay. I was hired by an interested party to find this priest killer. Jones seemed as if he were the probable next target. Turns out, we were right," Reed said.

She kept her perfect posture and hands folded — a veritable engraving of earnestness.

"Does your interested party not have faith in the task force specifically charged with finding this killer?" Langdon said.

"Of course, my client has faith in you all," Reed said.

Is she actually batting her eyelashes at me, Langdon thought, she's working me, and I can't help falling for it.

The detective shook his head, trying to re-focus.

"Pete, my client believes that the police have their resources and that I have mine," Reed said. "My client is doubling down on apprehending the killer."

"I guess that makes sense, but now that Father Jones is dead and the killer got away, what's your next move?" Langdon said.

"I can't really say," Reed said in a voice of earnestness squared.

"Hmm, all right, so why do you think these priests are being murdered?" Langdon said.

"I think it's Al-Qaeda," she said with faux sincerity.

Langdon couldn't help from laughing.

"I sure as shit hope not, Reed, then we'd have to add Homeland Security to the task force," Langdon said. "We'd need a bigger boat."

Reed laughed.

"Nice *Jaws* reference, Pete," she said.

"Thanks, but seriously, Reed, don't you think this is all the work of one seriously pissed off former altar boy?" Langdon asked.

Reed smiled at the detective, held up both hands, and said, "Truly, it's one possibility, but I don't know for certain at this point."

Then, right at that moment, Reed experienced an epiphany — she realized, while talking with this homicide detective at Tampa General Hospital, who the killers are.

"You okay, Reed?" Langdon said. "You seem distracted all of the sudden."

"No, I'm fine. Will there be anything else?" Reed said. She couldn't get this interview over sooner.

The detective pretended to study his notepad. He made some squiggly marks in his pad. He began tapping the notepad with his pen. Mostly, he simply was sneaking another glance at Reed's cleavage.

Man, what I would give to tap that, Langdon thought.

"Is there any way you'd tell me who your client is?" Langdon said.

"Really, Pete, I can't. You know that. Let's just say it's a concerned individual who wants this killer stopped," Reed said.

"All right, but if you catch the killer before we do, do you promise to turn him over to law enforcement?" Langdon asked.

"Absolutely, you have my word," Reed said. She held up her right hand as if she were being sworn in.

Chapter Fifty Eight

"Well, all right, then," Langdon said. "Oh yeah, you're carrying, aren't you?"

"Yes, Pete, I have a Browning nine millimeter in a holster on my right hip," Reed said. "I also have my concealed weapon permit in my back pocket. Would you like to see my CWP?"

"Yes, I would. Please." Langdon said.

Reed reached into the back pocket of her jeans and handed the permit to Langdon.

The detective carefully examined the permit.

"Looks good to me," Langdon said. "Now, may I see the Browning?"

"Why?" Reed asked.

"To make sure the permit and the weapon match," Langdon said.

Reed smiled slightly.

"I won't produce my sidearm out in full view," Reed said. "That's illegal and you know it. I can pull out my pistol only if I intend to use it to defend myself."

"Fine, fine," Langdon said. "Looks like the lawyer in you is coming out."

Reed shrugged.

I yam, what I yam, she thought.

"Tell you what, just open your jacket enough so I can confirm you're carrying a Browning."

Reed's smile broadened — she knew exactly what the detective had in mine.

"No problem, Pete," she said.

Reed unzipped her black leather jacket and opened it a few inches. Her right breast showed through her sheer white bra.

The detective appeared to look at the holstered pistol.

"That's a Browning, all right, and it's a beauty," Langdon said.

Reed closed her jacket and zipped it quickly.

"Which, Detective? My Browning or my right tit?" Reed said.

Langdon's face flushed.

"Both, actually," he said.

I think that was a major fucking mistake, he thought.

Reed sat straight up and put both hands in her lap.

"I think that concludes our interview, Detective," Reed said.

"Hey, I didn't mean anything there," Langdon said. "I was just being Henry David thorough — it's my job, you know."

Reed stared right into Langdon's eyes.

"It very well *could* be your job if I decided to speak with your superiors about this little sexual shakedown," Reed said. "Now piss off, shit bag."

Langdon shot out of his chair, stuffed his notepad in his back pocket, and left without saying a word.

Judi saw the detective briskly walk away. He appeared to mutter to himself.

The emergency room's glass doors swooshed open and the detective was gone.

"Game, set, and match, my dear?" Judi said to a still-seated Reed.

"Righto, Judi," Reed said.

Judi sat down next to Reed. She held two lattes, and handed one to Reed.

"Just what I needed," Reed said.

She popped the lid from her cup and took a healthy drink of coffee. Reed had a pencil-thin coffee mustache on her upper lip.

"So what happened?" Judi said, motioning to Reed to wipe her lip.

"Langdon tried to cause trouble, but he let his cock get in the way of his investigation," Reed said. She wiped her upper lip with a napkin.

"And did you have anything to do with getting him off track," Judi said.

"Maybe a little," Reed said.

"Maybe a lot?" Judi asked.

"Okay, maybe a lot," Reed said.

Judi laughed, then patted Reed's shoulder.

"That's my girl," Judi said. "A true feminist knows when to apply feminine wiles."

Reed took another sip of her latte.

"Didn't I read that somewhere on a tube of spermicide?" Reed said. "Or underneath a Snapple bottle cap?"

Both women laughed.

"And that idiot detective actually helped me to realize who the priest killers are," Reed said.

"Do tell," Judi said. She leaned toward Reed in a conspiratorial manner.

"First things first, let's check on Jake. I only hope he didn't hear us laughing out here," Reed said.

Chapter Fifty Nine

Reed got Jake back to the condominium by ten the next morning.

She had his prescriptions filled at Tampa General's pharmacy.

Now it was time to get him plenty of rest and recuperation.

"Jake, you need to get into bed and take your meds," Reed said. "You've had one helluva night."

"We both have . . . and Ravel, too," Jake said.

Reed nodded sadly. Ravel's situation weighed heavily on her.

With Reed's help, Jake crawled into their king bed. She pulled the white duvet up to his chest. Reed was tempted to crawl in bed with her man, but she knew she had important work to do.

She gave him tablets of antibiotics and painkillers, which he took with Acqua di Nepi mineral water.

"Those painkillers are going to knock you out in a few minutes, my handsome Frenchman," Reed said. "So I'm going to be quick here in what I have to tell you."

"It's about Ravel, I hope," Jake said.

"Yes, my love, it's about Ravel — we're going to get her back, alive," Reed said. "We're not going to do another fucking thing about the priest killers until we have Ravel home. Do you understand?"

Despite feeling groggy, what with the painkillers mixing with the remaining blow dart toxin, Jake fully understood Reed.

"Right, I got it," he said. "We're going to focus entirely on Ravel. You know, I want you back as much as she does . . . I mean . . . ."

Reed smiled at Jake, then held his large hand.

"I shouldn't have given you a painkiller before we talked, but I wanted you to be comfortable," she said.

Jake squeezed Reed's small hand.

"I'm a little loopy doopy, but I'll keep it together, no worries," he said. "Now, what have you decided to do about Ravel?"

"Ravel means more to me than Namaste," Reed said. "That's saying a lot, since we've helped so many women through Namaste."

"Right," Jake said, struggling to stay awake.

"We're going to give up half of Namaste to Petrov in exchange for Ravel," Reed said.

"Jesus, babe. I know we have little choice here, but Petrov as a partner?" Jake said. "In six months, he'll push us out and turn Namaste into a sleazy titty bar."

Reed now held Jake's hand with both of her hands. She appeared to be clutching a catcher's glove.

"First things, first," she said. "We get Ravel back. Alive and well. Whatever it takes."

"And what about Petrov?" Jake said.

Jake's head was starting to droop.

"I'll see to that, in time, Petrov will no longer be a problem for us," Reed said.

"What'd ya shay?" Jake said.

"Get some rest now, my love," Reed said.

Jake was sound asleep in seconds.

Reed left their bedroom to make the call to Petrov.

She hoped that she wasn't too late, in that Petrov couldn't control himself with Ravel.

Chapter Sixty

Father Angel had agreed to meet with Petrov at Bahama Breeze, a seafood restaurant at Rocky Pointe on the Tampa Causeway. Petrov sat by himself at an outdoor table. His bodyguards sat at a nearby table.

Petrov liked Bahama Breeze because it had decent food and attracted a lot of young women to the outdoor bar and dance floor.

Father Angel was running late, as usual.

Petrov's mind began to wander. He thought of an extraordinarily good night at Bahama Breeze about a month previous.

Jesus, it's big boner time every time I think of that bitch, he thought.

He had come across a woman who was by herself and, though probably in her early twenties, looked as though she were sixteen.

Despite Petrov being much older than she, the young woman was attracted to his good looks, his Russian accent, and his apparent wealth.

She noticed each time Petrov flashed his solid gold Rolex.

She noticed each time he pulled out a fat wad of Benjamins to pay for yet another bottle of Dom Perignon.

And she noticed every time his hand grazed her large facsimile breasts.

What she did not notice, however, was the packet of crushed Rohypnolor Roofies that Petrov slipped into her glass of Champagne.

Petrov knew he had less than five minutes to get her out of the restaurant and into his Audi.

Wouldn't look good dragging this bitch out of here by her two big feet, he thought.

He signaled to his two bodyguards.

With a bodyguard on each side of her, she wobbled out of Bahama Breeze. No one appeared to notice the quartet leaving.

She appeared as if she were a person who had too much to drink.

Petrov made certain not to make eye contact with anyone as he led his entourage out of the restaurant.

The bodyguards got the young woman into the Audi only seconds before she passed out.

Petrov drove to the storage unit in Clair-Mel City.

The bodyguards carried the young woman into the storage unit. They stripped her of her clothes, then hung her in shackles by her arms.

She was starting to regain consciousness.

Petrov was shirtless and barefoot.

He never spoke a word to the terrified young woman.

Slowly and deliberately, Petrov struck her with a hickory cane.

She emitted loud screams with each blow.

At first, Petrov focused on the young woman's torso, arms, and legs. Then he began striking her head.

After fifteen minutes of this horrible beating, she was dead. Petrov appeared to climax during her final breaths.

While toweling off his perspiration and her blood from his head and chest, Petrov instructed his bodyguards to put the dead woman's body into one of the four barrels lined up in the back of the storage unit.

After carefully folding her body into the barrel, which was half full of muriatic acid, the bodyguards welded shut the lid to the barrel.

Only one empty barrel remained. In a few weeks, it would be filled with yet another of Petrov's victims.

Then the bodyguards would have to make yet another late-night boat ride out into Tampa Bay. They did their best to dump the barrels in the same area of the bay. "Reef building" was how Petrov jovially described the barrel disposals.

"Hey, I'm all about the ecology," he said.

Petrov's mind wandered back to the present. He looked at his gold

Rolex: Father Angel was nearly thirty minutes late.

He was getting agitated, as he wanted to close the deal with Father Angel before the West Tampa business lunch crowd arrived at Bahama Breeze.

Petrov ordered another cappuccino.

Fucking Italians, he thought. Lazy and late, the whole bunch of them.

What's an Italian salute, he thought, oh yeah, hold up both arms straight up in the air. That's a Ukrainian salute, too. Hmm, what a handy, dandy joke.

Chapter Sixty One

Father Angel finally arrived at Bahama Breeze. Two young men, wearing polo shirts and khakis, walked behind the priest.

Probably a couple of those Swiss fairies that guard the Vatican, Petrov thought.

Petrov stood to greet the priest.

"Father Angel, I am Victor Petrov. Thank you for agreeing to see me on such short notice," Petrov said.

The two men shook hands.

Father Angel sat down at Petrov's table.

Petrov signaled for the waiter, who promptly came to the table.

"Bring us your best white wine," Petrov said. "And then bring us plates of crab cakes and those delicious coconut shrimp."

The waiter acknowledged the order, then stepped away.

There was no one else seated on the open-air deck, except for the four bodyguards, who shared a table.

Now we get down to fucking business, Petrov thought.

"Padre, I am the answer to all of your problems," Petrov said.

"Including my sciatica?" Father Angel said.

Petrov laughed a little too loudly.

"Sure, why not," Petrov said. "I'll give you one of my special treatments — get your mind off the sciatica."

"Thank you, but I'll pass on that offer," Father Angel said.

Fucking pervert sitting across from me, he thought.

"Ah, both our losses, then," Petrov said.

"You told me over the phone that you know who is killing our beloved priests, and that you could produce this killer," Father Angel said.

Petrov was about to speak when the waiter arrived with a bottle of pinot grigio and two wine glasses.

The waiter showed the wine to Petrov, who nodded his approval. The waiter opened the bottle, poured a small amount into Petrov's glass, then waited for Petrov to taste the wine.

Petrov drank the wine in a single gulp, smacked his lips, nodded his head, and held up his glass for the waiter to fill.

Father Angel subtly shook his head at Petrov's crudeness.

Petrov, though, caught the priest's disdain.

"Relax, padre, you can take the Cossack out of the Steppes, but you can't take the Steppes out of the Cossack," Petrov said.

This time, Father Angel laughed a bit too loudly.

"You were about to say something, Victor, before the server arrived with our wine," Father Angel said.

Petrov took a large gulp of wine, then wiped his mouth with the back of his hand.

"Yes, you see, I know who's the priest killer, which I have learned from a very reliable source," Petrov said. "And I can deliver this killer to you, with proper consideration, of course."

"Who is this very reliable source?" Father Angel said.

Petrov gulped more wine.

"That's proprietary," he said. "But I'll divulge that this source isn't a snitch. I happened upon this person and, in the course of enhanced interrogation, I extracted everything I needed to know about the killer of your six precious priests."

Father Angel took a modest sip of wine.

"And how much do you know about our deceased brothers in Christ?" he said.

Petrov slammed his wine glass on the table.

"Spare me the papist rhetoric, padre," Petrov said. "I know these boys had some hobbies that embarrassed your church. I know you've gathered the worst of the worst, or the best of the best, depending on your tastes, and plopped them right here in sunny Tampa Bay. 'Exodus' is what you call your little program, right? Thought you could keep a better eye on them if you had them all in one place, right? You plan on setting up these hinky kinky settlements all over the warm and sunny parts of these United States, right?"

Chapter Sixty Two

Father Angel was nonplussed at how much Petrov knew about Exodus, and what Petrov knew was entirely accurate.

"Just who was it that you interrogated so effectively?" Father Angel asked.

Petrov drank more wine, then smiled at Father Angel.

"Sorry, can't say," he said. "Besides, why do you care? Aren't you more concerned about stopping this vigilante?"

Father Angel took a larger sip of wine.

"Yes, of course," he said. "So, are you confident you can deliver this killer to me? Alive?"

"Absolutely," Petrov said.

"How much, Victor?" Father Angel asked.

"I'm not going to be greedy, padre. One million U.S. dollars will do. Half now, then the other half due upon delivery of the assassin. And that price includes disposal of the body, once you've had whatever fun you have planned for this person," Petrov said.

Petrov poured himself another glass of wine. He offered the bottle to Father Angel, who declined.

"Victor, I am not in the mood to negotiate your price. I don't want any more of my brothers to die," Father Angel said.

The waiter brought plates of crab cakes and coconut shrimp. He placed them in the center of the table and walked away briskly — this waiter knew instinctively that these men didn't want to chit chat with the hired help.

"That's good news, padre," Petrov said, as he piled crab cakes and shrimp onto his plate. He then offered the remaining seafood to Father Angel.

Father Angel paid no attention to the seafood. Instead, he took another small sip of the wine.

"Padre, wire me five-hundred grand this afternoon and I will give you your killer in forty-eight hours, alive of course," Petrov said. "Here's my business card."

"You have a deal, Victor," Father Angel said, as he took the business card from Petrov.

"Superb," Petrov said. "Just a few questions, then — simply for my edifaction."

"Edification," Father Angel in a tutorial manner.

"Huh?" Petrov asked.

"You meant 'edification,'" Father Angel said.

"Yes, '*edification*,'" Petrov said. "Thank you, padre, but the next time you dare to correct me, my price will double."

Father Angel sighed.

"What are your questions, Victor?" he asked.

"First, will you call off Reed O'Hara?" Petrov said.

"Why?" Father Angel asked.

"Answering a question with a question," Petrov said. "Seems like a technique more common with Jews than with mackerel snappers."

"But why should I call off Ms. O'Hara?" Father Angel said, ignoring Petrov's bigotry.

He clearly couldn't believe how much Petrov knew.

"Because I don't want her interference, and you don't want any more delays," Petrov said. "Think about it: inside of two days, if I can maneuver without that Irish bitch getting in my way, all of your problems will be over."

Father Angel totally capitulated.

"Fine, I'll terminate my agreement with Ms. O'Hara," the priest said.

"Thank you," Petrov said. "So what will you do with the killer once he's in your custody."

"Simply interview him, allow him to confess his horrible sins, then turn him over to the secular authorities," Father Angel said.

Petrov laughed so heartily that a piece of crab cake flew out of his mouth and onto the table.

"What complete bullshit," Petrov said, banging his fist on the table. All four bodyguards warily looked at Petrov.

"You know fucking well that you and those two faggots over there are going to put a bullet in his head, chop him up, and dump him in the bay," Petrov said.

Father Angel's bodyguards started to rise from their table, but the priest waved them off — he could see that Petrov's bodyguards making ready to confront his men.

"Victor, how can you say such a thing?" Father Angel said.

"Because, padre, it's what I'd do, in a Moscow minute. And you and me, we're not so different. I can read people, you know. You may be a little more classy than me, what with your holy robes and spouting fucking Latin, but you're still a stone-cold killer who will do whatever it takes to get the job done. You thought that bitch O'Hara could be your local connection. What a fucking disaster that was. But now you've got me. I'll deliver your priest killer. And I know full well you'll have me dispose of the body. See, soup to nuts, it's all going to work out now that Petrov is in the kitchen."

"I sure as fuck hope you're right, Victor," Father Angel said.

Petrov laughed heartily.

Father Angel rose from the table and left with his bodyguards. He didn't say goodbye to Petrov, who didn't seem to care about this slight.

"More goodies for me," Petrov said, as he tore into the remaining crab cakes and coconut shrimp.

Man, what a good fucking day this turned out to be, he thought.

Chapter Sixty Three

Reed and Jake were in their penthouse condominium in downtown Tampa when Father Angel called.

The couple was relaxing in the living room, drinking strong Italian roast coffee and listening to Vivaldi's *The Four Seasons*. Until Jake was back on his feet, Reed would play only classical music.

Jake was recovering well: no infection from the gashed forehead, the stitches were holding, and he was following the concussion protocol of resting with no physical activity.

It was a toss-up as to who was more disappointed, Jake or Reed, since they couldn't have sex for a week.

"Doctor's orders, I guess," Reed said. "but I've already calendared next Friday for having my way with you."

"Good, now I have something to live for," Jake said.

Reed's mobile phone rang; caller ID showed it was Father Angel calling.

Reed pressed the connect button,

"Hello, Father Angel, how are you?" she said.

"I am well, Ms. O'Hara, but I understand Mr. Dupree was injured while attempting to apprehend the killer," Father Angel said. He did his level best to connote sincerity.

"Yes, Jake is recovering from a nasty cut to his head and a fairly serious concussion," Reed said. "He's home now, and I expect him to make a full recovery. Thank you for inquiring about him."

"As the Spanish say, '*de nada*,'" Father Angel said.

"I sense, though, you called for reasons other than my husband's health," Reed said.

"Yes, I have," Father Angel said, "And let me say that I admire your directness — it's so classically American."

"As you know, I'm Irish-American, making me double the trouble sometimes," Reed said.

Father Angel laughed softly over the phone.

Finally, a woman worth fighting, the priest thought.

"Double the trouble, indeed, Ms. O'Hara," he said. "Allow me to be candid, then. As you might have surmised, I am upset that the killer took the life of Father Jones, and that you failed to capture this evil person."

"Yes, I'm troubled as well," Reed said. "It's as if the killer were waiting for us."

Proper use of the subjunctive tense, Father Angel thought, that's so intellectually sensual. Is it possible I'm succumbing to this woman's allure? No, no, no, put that thought in a tiny box and push it down, down, down.

"The only key people who knew of your stakeout plan was you, Mr. Dupree, and myself," Father Angel said. "I'm confident the killer did not learn of your plan from me. That leaves the possibility of a leak emanating from your camp."

Reed gripped the mobile phone tightly.

"Father Angel, I, too, am confident that the leak, if there were one, did not come from me or from my people."

"Then it appears we have a stalemate, Ms. O'Hara," Father Angel said.

"Yes, we do," Reed said.

"I cannot allow any more of my brothers in Christ to be murdered — six is quite enough, thank you," Father Angel said. "So I am afraid we need to go in a different direction."

"Father Angel, are you firing me?" Reed asked.

"I am afraid I am, Ms. O'Hara. You have not produced the results I expected," Father Angel answered.

"We've gotten very close, and we have new information that will aid us in planning the next stakeout," Reed said.

"There won't be another stakeout, Ms. O'Hara, but please be so kind as to give me this new information," Father Angel said.

You'll get some of it, but not all, you Vatican prick, Reed thought.

"It appears these murders are not the act of a single killer; rather there are at least three killers," Reed said.

"I see, that will be helpful — anything else?" Father Angel said.

"No, that's all," Reed said.

"In that case, you may keep the initial payment of two-hundred fifty-thousand dollars," Father Angel said. "Naturally, we will not pay the second quarter-million dollars."

"That's generous of you, Father Angel. I'm sorry we cannot move forward together," Reed said.

There was a pause, then Father Angel spoke.

"Move forward together? Am I to infer you will proceed with this matter on your own?" he asked.

"Absolutely, we'll proceed unilaterally. After all, you've paid us handsomely for a job not yet done. And besides, it's personal now, since they attacked my husband — it's an Irish thing, you know," Reed said.

"Ms. O'Hara, I absolutely forbid you to go forward with this matter. A requirement for your keeping the initial payment is that you go away, *pura e simplice*."

This time, Reed paused, then spoke.

"No, it is not pure and simple, Father Angel. As soon as we conclude this conversation, I will wire the initial payment to your Vatican account. No longer will I be beholding to you; I will then pursue this case as a private investigator acting on her own behalf."

Father Angel let out a guttural sound.

"Listen to me, you bitch, stay the fuck away! I have new people in place, and they won't like your interference. For your own personal safety, and that of your husband's, back off — completely."

Reed chuckled

"Such language for a man of God," she said. "Tell me, do you kiss your mother with that mouth? And you just threatened me. Diplomatic immunity will make for a lousy umbrella against the shit storm you're about to experience, you pimp for pedophiles."

Father Angel could only sputter over the phone.

"I promise you, Father Angel, I will find the killers before you do," Reed said. "And I'll turn them over to law enforcement before you can get your hands on them. Just for kicks, I might inform some journalists what I know about your Exodus program."

There was no pause this time.

"You fucking bitch, you wouldn't dare," Father Angel said. "Do you have any genuine idea with whom you are dealing? I am darkness incarnate."

"I do have an idea, Father Angel. I'm dealing with a worldwide religious organization so filled with hubris it cannot deal honorably with institutionalized perversion," Reed said.

"The Holy Church is addressing this problem," Father Angel said. "Can't you see that, you Protestant cunt?"

"Go to hell, Father Angel," Reed said.

She pressed the end button on her mobile phone.

Well, that went swimmingly, she thought, Jesus, why can't I control my temper?

Chapter Sixty Four

Jake overhead Reed's half of the conversation with Father Angel.

"Sent the old boy down the road to perdition, did you, my fiery Irish rose?" Jake said.

Reed was too angry to smile even slightly.

"That sonuvabitch fired me, then he threatened me," Reed said. "I could just choke him with a rosary."

Reed rarely exploded with such anger — she valued maintaining her composure in the worst of situations.

Sometimes, though, a woman has to explode, she thought.

Jake understood Reed's tempest would pass soon, so he gently reasoned with her.

"Choking him with a rosary is so apropo, Reed, but why risk going to prison over a sleaze bag like that?" he said.

Reed muttered to herself, then smiled at her husband.

"You're right, Jake," she said. "Say, would you mind sending that man's retainer to his Vatican Special Projects account?"

Jake opened his laptop and began typing on the keyboard.

"Done, and done, my love," Jake said.

"You, sir, are just grand," Reed said. "Now we are free of Father Angel, though I doubt we've seen the last of him."

"Yes, but let's concentrate on Ravel," Jake said. "You've called Petrov, told him you were willing to give up half of the Namaste in exchange for Ravel. What's next?"

Reed hugged Jake tightly. She truly didn't want to let go of him.

"We meet at Namaste at four p.m. today — only you, me, Petrov, and his attorney Jasper Conway, are allowed at the meeting."

"I take it there will be legal documents involved," Jake said.

"Yes, Conway is preparing them," Reed said.

"No one's allowed to bring weapons to this meeting, correct?" Jake said.

"That's right, I've agreed to our not being armed, and Petrov agreed to do the same," Reed said.

"Do you trust him?" Jake asked.

"God no, but he's got Ravel, so we'll play by his rules," Reed said. "After all, what choice do we have?"

"And what about Andre?" Jake asked.

"He's not happy about this arrangement, and Petrov demanded that Andre not be at the meeting," Reed said.

Jake sat forward, groaning slightly with pain.

"Tell me again, or for the first time — these damn meds have me so turned around — why the police won't be involved," he said.

"Because a police presence could further endanger Ravel," Reed said. "I've come to realize that Namaste is only bricks and mortar, dollars and cents, all of which pales against getting Ravel home."

"I understand, my love," Jake said.

"Thanks," Reed said. "Listen, I know this is extortion, and it makes me nauseous to consider Petrov a Namaste partner. But, baby, it's all about the process, one that we control, even though it might appear right now that we're not in control. And the first step of this process is getting Ravel back."

Jake perked up, as he was quite adept at reading between Reed's lines.

"Hmm, something tells me you have a plan," Jake said.

Reed ran her index finger down the length of Jake's prominent nose.

"Your French nose is so sexy," Reed said. "Goodness, I'm shocked at what I'm thinking of doing."

Jake gently moved Reed's finger from his face.

"Cut it out, Reed," he said. "You're trying to distract me for some reason, and I assure you that it's working, but what are you up to?"

"Fiddle dee dee, Rhett Butler, I've no idea what you're talking about," Reed said. "Is a lady not allowed to be provocative?"

Reed actually batted her lashes at Jake.

Jake took Reed into his arms, kissed her passionately, then said, "Baby, your power over me is inestimable, but I know you're cutting me out, *oui?*"

Reed sat back on the sofa and folder her arms across her chest.

Tears welled in her eyes, a rarity for Reed.

"*Ta,*" she said.

"Yes, indeed, I thought so," Jake said. "Let's have it Reed. First and foremost, we are a team. We have each other's back. It's our unified light that staves off the ugly, awful darkness. Let me hear your plan."

Tears rolled down Reed's high cheeks.

She sat silently, then uncrossed her arms and held Jake's hands.

"What I intend to do is unethical, immoral, and illegal, that's why I don't want the police involved, it's just . . . ." Reed said.

Reed cried so heavily that her body heaved.

"What is it, Reed, you can tell me anything," Jake said. "I don't judge you, I love you."

Jake wiped the tears from Reed's face with his hand.

"I don't want you to think I've given up on my principles, it's important you love me AND respect me," Reed said.

"I'll always respect you no matter what, and I'll always love you no matter what," Jake said. "I expect the same from you — *qui est notre grand compact.*"

"Truly?" Reed said.

"Truly," Jake said.

Reed lightly kissed Jake's lips, then bussed both of his cheeks.

"All right, Jake, we have four hours before we meet Petrov and Conway," Reed said. "Here's what we're going to do."

For the next twenty minutes, Reed laid out her plan to Jake, who sat in rapt attention. He held his chin with his right hand. Both he and Reed leaned toward each other as she spoke.

As Reed finished, she chopped her right hand into the palm of her left hand.

Serious business this is, Jake thought, let the deadly game begin. I only hope she is thinking clearly. Logic and emotion can make lousy bed partners.

Chapter Sixty Five

Reed and Jake arrived at Namaste at three p.m.

The couple settled into Jake's office.

Jake busied himself with preparing a pot of coffee, opting for a West Coast medium roast.

Reed sat at Jake's desk; she appeared lost in thought.

Namaste wouldn't open until seven p.m. The performers and staff would start assembling at the cabaret club no earlier than five p.m.

But Andre had been at Namaste since six a.m. He slept fitfully since Ravel's disappearance. He sat in his office, where he scanned the wall of security camera monitors, hoping against hope that Ravel would miraculously appear on one of the monitors, that she had come home to Namaste.

For Andre loved Ravel passionately, as if she were his daughter.

When Andre and Ravel first met, a tight bond developed instantly. They liked each other; they understood each other.

And why wouldn't they?

They were both castoffs — Andre was half Russian and half African American; Ravel was an unmoored, brilliant Swiss lesbian who was in the United States illegally and had no real home or family. They were a perfectly matched eccentric pair.

Namaste had brought together these two very different, yet similar, people.

Andre constantly fussed over Ravel, and he never made an untoward advance on her.

Ravel tolerated Andre's over protectiveness because she knew he meant well, that he sought nothing in return except for an occasional kind word from her or a gesture from her that suggested she appreciated him.

Ravel and Andre were always a formidable team, each bringing to the fight a fierce intelligence and a clear-eyed sense of the world.

So when Petrov kidnapped Ravel, Andre felt both a great loss and an uncontainable, seething anger.

It had been more than three years since Andre had killed a man. He knew that streak was in jeopardy with Petrov and his goons.

Reed had to use all of her persuasive powers to convince Andre that it was best for Ravel that he stay away from Petrov.

"There's a deal on the table to get Ravel back," Reed said to Andre, who had come in unannounced to Jake's office. By just marching into the office, without even a knock on the door, Andre clearly was distraught over Ravel. "We are going to hold up our end of the deal, Andre," Reed said.

"You're right, Reed," Andre said, "I don't think I could control myself with Petrov — he's hurt my baby bird."

"Which is exactly why you can't be at this meeting," Reed said. "I want you to drive over to St. Pete Beach, take a long walk on the beach, watch the sundown, and when you come back we'll have Ravel."

"Promise?" Andre said. A large tear rolled down his left cheek.

"We promise," Jake said, as he handed cups of coffee to Andre and Reed.

"You'll be safe with the Russians?" Andre said. He wiped off the tear from his face and regained his composure.

"We'll be safe," Reed said. "All of us have agreed to go unarmed to the meeting. I believe the proceedings will go peacefully, primarily because it's in everyone's best interest that there's no stupid gun play."

Tears welled up again in Andre's eyes.

"If you say so, Reed, then I'll do what you want and go to St. Petersburg," Andre said.

Turns out, it would be the first time that Andre had lied to Reed.

St. Petersburg be damned, Andre thought. I'll stay out of sight, but I won't leave Ravel and Reed and Jake exposed. I am on the Job.

Andre finished his coffee, said goodbye, and left Namaste.

Thinking all was resolved with Andre, Reed lingered over her coffee, all the while considering the myriad of details involved with the Petrov meeting.

"Jake, did you put our pistols in the safe?" she asked.

"Yes, dearest," Jake said.

"Surveillance system up and running?" Reed said.

"Yes, oh great one," Jake answered dutifully.

"Ready to stop being a smartass?" she asked.

"I am now," Jake said.

"Oh goody," Reed said.

Petrov and company were expected shortly.

Reed and Jake sat in silence and drank their coffee. Their shared quiet soothed each of them.

Chapter Sixty Six

Attorney Jasper Conway was twenty minutes late for his meeting with Petrov at the storage unit.

He hated visiting the place.

Talk about a steel box full of hell, he thought.

The first time he came there, he saw the row of four steel drums, and one drum already was sealed. He knew instinctively that one of Petrov's victims was inside the barrel. When he got home that night, he vomited uncontrollably, then he drank whiskey uncontrollably. He didn't get a good night's sleep for a week.

Conway was late for this meeting because he felt the need for several shots of whiskey to bolster his courage.

He pulled up to the storage unit in his leased Cadillac CTS. When he got out of his car, he immediately felt wobbly.

God knows how many fucking barrels are filled now, Conway thought.

He banged once on the sliding garage door, banged twice, then three times.

The door rolled up.

The larger bodyguard stood in the entrance way. He said nothing to Conway, who looked past him and spotted Petrov sitting on a folding chair.

The smaller bodyguard sat on another folding chair across from Petrov.

Ravel was between the two Russians. The tiny woman was chained to a heavy-gauged steel chair, which was bolted into the concrete floor.

Bloodied but breathing, Ravel sat slumped in the chair.

Thank you, Jesus, at least she's still alive, Conway thought.

"Why the fuck are you so late, shit bag," Petrov said.

Time to kick fat boy around, he thought.

The larger bodyguard slammed shut the garage door.

Conway jumped at the loud bang.

"Sorry, man, I had some stuff to take care of," Conway said. "Took me longer than I expected."

"What bullshit!" Petrov said. "You smell like a goddamn distillery. What'd you need, bourbon soaked balls to come here?"

"Maybe," Conway said sheepishly.

"You fucking pussy," Petrov said. "Good thing you're too fat to fit in that barrel. Course, I could have my boys chop you up real nice."

"Oh god, Petrov," said Conway, who thought he was going to get sick.

"You puke, fat boy, and I'll make you lick it up," Petrov said.

One day, this Russian creep is going to push me too far, Conway thought, and I'll see to it that he goes away forever.

"I'm sorry, Petrov, really I am," Conway said. "I won't get sick and I won't be late again."

Petrov chuckled.

"No worries, shit bag, I was only half kidding about chopping you up," Petrov said. "I still need you — for now."

Conway wiped perspiration from his brow.

"Sure, sure, whatever you say, Petrov," Conway said.

Petrov drank from a large plastic bottle of Publix spring water.

"Okay, fat boy, have you prepared the contract?" he said impatiently.

"You bet, the documents are in my Caddie," Conway said.

"You seem to have something on your mind, Conway," Petrov said.

Petrov and his bodyguards paid no attention to Ravel, who appeared semi-conscious.

Conway sensed that Ravel was feigning delirium and was listening to every word spoken. His instincts told him to be reticent around her.

"Yeah, well, I wanted to make certain about those last-minute changes to the contract," Conway said. "You're sure you're okay with them?"

Petrov threw his half-finished jug of water at Conway and hit him in the head.

First tennis balls, now water bottles, what's next, knives? Conway thought.

"Shit bag, how dare you question me," Petrov said. "Do as I say, and don't doubt me again. I know exactly what I'm doing, believe me, I got the vision thing going on."

Conway rubbed the welt on his forehead.

Both bodyguards laughed at him.

"Sorry, man, I guess I deserved that bonk in the head," Conway said.

You're gonna deserve it, Petrov, when I blow the brains out the back of your head, Conway thought.

"Whatever, fat boy, I could care less if you think you deserve my punishment," Petrov said.

Couldn't care less, you cretinous clown, Conway thought.

"Right, well, I'm ready to go whenever you are," Conway said.

"Whatever, lard of the ass," Petrov said.

Christ, is he doing this on purpose, is he baiting me into correcting him? Conway thought.

Petrov turned to his bodyguards.

"Get the computer set up," Petrov said in Russian to them. "Make sure the bitch is centered in the foreground, with the barrels in the background."

The bodyguards nodded in agreement.

"Just for the shits and giggles, cut up her shirt, so her titties are showing, and hang some chains directly behind her," Petrov said, continuing to speak in Russian.

"*Da, da, babushka,*" the smaller bodyguard said.

"That'll scare the shit out of O'Hara," Petrov said to no one in particular.

Conway nodded anyway.

He recalled to himself the ass kicking Reed inflicted on him in her law office.

Petrov, you're grossly underestimating that woman, Conway thought.

"Let's go to Club Nasty in that crappy Cadillac of yours," Petrov said.

Petrov and Conway left Ravel with the bodyguards, climbed into the Cadillac, and sped off for the night club.

Chapter Sixty Seven

At exactly four p.m., Petrov and Conway pulled up to Namaste.

It was pleasantly warm for a late winter afternoon in Florida. The sea breeze was coming in from the Gulf of Mexico, yet there was little chance for rain this time of year.

Petrov got out of the Cadillac, took off his sunglasses, and looked up to watch a pair of magnificent Sandhill cranes fly over Namaste.

"Crazy birds mate for life," Petrov said disapprovingly to Conway.

Andre was across the street at a small strip mall. He had parked in a space that was off to the left side of the strip mall businesses. With his back to Namaste, Andre watched Petrov in his rearview mirror. He wasn't worried anyone from Namaste would spot him, since he had borrowed a friend's pick-up truck. He wondered if this were the first time he had ever driven a pick-up.

That's right, Petrov, you watch the pretty birds and I'll watch you, Andre thought.

The only other car in the Namaste parking lot was Jake's Range Rover.

Petrov paused to study the Range Rover.

Love to give the Rover a cement bath, wouldn't you, Andre thought.

Finally, Petrov and Conway entered Namaste.

Let the games begin, Andre thought.

He speed dialed Sierra's mobile phone number.

"Hello, Sierra, it's Andre," he said.

Sierra said something to him over the phone. Andre nodded his head while keeping an eye on Namaste in the rearview mirror.

"Yes, I'm all set on this side," Andre said. "The calvary will be arriving shortly. And don't forget to contact Langdon."

Andre nodded in agreement again over what Sierra said to him on the phone.

"All right, my beauteous Swede, let's cross our fingers that this works out," Andre said. He pressed the "end" button on his phone.

Andre put his mobile phone in his leather jacket, then caressed the American Eagle fifty-caliber handgun holstered under his left shoulder. He had paid over two-thousand dollars for the handgun, and he felt it was worth every penny.

Time for a Sunday-come-to-Jesus meeting, he thought. Have to admit, sometimes I do love the Job.

Chapter Sixty Eight

Reed and Jake sat at a table in the center of the cabaret nightclub.

The stage was unlit, as was the long granite-top bar.

The only lights on were over Reed and Jake's table.

Petrov and Conway were doing their level best not to walk into chairs and tables as they made their way unsteadily to Reed and Jake.

"Jesus fucking Christ, O'Hara, your electric bill too high this month?" Petrov said.

Reed waved to Petrov and Conway.

"Walk toward the light, gentlemen," Reed said. "Don't be afraid, it isn't yet Judgement Day."

"Whatever, bitch," Petrov muttered.

Conway banged into a table.

"Fuck!" he shouted, rubbing his leg.

Eventually, Petrov and Conway made it to Reed and Jake's table.

"Anyone else hiding in this goddam potato cellar?" Petrov said.

"Nope, only me, Reed, you, and chubby," Jake said.

"I don't have to take that off of you, Dupree . . ." Conway said.

Petrov cut off Conway.

"Yes, you do, fat boy," Petrov said. "I'm letting you sit at the grown-ups table only because you've got paper shuffling to do."

Petrov and Conway sat down across from Reed and Jake.

"Let's get this freak show going," Petrov said.

"First, the preliminaries," said Reed, who was seething with anger yet staying controlled.

"Like what, sweetheart?" Petrov said.

"Are you armed?" Reed said. "And call me 'sweetheart' again and I'll tear off both your ears."

"Whatever, O'Hara," Petrov said. "No, we don't have any weapons, unless you're concerned I'd use porky's big gut as a battering ram."

Reed couldn't refrain from a slight smile.

God, he's an asshole, she thought, but sometimes a pretty funny asshole.

"Where is Ravel, Petrov? I need proof of life before I sign this deal," Reed said.

This time, Petrov smiled, though in a decidedly lascivious manner.

"No problem, O'Hara," he said. "Ravel is alive and . . . well, she's alive. Allow me to bring her up on my laptop. We have her safely tucked away. We'll bring her here as soon as we close the deal on Namaste."

"Whatever, Petrov, let's have a look at the documents while you attempt to use your computer," Reed said. Petrov nodded to Conway, who dutifully opened his briefcase, pulled out a file, and handed it to Reed.

"Everything should be in order here," Conway said.

Reed laid the file on the table, opened it, and began reading the contract agreement.

When she finished reading the first page, she handed it to Jake for his perusal.

Meanwhile, Petrov called up a streaming video of Ravel on his laptop.

Reed was into the third page of the agreement when she looked up at the image of Ravel on Petrov's laptop.

Reed was horrified at the image.

The bodyguards dutifully had set up a little shop of horrors exactly as Petrov had ordered.

Ravel remained taped to the chair that was bolted in the cement floor.

Her blouse and bra were shredded, exposing her scratched and swollen breasts.

Three steel chains dangled directly behind her.

The four barrels loomed in the background. The fourth uncovered barrel loomed ominously.

Ravel raised her head and looked directly at the camera. Her face was bruised and bloody.

Jake leaned forward in his chair and stared at Petrov.

"You asshole, you agreed to turn over Ravel as we sign the agreement," Jake said.

Petrov glared at Jake.

"What makes you think you can swear at me, Dupree?" Petrov said. "You're nothing but a bitch to this bitch." Jake was about to jump across the table and snap Petrov's neck, when Reed put her hand on his forearm.

"*Ne prenez pas l'appât, mon amour,*" Reed said.

Jake lowered his head for a few seconds. "You're right, Reed, he is baiting me — I'll try not to bite," he said.

Petrov smiled.

"That's a good boy, you fucking French poodle," Petrov said. "I'm going to deal only with your master."

"You'll need both of our signatures, Petrov," Reed said. "Play nice and let's get this over with, all right?"

"*Da, konechno, pochemu net,*" Petrov said.

"What did he say?" Reed said.

"He said, 'yeah, sure, why not,'" Jake said

Reed raised her eyebrows at Jake. She obviously was impressed with Jake's translation skills.

"Andre's been teaching me Russian," Jake said, as he shrugged his shoulders.

Suddenly, Ravel spoke into the camera.

"Reed, don't do this, Petrov's going to screw you over, then kill me and put me in that empty barrel — those barrels are already full of other women," Ravel said.

An off-camera voice said, *"Zatnut' sya, korovu,"* and a large hand slapped Ravel across her face.

"Tell them to stop, Petrov," Reed said. Her face was flushed, but there were no tears.

"O'Hara, I have no idea what Ravel is talking about," Petrov said. "And I don't have complete control over what my boys do. Let's just get this deal done."

"You hurt Ravel again and the deal's off," Reed said.

"And I get to kick your ass," Jake added.

"Stop, Dupree, your barking is scaring me, little puppy," said Petrov, who shuddered mockingly.

Reed looked at the laptop camera.

"Ravel, hang tough," Reed said. "We're going to get you home. Stay strong. Just nod your head. No more talking."

As tears streamed down her face, Ravel nodded her head in agreement.

Both Reed and Ravel realized they were staring right in the ugly face of complete and utter defeat.

Chapter Sixty Nine

Reed was reading the agreement when she stopped on page six.

"Whoa, Petrov, you said you wanted fifty percent of Namaste; it states here that we are to sign over seventy-five percent of the business — are you out of your goddamn mind?" Reed said.

Petrov furrowed his brow and turned up the palms of his hands.

"*Da, da*, O'Hara, a little last-minute change due to my understanding just how badly you want this Swiss bitch," he said.

"That's it!" said Jake, who lunged across the table at Petrov.

Though Petrov didn't react, Conway moved surprisingly fast for an overweight middle-aged man. In a flash, he pulled a revolver from inside his suit jacket and placed the barrel against Jake's temple.

"It's only a twenty-two caliber, Dupree, but at this distance I can scramble your brains with one shot," Conway said. "May not kill you, but it'll sure as hell turn you into one big eggplant."

"Big eggplant — I like that, fat boy," Petrov said. "And relax, Dupree, sit back down and behave yourself."

Petrov didn't notice it, but Reed did: as Jake appeared to calm down and return to his chair, he gave an odd glance to Conway, who had put away his small revolver.

Are Jake and Conway up to something, Reed thought.

Yet she didn't say anything. That was a golden rule of hers: don't speak until a situation is fully understood.

"Here's how this will go down, O'Hara," Petrov said. "First, you verbally agree to sign over control of Namaste to me for one dollar, then I'll have Ravel driven over here — as you sign the agreement, I'll release Ravel in the parking lot, then all of you mother fuckers get the hell off my new property. You can come back for the next board of directors meeting, which'll be never."

Reed smiled at Petrov while anger flared in her bright blue eyes.

Jake looked admirably at Reed.

That's it, my love, maintain your self-control, this should be over soon, Jake thought.

"Fine, Petrov," Reed said, "I agree to sign over Namaste majority ownership in exchange for Ravel."

"Good, and here's your dollar," Petrov said.

He handed a tattered dollar bill to Reed. The bill had been torn in two and was held together with a piece of shipping tape.

Petrov pulled out his mobile phone and called his bodyguards.

Over the phone, he spoke in Russian in a brusque manner.

Reed could see on the laptop video screen Petrov's bodyguards: the short one was on his phone with Petrov; the tall one stood next to Ravel.

As Petrov barked his commands over his phone, the short bodyguard nodded his head enthusiastically.

The phone conversation ended. The tall bodyguard, having received instructions from his shorter cohort, began cutting away the tape that held Ravel in the chair.

Reed and Jake watched on the laptop as the bodyguards handed Ravel a change of clothes, then motioned for her to get up and remove the filthy, torn clothes she was wearing.

Ravel cooperated — she took off her clothing and stood naked before the laptop camera.

Reed was horrified at the numerous cuts, abrasions, and bruises on Ravel's frail, small body.

She refused to show her horror in front of Petrov, who stared at Reed in anticipation of her gasping at Ravel's condition.

"Some of my better work, eh?" Petrov said. "Ravel was a tiny canvas, but I think I got in the right number of brushstrokes. I really should do more work with miniatures."

"Don't you mean breaststrokes?" Conway said.

"Shut the fuck up, fatty," Petrov said. "And by the way, who the hell told you to bring a gun to this party?"

"It's called taking initiative, Petrov," Conway said.

"No, it's called almost fucking up my deal, you stupid asshole," Petrov said. "I don't want to see that little girl gun again, got it?"

Oh, I got it all right, you Russian cocksucker, Conway thought, soon, maybe soon, you're gonna get it, too.

Conway nodded obediently to Petrov.

Reed studied the interaction between Petrov and Conway. She sensed a fissure developing between the two men. She considered how she might exploit this situation.

Curiously, Jake appeared not to pay any attention to the angry squall forming around Petrov and Conway.

Chapter Seventy

The tall bodyguard then made a gesture of kindness to Ravel: he handed her a clean hand towel and a bottle of water, then stood facing the laptop camera, thereby giving Ravel a modicum of privacy as she washed herself.

The short bodyguard sat in a chair. He paid little attention to Ravel.

"Thank you, Petrov," Jake said.

"Hey, don't thank me, Dupree," Petrov said. "Looks like I got more people taking the initiative, 'cause if it was up to me, I wouldn't let Ravel have one shred of dignity — go soft in this business and you get killed."

"Sounds like prophesy to me," Jake said.

"Huh?" Petrov said.

"Never mind," Jake said.

What a fucking moron, Jake thought.

Within five minutes, Ravel had cleaned herself and changed into fresh clothes.

The tall bodyguard stepped aside and Ravel stood before the laptop camera.

She wore a white tee shirt, gray sweatpants, and what appeared to be children's purple flip-flops.

Ravel was haggard and weak, though her spirit didn't appear broken.

"Look at that, good as new," Petrov said. "It's a gift of mine, really — inflict maximum pain, leave minimum damage. Truly, I'm a fucking artist."

"No, you're not an artist," Jake said. "You're a sociopath with a thumb for a penis who over compensates by hurting women."

Petrov flushed with anger.

"A tiny cock, huh?" he said. "Allow me to introduce you to my bullmastiff."

With that, Petrov reached for the zipper on his pants.

Reed held up her right hand.

"Please, Petrov, we don't need to see your penis," she said. "Let's do the exchange, *da*?"

Petrov shrugged and took his hand away from his pants zipper.

"Your loss," he said to Reed.

He called his bodyguards, again giving commands in Russian.

The laptop live stream showed the short bodyguard on his mobile and nodding vigorously.

He and the tall bodyguard each took one of Ravel's arms and led her off screen.

The laptop video screen showed only an empty chair, hanging chains, and the row of steel barrels, the entire scene resembling an abandoned set for a snuff film.

Petrov stood up from his chair. There was a Napoleonic air to his manner — he was in charge now, and everyone would obey his commands.

"It won't be long before Ravel and my boys arrive," Petrov said. "We'll all gather in the parking lot. You two sign the contract and at the same time we'll hand over the little Swiss shit." Then he sat back down.

For a quarter hour, Reed, Jake, Petrov, and Conway sat in silence. The only sounds were the usual creaks and groans of a nearly empty nightclub — the central air system clicked on and off as the ice re-settled in the bar bins.

Reed and Jake reviewed the agreement that, upon their signing it, would result in their nearly complete loss of Namaste.

"I see that you'll permit Jake, if he so chooses, to stay on as interim manager for forty five days," Reed said to Petrov. "How generous of you."

"Hey, I got a big heart, you know," Petrov said.

Despite the nightclub staying steady at a cool sixty-eight degrees, Conway kept wiping perspiration from his brow with a stained linen handkerchief.

Once again, Conway stole a furtive glance at Jake, who surreptitiously acknowledged the glance.

And once again, Reed picked up the signal exchanged between the two men.

Petrov, though, was so oblivious that he kept himself occupied with picking his nose and wiping the boogers on Conway's suitcoat sleeve.

Conway did not react to Petrov's crude bullying. Reed sensed an odd zen about the man.

Petrov's mobile phone lit up. He answered it, saying only, "*Da, da.*" Then he disconnected the call.

"My boys are outside with Ravel, so let's go," Petrov said.

Reed took out a small remote, pressed a button, and all the lights came up in the night club.

"Wouldn't want you two gentlemen to take a tumble on the way out," she said.

Jake chuckled.

"Kiss my ass, O'Hara," Petrov said.

"Never going to happen, Petrov," Reed said.

Zen master Conway stayed silent.

Chapter Seventy One

The foursome filed out of the nightclub and stepped into the glaring late afternoon Florida sunlight.

Petrov's Jaguar was parked in the middle of the Namaste parking lot.

Conway's Cadillac and Jake's Range Rover were the only other cars in the parking lot.

Traffic was getting heavier on Lois Avenue, as people were heading home from work.

No one appeared to notice Andre sitting in his friend's pick-up truck across the street.

Reed, though, spotted Ravel, who was leaning against the Jaguar, a bodyguard on each side of her.

Reed's impulse was to rush over to Ravel. Yet Reed and Jake both stood at the cabaret entrance, not wanting to provoke the bodyguards.

Reed stared at Ravel.

The poor soul, she looks even worse out in the daylight, Reed thought, but at least she's still alive.

The two women nodded to each other, acknowledging the awful indignity of the situation.

"Go ahead, O'Hara, blow her a kissy kiss," Petrov said pruriently.

"Up yours, Petrov," Reed said.

In her peripheral vision, Reed sensed that Jake winked to Ravel, who pursed her lips in acknowledgment of Jake's tell.

215

Again, she restrained herself from saying anything to Jake — after all, she didn't want to alert Petrov.

Besides, Conway had handed the agreement's signature page, which was attached to a clipboard, to Petrov, who hardly looked at the page before signing it.

Petrov handed back the signature page, then put Conway's pen in his shirt pocket.

"Think I'm gonna need the pen for O'Hara and Dupree to sign," Conway said sheepishly.

"Whatever, shit bag," Petrov said as he handed back Conway's pen.

Conway handed the pen and clipboard to Reed and Jake.

The couple carefully read the signature page, then signed it, thereby turning over majority ownership of Namaste to Petrov.

Conway placed the executed contract in a red-rope folder, tied it in a neat bow, and handed it to Petrov. Conway's work as an attorney had ended; his other work was about to begin.

Petrov waved the red-rope folder to the two bodyguards, who gave Ravel a gentle nudge toward Reed and Jake.

Only thirty feet now separated Ravel from her freedom.

"Come on, Ravel," Reed said. "Time to come home, sweetheart."

Then Jake stepped in front of Reed.

He reached behind and placed his right hand on Reed's right hip.

Reed didn't move or speak, waiting to learn what Jake's play was here.

She trusted her husband, and she knew instinctively that something was about to go down, that Jake was protecting her from whatever was about to unfold.

Suddenly, four Tampa Police cruisers swarmed into the Namaste parking lot.

None of the cruisers had on its siren and lights.

Also, Andre and Sierra, both carrying side arms, came running from across the street.

Completing this pincer movement, Jasper Conway pulled out his revolver and pointed it at Petrov's temple.

"Please do something stupid, Petrov," Conway said. "Nothing would make me happier than to cap your ass right here and now."

Chapter Seventy Two

"What the hell is going on?" Petrov said. He seemed genuinely worried.

Conway poked him in the temple with his small revolver.

"Party's over, that's what's going on, you prick," Conway said. He spoke with a confidence that Petrov had never heard before.

The police cruisers formed a semi-circle around Petrov's Jaguar.

Eight officers, including Detective Peter Langdon, jumped out of the cruisers. All the officers were brandishing service weapons: four of the officers held assault rifles, while Langdon and the other officers had semi-automatic pistols. All of them wore Kevlar vests marked "POLICE" on the front.

The officers spread out behind the cruisers.

Detective Langdon clearly was in charge.

"All right, assholes, get your hands off the lady, get face down on the ground, and spread your arms," Langdon shouted to Petrov's bodyguards.

The two men froze — they appeared not to understand the detective's commands.

Ravel understood, though.

Having spotted Andre and Sierra standing within the semi-circle of police officers, Ravel shook free of the bodyguards and bolted to Andre and Sierra, both of whom grabbed Ravel and got her behind a police cruiser.

The two bodyguards were at a loss over what to do: Ravel had gotten away from them; their boss was being held at gunpoint by Conway; and eight police officers and two armed civilians were drawing down on them.

Embroiled in a showdown so lacking in options, the bodyguards simply went with their baser instincts.

Kidnapping charges would be only a starter. Eventually, the police would learn about the tortured and murdered women.

The bodyguards realized instantaneously that they would be arrested, convicted, and probably executed in Florida.

So they took the course that made the most sense to them: they pulled out their large revolvers.

The short bodyguard aimed his revolver at Conway and fired.

Conway's right shoulder exploded into a bloody mushroom cloud, splattering Petrov, who dropped to the asphalt.

The short bodyguard aimed his revolver at the police and began firing. The tall bodyguard joined him in firing at the police.

The two Russians got off only one round each before the police unleashed a devastating barrage.

Taking multiple rounds into their heads and torsos, the two bodyguards performed an abstract expressionist dance, their legs wobbling, their arms flailing, their heads bursting into gory halos.

After twice spinning completely around, the two Russian bodyguards collapsed on the asphalt. They were dead as Lenin. The blood-sprayed asphalt around the bodies resembled a Jackson Pollock painting.

"My boys, you mother fuckers murdered my baby boys," Petrov screamed. He reached out to the still bodies of his bodyguards.

Petrov, though, wisely remained flat on the ground.

Conway lay bleeding next to Petrov. He was still breathing.

His revolver was on the ground and within Petrov's reach. But Petrov made no attempt to grab the gun. Again, another smart move on Petrov's part — after all, this wasn't Petrov's first rodeo.

Reed got off the asphalt.

"You okay, Jake?" she said.

Jake also got up and brushed himself off.

"Yes, I'm fine," he said. "And you, are you injured?"

"I'm not hurt, just a little scraped up," Reed said.

While Andre and Sierra stayed with Ravel, Detective Langdon and the other police officers converged on the dead bodyguards, Petrov, and Conway.

First, the officers gathered the bodyguards' revolvers, then checked for pulses, finding none.

Langdon and two other officers set upon Petrov and Conway.

While Langdon cuffed Petrov, the two officer's picked up Conway's revolver, then began administering first aid to the wounded lawyer. Over his radio, one of the officers called in for medical assistance, which was waiting nearby.

Meanwhile, Sierra and Andre consoled Ravel. Sierra held Ravel in her arms. Both women were weeping. Sierra was trying not to squeeze Ravel too tightly.

Andre was down on one knee. He gently and lovingly rubbed Sierra's back while he spoke softly to Ravel.

He, too, was crying.

Chapter Seventy Three

Andre yelled to the police officers, "Get an ambulance for Ravel, and please hurry!"

Detective Langdon nodded affirmatively.

Supported by Andre and Sierra, Ravel rose unsteadily from the ground.

Ravel immediately collapsed into Sierra's arms.

Sierra helped Ravel walk slowly toward Namaste.

Andre ran ahead of the women to retrieve the fully stocked first-aid kit inside Namaste. He waved to Reed and Jake as he passed the couple.

As Ravel and Sierra walked by Reed, Ravel caught Reed's eye and smiled weakly at her.

"I'll be inside in a little while to check on you, okay, Ravel?" Reed said.

"Yes," Ravel said in a faint whisper.

In the near distance, Reed could hear sirens; the ambulance was getting closer.

Reed crossed her fingers that there were two ambulances on the way.

The police officers were doing their best to stanch Conway's bleeding.

Conway remained conscious. He was alert and not moaning or whining about his condition.

Detective Langdon and another police officer kept Petrov face down on the asphalt. Having handcuffed his hands behind his back, they searched him for weapons, finding none.

Then the same pair of Sandhill cranes flew back over Namaste.

Petrov peered up at them.

"Nice birds," he said.

The birds flew west, toward Tampa Bay.

With emergency lights flashing and sirens blaring, two ambulances rolled into the Namaste parking lot.

Detective Langdon waved the ambulances over to him.

Carrying large medical kits, paramedics rushed out of the ambulances.

A paramedic immediately tended to Conway.

Detective Langdon instructed one of the other paramedics to tend to the fallen bodyguards and another one to go inside Namaste to check on Ravel.

Within five minutes, Conway was stabilized, placed on a stretcher, and loaded into an ambulance, which sped off to Tampa General's trauma center, one of the best in the country. Conway was alert and stoic.

Two unmarked cruisers, a medical examiner's van, and a forensics crime lab van all arrived at Namaste.

A third ambulance and a Tampa Fire Department ladder truck arrived as well.

After conferring with Langdon, the two homicide detectives, who had arrived in the unmarked cruisers, verified with the paramedic that the two Russian bodyguards were deceased.

Meanwhile, Ravel had been placed on a stretcher and was being wheeled out of Namaste and toward the second ambulance.

Just before Ravel was about to be placed in the ambulance, Reed and Jake walked over to her.

Reed held Ravel's hand.

The two women smiled warmly at each other.

"Welcome home, sweetheart," Reed said.

Then Ravel motioned for Reed to lean closer to her, which she did.

For a full minute, Ravel whispered into Reed's ear. Reed nodded occasionally. Then Ravel gently placed her small, battered hand behind Reed's neck and kissed Reed softly on the lips. Reed fully and unabashedly returned the kiss.

Ravel collapsed back into the stretcher. The two paramedics carefully put her in the ambulance, which then left Namaste for the Tampa General emergency room.

Reed, Jake, Andre, and Sierra stood together, watching the ambulance pull away.

The sun was beginning to set, creating a soft pink hue to the western sky.

"Looks as if it's going to be another beautiful sunset," Reed said.

Jake put his arm around Reed, who leaned her head on her husband's shoulder.

Chapter Seventy Four

Detective Langdon appeared too involved with the investigative team to speak with Reed and Jake.

Reed thought Langdon, for some reason, was avoiding her and Jake.

Meanwhile, the bodies of the two dead bodyguards had been covered in opaque heavy plastic sheets.

Yellow crime scene tape formed a large oval around the area of the shoot-out.

The medical examiner was busy with her work inside the oval. She already had photographed extensively the bodies.

The fire truck remained at the scene.

There were now ten marked and unmarked police cruisers in Namaste's parking lot.

Uniformed officers were directing the Namaste performers and staff, who were arriving by cars, motorcycles, and bicycles, through the gauntlet of news trucks, reporters, and cameras that had gathered on the street in front of Namaste.

Reed and Jake stood at the entrance to the nightclub. Their employees simply nodded to them as they quietly entered the night club.

"Just go inside and chill," Reed said to them. "We'll have a staff meeting in a bit, and don't bother setting up — we won't open tonight."

Jake again put his muscular arm around Reed's shoulders.

"Reed, we should pay all of them as compensation for closing tonight," he said.

"I agree," she said.

Once Andre and Sierra had been interviewed by the homicide detectives, they walked over to Reed and Jake.

"You two have some explaining to do," Reed said. Her hands rested on her hips; her right foot was tapping. Her anger was the genuine article.

"Well, to be perfectly succinct, Andre and I made arrangements with Detective Langdon to ambush Petrov," Sierra said.

"Langdon? Really?" Reed said. "That's quite a surprise, since I thought he was still put out at me for calling him a shit bag."

"Tell me about it — Langdon called Andre completely out of the blue," Sierra said.

Reed looked at Andre.

"It was Judi Ploszek's doing," Andre said. "After your run-in with Langdon at the hospital, Judi called him up and rimmed him out thoroughly for his unprofessional behavior with you. Judi told Langdon that Notre Dame would be so ashamed of him, and that he needed to make a pilgrimage to the Grotto, whatever that means."

Reed smiled.

"Oh, I think I know exactly what that means," she said. "The end result was that Langdon was completely in Judi's pocket."

"Exactly," Andre said.

"What a smart move on Judi's part," Jake said. "Just what you'd do, isn't it."

"Better believe it," Reed said, though privately she was impressed with how quickly Judi moved on Langdon.

Playing the Grotto card was brilliant on Judi's part, she thought.

"So when Judi found out that Ravel was going to be turned over to you in exchange for Namaste, she approached me and Andre," Sierra said.

Crap, I gotta stop telling Judi everything, Reed thought.

Reed was trying to absorb the multitude of details involved in pulling off an operation of this complexity, all the while keeping her shut out.

"Why didn't you talk to me about getting the police involved?" Reed asked. Her anger was beginning to ebb.

"Please believe me, Reed, we agonized over not telling you," Andre said. "Ultimately, we agreed you'd probably be against the plan, and even if we could talk you into it, you might have been distracted going into your meeting with Petrov and Conway."

"And Reed, this was all about getting Ravel back," Jake interjected. "Getting back Namaste and bringing Petrov to justice were secondary."

Reed stared at Jake for about twenty seconds. No one spoke.

"That's right, baby, I knew all about it," Jake said. "My job was to see to it that you didn't get hurt. And Petrov knows I hate his guts, so if he sensed something froggy about me, we figured he'd think I couldn't stand it that they'd won."

Reed continued to be silent. Again, no one spoke.

Finally, she broke her silence.

"My husband and key members of Namaste went behind my back to ensnare Petrov?" she said.

Jake, Sierra, and Andre nodded in unison.

"And what was the end result?" Reed said. "Ravel is safe and relatively sound; Petrov is in custody; his own attorney turned on him; his bodyguards are dead; and we keep Namaste."

The trio smiled eagerly.

"Even though I'm royally pissed at you all, you made the right decision — I was working in a silo, and that was a mistake," Reed said. "I couldn't be more proud of you all."

Jake, Sierra, and Andre beamed with pride.

Reed took Jake into her arms.

"And, Jake, my loquacious Frenchman, how you kept all of this to yourself is an absolute wonder," she said. "You are a complex and wonderful man."

The couple embraced and kissed passionately.

Andre and Sierra politely looked away, though Andre furtively smiled and winked at Sierra. Both understood that they had escaped the woodshed.

As Jake was holding Reed, he reached around and felt the metal object placed in the small of Reed's back.

Jake knew the metal object was Reed's handgun.

He whispered to Reed, "I'm glad we didn't go with your plan."

Reed whispered back, "Funny isn't it — Petrov was the only person not armed at the meeting, so I don't think my shooting him out of self-defense would have worked. So much for the best laid plans."

The quartet headed inside Namaste to meet with the staff and the performers.

The police continued their work. Langdon and his fellow officers knew they would remain at the crime probably until midnight.

Glad I sidestepped O'Hara, for now at least, Langdon thought, would hate to see her gloat over Judi making me her bitch — goddamn Notre Dame, goddamn Grotto, and goddamn Judi Ploszek. No, no, that's not right — really, it's God bless Judi Ploszek.

Chapter Seventy Five

Within twenty four hours, Reed O'Hara's world had righted itself considerably.

Namaste re-opened to a capacity crowd on Tuesday evening. Reed and Jake took the night off, allowing Sierra and Andre to manage the cabaret.

Reed and Jake knew full well that Benecio, Andre's assistant, was involved in Ravel's kidnapping. Initially, Reed was suspicious of Benecio's story, that he was completely ambushed by Petrov's bodyguards and was totally helpless in preventing Ravel from being kidnapped. The clincher, though, was Ravel whispering to Reed: Ravel overheard Petrov talking to Conway at the storage unit — Petrov's reward to Benecio was to make him head of security of the new Namaste, even though Benecio told Ravel that Petrov would make him general manager.

Reed and Jake considered having charges filed against him, but they knew there wasn't enough concrete evidence. Better to just remove Benecio, they concluded.

Jake instructed Andre to give Benecio five-hundred dollars in severance pay, drive him to the bus station in downtown Tampa, and purchase him a one-way ticket to anywhere outside of Florida. Benecio was forced to sell his truck.

Benecio chose Paris, Texas, his hometown. He was totally cooperative with Andre, an unspoken admission of guilt on Benecio's part.

"And don't let me catch your sorry ass anywhere in Tampa Bay," Andre said to Benecio, who was first wanded by security before stepping onto the bus.

"I don't know, Andre, you might need me someday," Benecio said.

"I sure hope not," Andre said. "Safe travels straight to hell, asshole."

Andre remained at the bus station until Benecio's bus pulled out.

With Benecio gone, Reed and Jake promoted Sierra to assistant manager for security. Sierra still could perform on stage while coordinating with Andre on her off days.

Reed and Jake felt totally confident that Andre and Sierra would make a great security team.

As soon as she was strong enough, Ravel would return to Namaste as Jake's assistant manager.

And Ravel was recovering nicely.

Though Petrov had beaten her severely, Ravel was one tough Swiss. While she agreed to using antibiotics and topical analgesics to aid her recovery, she refused painkillers. Having abused prescriptive and street drugs in the past, she was determined to avoid pain medication because of its powerfully addictive quality.

Besides, pain and discomfort reminded Ravel of the sheer, utter vitality of life itself, that her previous life of narcotic numbness no longer had hold of her. With pleasure or pain, Ravel felt alive.

Reed restored herself by making love to Jake at dawn, her favorite time to have sex. She had had a great night's rest, sleeping a full eight hours. When she awakened, the early sunlight outlined the bedroom drapes.

She took off her Golden State Warriors tee shirt and her sheer amber panties, tossing them on the floor.

Jake was still asleep, though not for long.

Reed kissed his forehead and both cheeks, then darted her small tongue in his mouth.

Fully awake now, Jake became aroused immediately.

He cupped her breasts and slowly licked each of her erect nipples.

Reed gently straddled Jake. She stroked his large, engorged penis —
before mounting him ever so slowly. As she moved her hips
rhythmically, she arced her back while touching her breasts and lightly
pinching her nipples.

Jake held Reed's round, muscular buttocks and pulled her forward
with each of her lunges.

A well-oiled love machine, they climaxed together.

Reed breathed heavily and glowed in perspiration. A single drop of
sweat fell from the top of her nose onto Jake's chest.

Having caught her breath, Reed leaned down and kissed Jake.

"Now go back to sleep, lover," Reed said. "Rest for a little longer."

"Yes, ma'am," he said, then turned on his side and was asleep in just
seconds.

Reed studied her husband's nude muscular body, then curled up and
fell into a deep, sweet sleep.

Chapter Seventy Six

Ravel awakened at nine in the morning. Reed and Jake were still sleeping. She wore Reed's Memphis Grizzlies tee shirt, gray sweat pants, and bright red fuzzy socks.

She had found the Grizzlies tee shirt in Reed's laundry basket. She wanted to rest in the shirt so as to be enveloped in Reed's scent — no pharmaceutical painkiller could soothe her more.

As she climbed out of bed and walked to the en suite bathroom, she felt as if she were an eighty-year-old woman racked with osteo-arthritis. She dutifully took her antibiotics, then bunched the Grizzlies tee shirt into her face and breathed in deeply. She ended up taking five deep breaths.

My god, her scent is turning me on, Ravel thought.

By lifting the tee shirt to smell Reed's scent, though, she exposed her breasts and flat, muscular stomach.

She looked at herself in the mirror above the vanity. The multiple lacerations, inflicted with such perverse enthusiasm by Petrov, resembled a surreal tic-tac-toe grid. The bruises on her torso were a deep purple.

Smoke on the water, fire in the sky, she thought, man, I miss Montreux.

Ravel knew there would be scarring on her chest, and it would be at least a month before the bruises and cuts healed, then dissipated. She realized she would carry the marks of torture for the rest of her life.

No matter, she thought, makes me look like the tough little shit I am.

She gingerly walked out to the kitchen.

She stepped carefully in her sock feet, as the last thing she needed was a slip and fall.

She busied herself in the kitchen by making a *café con leche* with a double short of espresso. She tried not to use the milk steamer for too long, as the noisy steam wand might awaken Reed and Jake.

Ravel walked into the expansive living room and sat down on the long leather sofa.

Reed had charged Ravel's laptop, then left it on the smaller teakwood coffee table. Reed had told her that she loved the coffee table because it reminded her of the teakwood promenade decks on cruise ships.

Ravel set down her cup of *café con leche* and reached for her laptop. She winced from sharp pain emanating from her rib cage.

Fuck, fuck, fuck, she thought, Petrov put one hell of a hurt on me. Suck it up, baby, suck it up. At least the Russian monster is now in very deep shit.

Shortly after checkout out of Tampa General Hospital, Ravel learned from Reed that Petrov wasn't allowed to bond out of jail.

As Reed explained it, Petrov's initial charges, which came down the day after the shoot-out at Namaste, were kidnapping and torturing Ravel.

Yet more charges were forthcoming, thanks to Jasper Conway, Petrov's attorney.

Conway had survived being shot at Namaste. And he was talking. A lot.

From his hospital bed, Conway told the police investigators that Petrov was a sexual predator, a sadist, and a serial murderer of the most perverse order.

The investigators couldn't believe what there were hearing from Conway.

The two detectives had paid a visit to Conway to compile damning evidence of Petrov kidnapping and torturing Ravel and his attempted extortion of Reed and Jake.

Conway obliged them by providing all the details about the kidnapping, Benecio's involvement, the location of the storage unit, and even the entry code to the storage unit's door. Taking notes, the detectives had to tell Conway to slow down, so as to not miss any details.

He explained how Petrov had planned the kidnapping, paid Benecio to turn on Ravel, then brutalized Ravel.

"Even when Petrov got all the information he needed from Ravel, he still beat her some more — not enough to kill her, of course, but more than enough to inflict serious pain," Conway said to the investigators.

Conway also explained how he prepared the legal documents designed to wrest control of Namaste from Reed and Jake.

"I knew this was flat out extortion, but I did it anyway," Conway said in a disgusted tone of voice.

He had more to say to the investigators, but he reiterated he did not want immunity from prosecution. He wanted no consideration for his cooperation.

"None, not one iota," Conway said. "I'm telling you the full unvarnished truth and the only thing I want in exchange is a clear conscience."

Then Conway dropped the atomic bomb, mushroom cloud and all.

He inhaled deeply, then let out a slow breath.

Tears began to well up in his eyes.

"Petrov abducted, tortured, raped, and murdered eleven young women, all of them from around these parts," Conway said.

The two investigators sat in their chairs in stunned silence. One detective made certain the tape recorder was still on.

"How do you know this?" the investigators said in unison.

Tears streamed down Conway's broad face.

"I saw him do all eleven women," Conway said in a whisper. "Petrov made me watch every one of them. I used to throw up at first, which Petrov just loved. After the third or fourth one, I simply went all numb."

Conway wiped his face with the bed sheet.

"I swear, Petrov would tear into the girls just to get me to convulse," he said. "He and his goons laughed and laughed as the girls bled out, and I whimpered like a scared hound dog."

Conway sat up in his hospital bed and described to the detectives how Petrov and his two bodyguards would find their victims in Ybor City nightclubs, in hip Central Avenue bars in St. Petersburg, and in bikini bars up and down Clearwater Beach. One of Petrov's favorite spots was Bahama Breeze at Rocky Point, Conway said.

He also described how the women always ended up in Petrov's storage unit, tortured and raped for what seemed liked hours, then ultimately beaten to death by Petrov.

Finally, Conway described how Petrov's bodyguards would dutifully dump the tortured bodies, under Petrov's direction, into large steel drums. Once they had amassed four filled drums, the bodyguards took them by boat to Egmont Key and unceremoniously dropped them into Tampa Bay.

"Reef building, Petrov called it," Conway said. "The sick fucker."

Conway said the bodyguards had made two trips to Egmont Key, dumping a total of eight bodies.

"Three of the four remaining drums at the storage unit are filled. Petrov kept the fourth empty drum available, reserved for Ravel," Conway said.

"Luckily for that little girl, Petrov decided to have Ravel taken to Namaste to close the deal," Conway said, speaking now with a stronger timbre. "Besides, he's already had some fun with Ravel, so he wanted to save the fourth drum for a 'fresh sturgeon,' he liked to say."

Conway and the two investigators sat in silence.

Though sunlight streamed into the hospital room from the large picture window, there was a dark pall cast over the three men.

"Sturgeon . . . can you believe that?" Conway asked. "For me, it's more like an albatross, and I'm ready for the albatross to drop off my neck, Detectives."

"What do you mean?" said the older investigator, though he knew full well the significance of Conway's reference to Coleridge's poem *The Rime of the Ancient Mariner.*

"I'm ready to help in any way I can, and I'm ready to take the punishment I deserve," Conway said. "Who knows, maybe I'll get back a scintilla of humanity in the process. I want to tell my horror story in court and to anyone else who will listen."

Conway began weeping uncontrollably.

The younger detective also teared up — not for Conway, but for the eleven women who apparently met such a horrific and ghastly death.

Ravel, still sitting on the living room sofa in Reed and Jake's condominium, thought of those poor eleven souls as well.

Her *café con leche* had grown cold, yet she still gripped tightly the large ceramic coffee mug.

Thinking of those murdered women, and of how close she came to being Petrov's twelfth victim, made her feel cold and numb.

Ravel began to cry uncontrollably.

Reed heard her from the bedroom and came out into the living room.

She sat down next to Ravel and gathered the tiny Swiss woman into her arms.

"There, there, my sweet baby, you're safe now," Reed said. "I'm never going to let you out of my sight ever again. I love you so much."

Ravel gained control of her emotions enough to realize that Reed was overstating a bit to make her feel better.

So she was not going to miss this rare opportunity.

Ravel kissed Reed's lips.

Reed responded by kissing Ravel passionately.

Their tongues darted between each other's lips.

Ravel caressed Reed's breasts. She slipped her hand under Reed's tee shirt, cupped her breast, and gently squeezed her erect nipple.

Both women were breathing heavily.

When Ravel reached down to Reed's panties, Reed took her hand and placed it on her hip.

Ravel made an archly pouty face.

"Are you afraid we're going to wake up Jake?" Ravel said.

"Not at all, my dear," Reed said. "I just sense I've violated my marriage vows enough for one day."

Both women giggled.

"Okay, I understand, baby steps, right?" Ravel said. "Your kiss was simply delicious, and I can't wait to taste all of you."

Ravel smiled and arched her eyebrows.

"Hmm, well, you want some pajamas to go with that dream?" Reed said.

Again, both women laughed, this time loud enough to awaken Jake.

Chapter Seventy Seven

The women's laughter awakened Jake shortly before eleven. Normally, he arose at dawn. When he looked at the clock on the night stand and realized he'd been sleeping for ten hours, he felt guilty and disoriented. Yet he also felt refreshed and eager to learn what the women were laughing about.

Throwing on a white tee shirt and long black workout shorts, Jake strode out into the living room. Normally, the outfit would be inappropriate for Jake: entirely too casual and more appropriate for a workout. However, he thought of his selection as recovery togs.

Ravel and Reed were busy reading from Ravel's open laptop on the coffee table.

Reed looked up at her husband. She was surprised to see him in shorts and a tee shirt.

"Good morning, my sexy French man," she said. "*Comment allez-vous?*"

Jake smiled at his wife.

"*Je suis bien, ma petite fleur,*" Jake said. "*Comment allez-vous tous?*"

Jake noticed that Reed's nipples were exceptionally erect and quite noticeable in her thin tee shirt.

He glanced at Reed, who spotted him looking at her chest.

She gave Jake a subtle shrug, then a winsome smile.

Jake returned her smile.

God, those two are something else, he thought.

Without looking up from her laptop, Ravel said, "I think I can speak for both of us, Jake — we're doing great."

Ravel tapped her computer and a file appeared on the screen.

"Yes, I want to look very carefully at this dossier," Reed said, striking an all-business tone.

The two women slumped shoulder to shoulder over the laptop. They resembled a pair of blue herons standing motionless in the brackish shallows, waiting for sunfish to swim a bit closer.

"Digital fishing, are we?" Jake said.

"Um, uh," Reed said This time, she did not look up at Jake when she spoke to him.

The herons were in maximum predator mode.

Jake was starting to feel excluded.

"So do we have a game plan?" he asked.

Are they not taking me seriously because of how I'm dressed, he thought.

Reed picked up on Jake's irritated tone.

Time to be inclusive, she thought.

"Yes, there's a plan, Jake, but I need your input," she said.

Nice recovery, Reed, Jake thought.

Reed actually did not have a concrete plan of action, only a couple of loosely strung together ideas. But she understood instinctively that part of being a leader was bluffing a bit occasionally. And this was one of those occasions.

Reed patted the sofa and held up her right arm, a signal that she wanted Jake to join her.

Ravel was oblivious to Reed's overture to Jake. Instead, she stared intently at the laptop screen.

"Sure, baby, I'll join you but how about I first fix all of us some coffee?" Jake said.

Ravel looked at Jake.

"Jake, you are *the* absolute fucking man," she said.

"Why thank you, Ravel," Jake said. "I didn't know you cared so much."

Ravel guffawed, then said, "What I care about, dear boy, is getting more coffee."

Amazing, Jake thought, after everything she has been through, Ravel endures — still sarcastic and contentious as ever.

"Ravel, I live to serve," Jake said.

The two exchanged tentative smiles.

They are so damn cute, Reed thought. Cute as a pair of pitbull puppies.

Jake headed off to the kitchen to make a pot of coffee with the French press.

Once Ravel and Reed were alone, Ravel casually slid her small, delicate hand down Reed's inner thigh.

Reed deftly grabbed Ravel's hand and placed it in Ravel's lap.

"Now none of that, little missy, I am a married woman after all," Reed said.

"Oh, come on, Reed, does it really count if your seducer is another woman?" Ravel said.

"Yes, Ravel, it does matter," Reed said.

Reed was starting to get annoyed.

Jake called out from the kitchen, "One of the foundational tenets of feminism is inclusiveness — cheating is cheating, regardless of gender, so cut it out!"

Ravel looked sheepishly at Reed.

"Better watch it, baby, that boy has freakishly good hearing," Reed said.

"I heard that," Jake said from the kitchen. "And thank you, my love."

Jake came into the living room. He carried a tray with three cups and saucers, sugar and cream bowls, and a large pot of freshly pressed French roast coffee.

"God, that smells so good," Reed said.

Ravel nodded eagerly in agreement.

"Just a small, yet very important, aspect of my job description," Jake said.

For the next few minutes, the trio sat in the living room, sipping on the strong coffee, not speaking.

Finally, Reed set her empty cup on the saucer, bringing the meeting to order.

Chapter Seventy Eight

"Okay, Petrov's out of the picture, but we don't know if he communicated with Father Angel before getting arrested," Reed said. "I'm going to assume that Father Angel knows that the priest assassins are three nuns."

"Yes, three nuns with very bad habits," Jake said. He seemed very pleased with his pun.

Ravel almost did a spit-take with her coffee.

"That's actually fucking funny, Jake," Ravel said, wiping her chin. "And, Reed, smart assumption that Father Angel knows about the nuns — even if Petrov hadn't told him previously, that slithery priest probably has already visited Petrov in jail, you know, to provide Petrov spiritual guidance."

"True that," Jake said.

Reed looked at Jake and Ravel.

"So we all agree that Father Angel knows about the nuns," Reed said.

Jake and Ravel nodded affirmatively.

"He's going to start looking for the nuns on his turf." Ravel said. "It won't be long before he finds them."

"Why do you say that?" Reed asked.

"As usual, I'll spare you the gory details, so as to avoid assaulting your delicate moral sensibility, but I checked up on Father Angel," Ravel said.

"What'd you find out?" Jake said, as he re-filled the three coffee cups.

"Clearly, he figured out too late that someone was eavesdropping into his secured e-mail," Ravel said. "For quite a while, he communicated with his assistants in Rome — their names are Antonio and Bumandi — in an encryption code that a high school gamer with half a brain could break in five minutes."

"So with a false sense of security, he communicated freely with his assistants," Reed said.

"Exactly," Ravel said.

"And?" Jake said.

"Father Angel told his assistants that Petrov wanted to meet with him and that he wanted Antonio and Bumandi to travel to Tampa and assist him," Ravel said.

"I doubt Petrov gave Father Angel all of the details that Petrov tortured the shit out of you, Ravel," Reed said. "But Father Angel is a smart guy, and I'll bet he got enough pieces of the puzzle to fill in the blanks himself after meeting with Petrov."

"I think you're spot on, Reed," Jake said. "So Father Angel fires us and puts Petrov on the trail to finding the priest killers."

"Bingo, Jakester," Ravel said. "Only Petrov's out of the picture now, so now it's only Father Angel and his two assistants trying to find these very naughty nuns."

"And how do you know Father Angel is aware of someone — who shall go unnamed — has been hacking his e-mail?" Jake asked.

"Because, all of a sudden, he stopped using the encryption code, and the content of his current e-mails is as innocuous as it is useless," Ravel said. "He also deleted his encrypted e-mails, thinking they'd disappear into the cyber ether."

"You retrieved them, didn't you, my clever girl," Reed said.

"Absolutely," Ravel said.

"Do you think Father Angel realizes it's us doing the eavesdropping?" Jake said.

"Of course he does," Reed interjected. "As a result, he's going to move with all deliberate speed to find these nuns."

"Why don't we conduct a similar search, Reed?" Jake said.

"Because we don't have the physical access Father Angel has," Reed said. "Believe me, he'll find this trio rather quickly."

"This unholy trinity?" Ravel said.

"Hey, woman, don't be piggybacking my witty repartee," Jake said. "So, Reed, we've got to come up with a different strategy to find these nuns."

"Any ideas?" Reed said.

"Yeah, baby, continue doing what you and Ravel were doing before I got up," Jake said.

"Fucking?" Ravel said.

"No, sweetest, try to guess who is next in line for a papal smoking," Jake said. "Isn't that what you all were reviewing — the priest files that we acquired from the Vatican?"

Reed pinched Ravel lightly on her ear.

"Ravel, we weren't fucking and you know it," Reed said. "I simply was comforting you."

Ravel chuckled.

"My recovery is weeks away, so you'll need to keep up that comfort protocol," she said.

"Want me to pitch in, Ravel?" Jake said.

"I'll pass," Ravel said. She shuddered slightly at Jake's tongue-in-cheek suggestion.

Jake and Ravel scrunched their noses dismissively at each other.

"All right, people, let's focus," said Reed, who surreptitiously stuck her tongue out at Ravel. "Jake, I get the idea you want to fine-tune our approach."

"I do," he said.

Ravel giggled.

"You may now kiss the bride," she said.

"Ravel!" Reed exclaimed.

"Sorry, Reed, but he keeps setting them up for me to knock out of the court."

"It's a 'ballpark', Eurogeek," Jake said. "And I do think we should try to think as the nuns are thinking."

"How are they thinking?" Reed said.

Jake poured himself another cup of coffee and took a large drink of the brew.

"First, the nuns came close to getting caught the last time they assassinated a priest," Jake said. "Second, it has been while since they've struck again – why the pause?"

"Said the mouse to the kitty," Ravel said.

This time both Jake and Reed laughed.

"Because, and this is my third point, the nuns are sensing the end," Jake said. "They're probably aware that Father Angel is a cold-blooded operator who's now aware of them, and while they may or may not know who we are, they know someone is out there tracking them — and getting closer. Their time of sitting at this table is getting short, and it won't be long before they're on the menu."

"You think the nuns have only one more opportunity to kill a pervy priest," Ravel said.

Jake re-filled Ravel's and Reed's coffee cups.

"*Absolument*," Jake said. "In some quirky way, the nuns want to be caught and be done with the killing."

"Probably stressful and exhausting for them," Reed said.

"Yes, believe me, it takes a lot out of you being judge, jury, and executioner," Jake said. "Makes it hard to sleep."

Ravel gulped down her coffee.

"How would you know that?" she said.

"Trust me, Ravel," Jake said. "I know, all too well."

Jake hung his head slightly, seemingly lost in thought.

Chapter Seventy Nine

"All right, here's what we do," Reed said, breaking the uncomfortable silence. "We approach this situation from the nun's perspective — we acknowledge that there's probably only one more execution left, then we choose the most likely target not by quantity, but by sheer perversion."

"Right, right, right," Ravel said excitedly, the caffeine now kicking in full bore. "Maybe a priest connected with a single child, one who disappeared, later found having been tortured and murdered, but the church provided the priest a solid alibi."

Reed read from the laptop while listening to Ravel's riffing.

"You're on the right track, Ravel," Reed said. "And I think we have here our likely prospect, although I may get sick to my stomach if I look at this file much longer."

Reed's rapidly whitening face concerned Jake, so he gently slid the laptop over to himself.

"Think I'll take a look for myself," he said.

He clicked through the entire file.

Jake bit down on the knuckle of his right index finger, clearly attempting to not let forth a string of obscenities. He actually drew blood on his knuckle.

"That's the one, Reed, he has to be," he said.

Ravel finished off her third cup of coffee.

"What, what, what?" she said.

"I'll tell you, Ravel, if you'll stop drinking coffee for a while," Jake said.

"Deal," Ravel said. She shook her head, as if trying to hit the temporal refresh button.

She actually sat up straight and put her hands in her lap, as if she were a pupil in a Bern finishing school.

"Father Colin Joyce, what a first-class piece of garbage," Jake said. "Assigned to a Catholic mission right in between Tucson and Nogales in Arizona."

"Fluent in Spanish, I take it," Ravel said.

"Yes," Reed interjected. "In fact, he was heavily involved with helping Mexican illegals, providing food and shelter at the mission, even carting water jugs out to the Sonoran desert."

"Sounds like an amazing person, so why is his file in this group of deplorables?" Ravel asked.

"Because . . . . because . . . I can't say it," Jake said.

"Because Father Joyce was suspected of snatching a three-year-old Mexican girl, raping and torturing her for three days, then murdering and burying her in the dessert," Reed said. She spoke in an emotionless, resigned manner.

First, there was a lengthy pause, then Ravel said, "Fuck me."

Jake had collected himself by now.

"The family was distraught over their missing child, upset enough to go to the border patrol," Jake said. "The authorities and the community of illegals suspected Father Joyce, but the church provided him an air-tight alibi."

"And the end result?" Reed said. "Father Joyce never was charged, the family was deported to Mexico. The church refused to allow the little girl to be buried in their cemetery, though they did pay for her body to be transported to Mexico."

"Talk about the cover-up being just almost as bad as the crime itself," Ravel said.

"Indeed," Jake said. "Not long afterwards, Father Joyce was admitted into Father Angel's Exodus program."

"That's the nun's final target," Reed said.

"I agree," Ravel said.

"So do I," Jake said.

"Really, Jake?" Reed said.

She had come to recognize Jake's gift for assessing a situation and making a sound judgement, sometimes based exclusively on his intuition.

"Yeah, baby, this guy is their next target," Jake said.

"Then Father Colin Joyce is our target, too," Reed said. "I need to go to my law office today, and you two need to get over to Namaste. Let's meet with Andre and Sierra at Namaste later on tonight."

"Roger that," Jake said.

"So we have a plan?" Ravel said.

"Yes, we do, though right now it's more of a work in progress," Reed said. "But it's time once more for us to draw the sting."

"So can I have more coffee," Ravel asked.

"You betcha, Ravel," Jake said. "In fact, I'll fix you a fresh pot."

Chapter Eighty

Reed sat at her large desk in her law office in downtown Tampa. Since she had been away from her law practice for several days, she was attempting to get re-organized and caught up.

After sifting through over a thousand e-mails, she waded through the regular mail that her office manager Roman had stacked neatly on her desk.

Reed eyed the elliptical trainer over in the far corner of her large office.

Tempting, she thought, but I should stick with this administrative hooey.

Besides, she was wearing a yellow Nara Camicie silk blouse, black slacks, and black Franco Sorto woven flats.

So she'd have to change into a workout outfit and, if she were to do that, would commit at least an hour to the elliptical trainer. An hour, minimum.

Nope, gonna get through this stuff, she thought, since we've got a big night tonight.

Happily, Roman interrupted this drudgery by buzzing her that Andre was calling.

"Put him through, Roman," Reed said eagerly.

"Hello, Andre, how are you?" she said.

Andre's deep voice boomed through the speaker.

"I'm well, Reed, and you?" he said.

Reed sat back in her high back leather chair.

"Swamped with office chores, and my 'to do' list includes several calls to clients this afternoon," Reed said. "My goal is to get everything ship-shape by late afternoon."

"Good plan, and Jake and Ravel are pretty much doing the same thing here at Namaste," Andre said. "So we're still on for tonight?"

"Yes, we are still on for tonight," Reed said. "Did Jake provide you and Sierra with all the necessary details — location, gear, perimeter points?

"Yes, Jake filled in both me and Sierra," Andre said. "It sounds like an excellent plan, though I don't think we should be talking in any more detail about this matter over the telephone."

"Good point — funny, isn't it, in this age of transparency, we don't seem to have secrets anymore, do we?"

"No, we don't, which is why I prefer to hide in plain sight — no small task for a black man in America," Andre said.

"So you simply make Ralph Ellison's notion of the invisible man work for you, right?" Reed said.

"Yes, ma'am, I do," Andre said.

"All right, Andre, we'll see you all tonight," Reed said.

"Yes, ma'am," he said.

Andre hung up.

Reed returned to her mail. To her right was a large stack of legal documents that needed her attention before she could make client calls.

Once more into the legal breach, she thought.

Chapter Eighty One

Roman buzzed again.

"Yes, Roman?" Reed said. She had just gotten into the flow of reading the legal documents.

"A Detective Langdon on the phone for you," Roman said.

"Put him through, please," Reed said impatiently.

Now she was starting to feel frustrated.

Reed picked up her phone.

"Good afternoon, Detective," Reed said.

"Hello, Mrs. O'Hara," Langdon said.

"'Reed,' please."

"Then 'Pete,' please."

"Okay, Pete, what can I do for you on this beautiful Florida day," Reed said.

"Well, I need to talk with you about three things," Langdon said.

"Let's do this, then," Reed said.

"First, are we okay now?" Langdon said.

"Pete, I don't like to be coy with people, I much prefer to be direct," Reed said. "So yes, we are okay."

"I'm relieved to hear that," Langdon said. "You know, Judi Ploszek set me straight after my ignorant behavior that night at Tampa General. I really am sorry."

"Apology accepted, Pete. Besides, you were instrumental in saving Ravel and apprehending Petrov. Thank you from the bottom of my heart," Reed said.

"You're very welcome, Reed," Langdon said. "And speaking of Petrov, he's the second thing I wanted to talk about."

Though Reed was an enthusiast of precise language, and it truly bothered her that people used the clunky, amorphous noun "thing" all too often, she knew better than to give Langdon a style tutorial — right now, at least, she was in complete control.

"Okay," she said "What's going on with Petrov?"

"I've talked to him a few times over at the Orient Road jail," Langdon said. "He knows we've recovered all of the barrels. And he's aware that the state attorney will soon bring multiple kidnapping, extortion, and homicide charges against him. He's dead in the water — sorry, that was an unintentional pun — and he knows it. His reaction, though, it's just so odd."

"How do you mean 'odd'?" Reed said.

"Well, he told me he plans on pleading guilty right up front. No trial. No steadfast defense. He's just giving up. All he asks for is a life sentence with no chance for parole. He wants to avoid the death penalty," Langdon said.

"So you think it's out of the ordinary for a hardened criminal such as Petrov to roll over without a fight?" Reed asked.

"No, it's not so much that," Langdon said. "Listen, I've seen plenty of guys like him pack it in because the deck is stacked against their getting off," Langdon said.

"So what is it, then?" Reed asked.

"He actually seems kind of content," Langdon said. "Petrov says that an American prison is like a luxury resort compared to the Russian prisons he has been in. Besides, he told me he screwed up big time in the eyes of his Moscow bosses, who think Petrov should have left those women alone and stuck to running their businesses in Tampa Bay."

"Makes sense, I guess," Reed said.

"Yeah, Petrov figures his bosses will have a harder time getting to him in a Florida prison."

"And Petrov isn't afraid of living in a cage for the rest of his life?" Reed said.

"Nah, he figures he'll have three hots and a cot every day for decades," Langdon said. "He said his philosophy on life is that he doesn't want to live forever, just one more day."

"What a slimy bastard," Reed said. "I take it he hasn't expressed remorse over kidnapping, torturing, and murdering those eleven women?"

"No, Reed, not a single word of regret or remorse," Langdon said. "He told me he has lots of nice memories to get him through his days in prison. He's a sociopath through and through."

"At least he's behind bars, Pete, and we have you to thank for that," Reed said. "Again, thank you."

"And again, you're welcome," Langdon said. "Now we come to the third thing."

Reed gritted her teeth.

"Are you saving the best for last?" she said.

"I guess so," Langdon said. "It's about the priest, Father Angel."

There was a long silence over the phone.

"How do you know about Father Angel," Reed said.

"Petrov had told me about him. Then I happened to be at the jail at the same time Father Angel was visiting Petrov," Langdon said. "I spoke with Father Angel long enough to realize he's a dangerous wolf in sheep's clothing, a real piece of work, that guy."

"Tell me more, Pete," Reed said. She noticed there was a slight sultry tone in her voice.

Shameless, you are absolutely shameless, Reed thought.

"You're aware, right, that Father Angel hired Petrov to locate the priest killers," Langdon said.

"Yes," Reed said. "Right after Father Angel fired me."

"No kidding?" Langdon said.

"No kidding," Reed said.

"You know, that makes sense. Father Angel must have figured Petrov wouldn't be restrained by ethics or morality or the law, that the shithead would just get the job done, no matter what it took."

"Yes, you're right, Pete," Reed said. "So you're aware, aren't you, that Petrov tortured Ravel after he kidnapped her, that he found out the priest killers actually are three nuns who are, pardon *my* pun, taking aim at the patriarchal system that is the Catholic Church."

"Petrov told me about it," Langdon said.

"So what are you going to do, Pete, bring in the task force?" Reed said.

"Believe me, Reed, it's tempting," Langdon said. "Be quite a feather in my cap if I could point the task force in the direction of the priest killers."

"You seem to be hesitating, though," Reed said.

"I am," Landon said.

"Why?" Reed asked.

"Because, Reed, my very big gut is telling me you've got a plan for catching these nuns," Langdon said. "I'd bet you'll catch 'em before we do, and I feel sure you'd turn them over to us."

"You're right on both counts, Pete," Reed said. "So why did you bring up Father Angel?"

This time, Detective Langdon paused over the telephone.

"Listen, I was raised in a good Catholic family, I went to Jesuit High School," Langdon said. "Hell, I went to Notre Dame with Judi, who was one of the first women to attend the university. She and I used to pray together at the Grotto of Our Lady of the Lourdes on campus. We were good friends, but nothing romantic, you know? And so I know all about priests and nuns."

"Let's hear more, Pete," Reed said.

"Strictly off the record, Reed, I really understand these nuns. They see the church letting these asshole priests getting away — literally — with murder and all sorts of other perversions. The nuns feel helpless in saving these children. So these three nuns are taking matters into their own hands. And this Father Angel, he's on a mission from God to protect His turf. If he gets to the nuns before we do, we'll never see those women again."

"That's what worries me the most," Reed said. "You're a good guy, Charlie Brown. Let me put my plan into action. And let's get off the phone so that I can get ready."

"You got it, Reed," Langdon said. "Good luck and God bless."

Reed hung up the phone.

God bless, huh, she thought, yeah well, one of these days I'm going to have to have a chat with Him over his fucking indifference to all this insanity.

Chapter Eighty Two

Reed made it through the stack of legal documents, then called her clients. Finally, her desk was clear and her law practice in good shape.

She felt ready for tonight.

Then Roman buzzed her.

"You've got to be kidding me, Roman," Reed said.

"Reed, Father Angel just walked in," Roman said over the phone. "He said he apologizes for not calling first, but there's a pressing matter he wishes to discuss with you."

I bet he does, Reed thought, I knew it was too good to be true that I have everything in order.

"Send him in, Roman," she said.

"Yes, ma'am," he said.

Father Angel strode confidently into Reed's office.

Reed rose from her desk, walked over to Father Angel, and shook his hand.

"Father, it's good to see you again," Reed said. She hoped she had disguised her insincerity.

"And you as well, Ms. O'Hara," Father Angel said. "Thank you for seeing me on such short notice."

"Or no notice at all, Father," Reed said.

Father Angel grinned at Reed's slight.

"*Touché*, Counselor, *touché*," he said.

Father Angel bowed his head, then sat in a chair in front of Reed's desk. She noticed that the man never waited to be asked to take a seat.

Reed returned to her desk chair.

"I am rather pressed for time, Father, so, as we sometimes say in the Deep South, what's on your mind besides your hat?"

Father Angel instinctively touched the top of his head, then began to laugh.

"I promise not to keep you long, Ms. O'Hara," Father Angel said. "I come here both chaste and repentant."

Yeah, I bet you do, Reed thought.

"Whatever do you mean, Father Angel," said Reed, who suddenly realized that this was the first time she had been coy with a Catholic priest.

"Since our time is limited, I shall be succinct. I deeply regret our previous conversation, and I hope you will forgive me and be receptive to our working together again," Father Angel said.

Reed's Mona Lisa smile appeared.

"There's nothing to forgive," she said. "You simply wanted to go in another direction, and I accepted your decision."

"Yes, yes, and you were courteous and professional to return the retainer," Father Angel said.

"It was the honorable thing to do, wasn't it," Reed said.

Jesus, did I just use "thing," she thought.

"Indeed, it was an honorable act on your part, yet might I entreat you to accept a new retainer, say five-hundred thousand dollars?" Father Angel said.

The balls on this man of God, Reed thought.

"You've got to be kidding me," she said.

"'Kidding'?" Father Angel said. "I don't understand . . . wait, 'kidding' is 'joking,' right? No, I am not kidding. I am as serious as a stroke."

"'Heart attack,'" Reed said.

"Pardon?" Father Angel said.

"You meant, 'I'm as serious as a heart attack,'" Reed said.

"All right, Counselor, thank you for that clarification," Father Angel said. "I am one of those rare people who appreciate being corrected."

My very nice ass, Reed thought.

"Whatever, Father Angel," Reed said, "I'm tempted to sit here in silence because sometimes by saying nothing, we say everything. But I sense you might miss my point, so let me be perfectly clear: I do not want your retainer, and I no longer wish to work for you. *Capiche?*"

Father Angel sat forward in his chair.

"Yes, I understand, but why, Ms. O'Hara?" he said.

"Really?" Reed said. "Do I have to explain myself?"

"Please do so, perhaps we can clear up any misunderstandings," Father Angel said.

"All right, your agenda is to find the priest assassins before your Exodus program is exposed and possibly shut down," Reed said. "Once you have these vigilantes, you'll eliminate them. That way, the executions cease, and Exodus can continue to operate. Is that a fair and accurate assessment?"

"Fair, yes, accurate, not entirely," Father Angel said. "I only want to bring these three murderers to justice. It is not my intention to hurt them in any way."

"Padre, that is such complete bullshit," Reed said. "And don't think I didn't catch your reference to 'three murderers.'"

"Truly, Ms. O'Hara, such bluntness in a woman is an unseemly as it is unbecoming," Father Angel said.

This admonishment from such a hypocrite, she thought.

"Don't presume you can comment on my femininity, Father Angel," Reed said. "Besides, you're avoiding the issue at hand."

"And that is," Father Angel said.

"We're both aware that the priest assassins are Catholic nuns," Reed said. "You haven't yet found them within your domain, so you're doubling down by trying to re-enlist me in finding them."

"'Doubling down,'" Father Angel said. "Now that's an allusion I understand, so I will tip my cards just a bit. Yes, I haven't yet found these deranged sisters, but it should not be much longer — meanwhile, what's the harm in your searching for them in the secular world?"

"There would be great harm, for the nuns," Reed said. "No, I will not do it on your behalf."

Father Angel raised his bushy black eyebrows.

"So you are still tracking them," he said.

"None of your business, padre," Reed said.

Father Angel exhaled in frustration, then he intertwined his fingers and placed his hands in his lap.

"A final offer, then, Ms. O'Hara," Father Angel said. "If you were to assist in apprehending these, women, then I will make a one-million dollar contribution to the local Planned Parenthood — you are a board member, are you not?"

"Yes, I am," Reed said.

The Catholic Church giving a million dollars to Planned Parenthood, Reed thought, it stretches the concept of fungible money beyond credulity.

"Are you saying that there is a chance you'll accept?" Father Angel said.

"No chance, padre, no chance at all," Reed said.

Father Angel exhaled again.

"Then allow me to give you a heartfelt warning, Ms. O'Hara," he said. "If we cross paths in the course of these three women being brought to justice, do not interfere with my mission, or there will be consequences of Old Testament proportions."

Jesus help me, I want to reach across my desk and snap this asshole's neck, Reed thought.

She buzzed Roman, who promptly came into the office.

"Roman, escort Father Angel out of the building," Reed said. "If he gives you any trouble, you have my permission to persuade him to leave in any fashion you see fit. Head first, feet first, ass first, doesn't matter to me."

"With pleasure, Reed," Roman said. "Father Angel, time for you to hit the bricks."

No longer interested in learning American colloquialisms, Father Angel simply rose from his chair, turned, and walked out of the office with Roman at his side.

The priest didn't utter a word.

By saying nothing, he said everything, Reed thought, so the race is on, and his threat is duly noted.

Chapter Eighty Three

Reed's plan was in place to take down the crossbow-bearing nuns.

First, Reed had to convince Ravel not to join the dragnet, even if it had been Ravel's uncanny intuition that indicated strongly this was the night to apprehend the nuns.

"Ravel, I need you to manage Namaste while we're out," Reed said. "I know you set this operation in motion, but you need to continue to heal while overseeing the club. Can you do that for me, please?"

Ravel stomped her left foot on the living room's wood floor.

"That's so fucking unfair, Reed," she said. "I had the vision earlier this morning while I was sleeping. Granted, the setting was pure American Gothic — South Tampa about 1900, I think — and we were wearing high-collared dresses with cameo brooches, and Jake was a Cudan house servant and Sierra was a miniature mermaid swimming in our immense fountain and . . . ."

"A colorful dream, but what's the point other than you've been studying your Art Deco books again?" Reed said.

Ravel shook her head derisively.

"The point? The point is I saw US capturing the nuns, you know, just after they kill the pervy priest," Ravel said. "And it's all happening tonight."

"And I thank you for sharing your vision, though I trust that Jake and I will prevent the nuns from executing the priest," Reed said.

Ravel smiled.

"A girl can dream, right?" she said. "So do I really have to stay at Namaste?"

"Absolutely, end of discussion," Reed said.

Ravel scowled and marched off to her bedroom.

Reed and Jake had spent the better part of the afternoon cleaning their handguns and making certain their stun guns were charged and operational.

"So Ravel thinks this is the big night, huh?" Jake said.

"Yup, and do you realize she's never been wrong with her visions?" Reed said. "A detail here and there has been off, but overall she's spot on. Jesus, it's as if she and Sierra are psychic twins."

"Amazing. Do you really think they're psychic?" Jake said.

"I wouldn't doubt it," Reed said.

The couple put the safeties on their pistols, then popped full ammunition clips into them. Locked and loaded, ready to unleash hell.

Andre and Sierra arrived at the penthouse apartment at six p.m.

They both were packing sidearms in shoulder holsters, and were dressed in black leather jackets, dark tee shirts, black jeans, and black running shoes.

Jake chuckled.

"You two look as if you're ready for your Michigan Militia Christmas photo," he said.

Jake gave walkie talkies to Reed, Sierra, and Andre.

"Clip the transmitter to your waist, and don't forget the earbud," Jake said.

"Roger that," Andre said. "So Sierra and I are outer perimeter."

"Yes," Reed said.

"How's Ravel doing?" Sierra said.

"Royally pissed she's not coming," Reed said.

"Well, it was decent of you two to let her recuperate at your home," Sierra said. "I'm telling you, once this is over and Ravel has fully recovered, I'm going to show her some absolutely wicked moves in bed."

"You go, girl," Reed said.

Andre shook his head in mock disapproval.

"Back to the matter at hand," he said. "Is everything else in place?"

"Yes, since Father Joyce lives in Seminole Heights, I called Nat Doliner to give him the heads up that the four of us will be lurking about that neighborhood tonight."

"Doliner's the district neighborhood watch captain, right?" Sierra said.

"Yes, and one hell of an attorney, too," Reed said.

"And a fine athlete, as well," Andre said. "He sometimes works out with me at the gym — built like a brick shithouse. Not bad for being nearly seventy."

Reed raised her eyebrows at Andre.

"Forget it, buddy, I know what you're up to, and we are not adding Nat to this operation," Reed said. "Perhaps one day we'll add him to the team, but not tonight"

"Fine. I was only brainstorming," Andre said, pretending to pout.

"No worries, my man," Jake said. "Nothing wrong with that."

"What about the police?" Sierra said.

"Detective Langdon is on board with our plan, and we'll bring him in as soon as we have these habitual offenders in custody," Reed said.

There was a pause, then Jake, Sierra, and Andre laughed at Reed's pun.

"Whatever, *mis tres amigos*," Reed said. "It's time to rock and roll."

Chapter Eighty Four

Ravel's intuitions were panning out beautifully. The plan was progressing smoothly. Reed sensed that she and her team were about to strike gold.

Just don't let it be goddamn pyrite, Reed thought.

All four members of the tracking team were in place by ten p.m. Reed and Jake were in the inner perimeter. Andre and Sierra secured the outer perimeter.

Having been given the heads up by Reed, Nat Doliner arranged for his neighborhood watch volunteers to patrol normally, yet stay away from the block on which Father Joyce lived.

Detective Peter Langdon was ready for Reed's call, which he wouldn't receive until the priest killers were captured. He sat on the outside patio of a nearby Starbucks café. Langdon and his partner were sipping on large cups of Komodo Dragon. Langdon had apprised his captain of his plans, though he left out the part about waiting for Reed's signal.

If this doesn't work out, my ass is in the fucking ringer, Langdon thought.

For some odd reason, there was no private security watching over Father Joyce.

Since there was a streetlight near the front of Father Joyce's bungalow, Reed did not need night vision goggles. So she hid behind a tall hedgerow of podocarpus.

She waited. Impatiently.

Jake was hidden behind viburnum hedges in the backyard of the priest's home.

He, too, waited. Not impatiently, but with a perfect zen calm, since being alone in the darkness, after all, was his *métier*.

It was 10:30 p.m., and the priest appeared to be turning off the lights in his home.

Beddy bye time for the bonzo, Jake thought.

Then Father Joyce turned on the back porch light and looked out the rear door window.

Less experienced operators would have bent down abruptly, but Jake knew it was better to remain motionless.

Looks as if the old perv is getting a little nervous, Jake thought.

Then the porch light went off.

Father Joyce appeared settled in for the night.

All was quiet, except for a few frogs chatting with each other.

Then everything seemed to happen at once.

Sierra signaled to Reed and Jake that three figures wearing black and carrying rucksacks had entered the outer perimeter.

"They're heading right to you, Reed," Sierra said over the transmitter.

"We're ready for them," Reed responded.

"Roger that," Jake said over his radio.

Hardly two minutes went by before the three figures appeared across the street from Father Joyce's bungalow.

Two of the dark figures moved quickly and silently across the street.

The third figure stayed across the street and hid behind a large hibiscus hedge.

"Two of the nuns are coming your way, baby," Reed whispered to Jake over the walkie talkie.

"Roger that, my Irish wild rose," Jake responded.

The third nun, obviously the lookout, was not thirty feet from Reed. Fortunately, the traffic noise from nearby Interstate 275 gave Reed a bit of sound cover to contact Andre and Sierra.

"Listen up, Sierra and Andre, it's happening right now," Reed said. "Start moving in slowly, weapons drawn."

"Roger that," Andre said.

"Sounds good," Sierra responded.

Reed maneuvered stealthily behind the lookout. She came within ten feet of the nun, who was focusing almost entirely on the priest's house.

Reed drew her Taser.

"Don't move, Sister," Reed said. "Your new vocation is over."

The nun reeled around and raised the blowgun to her mouth.

Reed fired her Taser at her. Both electrodes hit the nun in her chest.

With fifty thousand volts surging through her body, the nun dropped the blowgun and fell backwards.

"It's over, Sister, it's over," Reed said. "Don't make me give you another charge."

The nun was on her back and gave up trying to rise.

"No more, please," she said.

Reed kicked away the blowgun, put her knee on the nun's chest, then checked her for other weapons. Finding none, Reed turned the nun on her stomach and applied flex cuffs to her wrists and ankles. Reed rolled her back over, helped her to sit up, then gently pulled the electrodes from her chest. The nun winced at the electrodes extraction. Reed was nonplussed at how tiny the nun was.

"I'm sorry I hurt you, but you're going to be fine," Reed said. "Now, are you going to keep quiet, or do I have to gag you?"

"I'll be quiet, I promise," the nun said in an alarmingly juvenile voice.

Reed turned on her smart phone flashlight to illuminate the nun's face.

"My god, how old are you?" Reed said.

"I'm nineteen," the nun said.

Reed pulled the black baseball cap off of the nun's head. Her long hair was a bright fuchsia red and in a braid. Her skin was a Victorian porcelain hue. There was more fear than defiance in her green eyes. Her thin body shook.

My God, this is the face of a killer? Reed thought.

"I'm not going to harm you," Reed said. "What's your name?"

"Chenoa, Sister Chenoa," the nun said.

"Okay, Sister Chenoa, I'm going to leave you here for a little while," Reed said. "Do not attempt to crawl or hop away, all right? You wouldn't get far and, besides, you'd look absolutely ridiculous."

Sister Chenoa smiled slightly, then nodded in agreement.

"And you'll keep quiet?" Reed said.

The nun nodded again.

"Excellent," Reed said. She patted the nun on her shoulder, then got to her feet.

Reed walked with deliberate speed toward Father Joyce's bungalow. As she walked, she pulled out her phone to call Detective Langdon. Everything now was happening very quickly.

Suddenly, three gunshots rang out behind the priest's house. A few seconds of silence, then two more gunshots rang out. In the absence of other noise, the gunshots sounded like cannons firing.

Reed sprinted to the priest's backyard.

The carnage before her was illuminated by the back porch light.

Two nuns, clad in black, were sprawled on the lawn. Each nun had died from a perfect headshot between the eyes. The crossbows lay next to the lifeless bodies.

Jake sat nearby. He was conscious and clutching his forehead with his left hand. His right hand still held his pistol.

On the back porch, a lifeless figure was sprawled out on the deck.

It was Father Angel. He was dressed in pajamas, a bath robe, and slippers. Thoroughly dead — he had gunshot wounds to his forehead and chest — he still clutched his revolver.

Reed rushed over to Jake.

"Are you okay, baby?" Reed said.

"I'm fine, just a crease," Jake said. "I'm one lucky son of a bitch, because Father Angel was a helluva shot."

Reed examined Jake's head. The wound was a minor scrape.

"I'm glad it was a head shot, so nothing really important got damaged," Reed said.

"That's so fucking funny," Jake said.

Husband and wife smiled at each other.

"Listen, Jake, I'll be right back," Reed said. "Sierra and Andre will be here any moment. In exactly five minutes, call Detective Langdon and Nat Doliner to give them an update, okay?"

Jake used the back of his hand to wipe away the small amount of blood on his forehead.

"Where are you going?" he said.

"I have to take care of something very important," Reed said. "Won't be long, but make the calls in five minutes, right?"

"Roger that, sweetums," Jake said

Dogs were barking throughout the neighborhood. Lights were coming on at the surrounding bungalows.

Reed ran to the front of the priest's house, crossed the street, and came upon Sister Chenoa, who hadn't budged.

"Look, young lady, the other two Sisters are dead," Reed said. "I'm sorry for not being more delicate, but we're out of time. The police will be here soon."

"Oh god, oh fuck!" Sister Chenoa exclaimed. "I can't believe they're gone."

She closed her eyes and her lower lip quivered.

"What were their names?" Reed said gently.

"Olivetti and Elizabeth," the young nun said.

"Thank you," Reed said. "Now listen carefully: I can't believe I'm doing this, but I'm going to let you go, after you answer a couple of questions."

"Why are you letting me go?" Sister Chenoa asked.

"Because too many people are dead, all right? And you're too damn young to go on death row, which is exactly where you'd be heading," Reed said.

Reed used a pocket knife to cut both sets of stretch cuffs.

Sister Chenoa rose, then rubbed her wrists.

"What did you want to ask me?" she said.

"First, why did you take it upon yourselves to murder these priests?" Reed said. "And be succinct."

Sister Chenoa lowered her head.

"The three of us felt that these men of God had betrayed their vows and the Holy Church, and that they were going to avoid any secular punishment for their horrible acts against innocent children," Sister Chenoa said. "When we found out about the Exodus program, we thought this was an opportunity to step forward and take action."

"Did you know we were tracking you?" Reed said.

"Absolutely," the nun said.

"How?" Reed said

"Computers, Ms. O'Hara," Sister Chenoa said. "They're now as important as crosses and rosary beads in my former calling."

Clever little snit, Reed thought.

"Do you regret what you've done?" Reed said.

"Not at all," Sister Chenoa said. "We were avenging warriors trying to shake up this chauvinistic system that is the Holy Catholic Church. We took abuse for too long from these supposed men of God. I know I'll burn in eternal hell for my acts, but I take solace in knowing we got a few despicable priests to pay for their horrific acts."

There was a silence between the two women.

"Last question: why the crossbows?" Reed said.

"Because they're so fucking cool," Sister Chenoa said. "Thank you for letting me go. Don't worry, I'm through with killing priests. I'll pray for you."

"Save your prayers, Sister," Reed said. "Now get the hell out of here."

Sister Chenoa slipped off into the darkness.

Reed stood on the sidewalk and saw two cars approaching her on each side of the street.

To her left, an unmarked Crown Victoria, blue lights flashing in its grill, came speeding toward her. To her right, Nat Doliner's white Lexus sedan was moving toward her just as quickly.

The cavalry had arrived.

And Reed decided right then and there to tell Langdon and Doliner that the lone surviving nun somehow had slipped through their net.

Chapter Eighty Five

In the seven days after the shoot-out at Father Joyce's bungalow in Seminole Heights, a lot more had happened — and not happened — than the hundreds of azalea shrubs in Tampa Bay exploding with purple, pink, and white blossoms. The azalea blooms were a sure sign of the start of bay area's shoulder season.

The law enforcement task force, which was charged with apprehending the priest assassins, judged that the two dead nuns were indeed the assassins. No mention was made of a possible third nun involved. If Detective Langdon were aware of Chenoa, he said nothing. From the task force's point of view, the case was closed. The task force considered Detective Langdon instrumental in solving this case.

The state prosecutor did not pursue charges against Jake for shooting and killing Father Angel. The prosecutor based her conclusion on the detailed police reports: Father Angel had fired on Jake, possibly thinking Jake was one of the assassins, and Jake retuned fire in self-defense. Sometimes, she decided, mistaken identify can have very lethal consequences, but no one will be prosecuted.

As to Father Angel firing upon the two nuns, the prosecutor felt she was in more of a gray area — posing as Father Joyce, Father Angel appeared to have every intention of killing the priest assassins. But wasn't he simply protecting a fellow priest? After all, the Vatican had instructed Father Angel to put an end to these murders. And the nuns showed up with their cross bows. Ultimately, the prosecutor concluded

Father Angel had acted appropriately, tainted as it was with extreme prejudice. Father Angel acted as an official agent for the Catholic Church, but once again the Vatican would escape culpability.

Antonio and Bumandi, Father Angel's loyal assistants, oversaw the return of Father Angel's body to Italy — more precisely, to the Vatican state. Father Angel's burial ceremony was subdued, discreet, and brief. Antonio, always the more politically astute of the two assistants, was appointed head of special security.

The Exodus program, however, met the same fate as Father Angel. Through Ravel's efforts, all done anonymously, a wide array of news media reported on the program. All of its ugly details emerged from news outlets around the world. The Vatican's take was that Exodus was created with the best of intentions, then the program was disbanded very quietly. There were no admissions of bad judgement. No apologies. Nothing. Like Father Angel's ceremony, Exodus' burial was subdued and immediate.

These developments were on the minds of all the people assembled at Namaste.

Reed and Jake, Ravel and Sierra, and Andre had gathered at the cabaret. It was four a.m. Namaste was closed down for the night. Everyone was sipping on cappuccinos prepared by Jake. The plan was to talk and commiserate for an hour or so, then head out for breakfast at 2 Minutes Restaurant in Zephyrhills while the sun rose slowly and confidently.

"So how the heck did Father Angel end up at Father Joyce's house?" Andre said. His giant hand dwarfed the coffee cup.

Jake wore only a small bandage now on his forehead. He absent mindedly touched the bandage every few minutes.

"Turns out," he said, "the asshole used his two assistants — Bumandi and Antonio, right? — to bug our condo. When we swept the place a couple days ago, the sweeper beeped like a swarm of crickets gone Godzilla."

Jake finished his cappuccino. Again, he touched his forehead.

"Father Angel seemed more like a covert operative than a priest," he said.

"You'd know all about that, wouldn't you," Ravel said.

Jake glared at Ravel. He didn't appreciate her poking at him. And only he was allowed to bring up his past.

Reed reached out to hold Jake's hand. He took hold of her hand.

"I'm really glad the state attorney won't charge you for shooting Father Angel," she said. "As Detective Langdon said, it was a clear cut case of self-defense."

Jake stopped glaring at Ravel and smiled at Reed.

"Well, she started it," Jake said with an impish grin.

Everyone laughed heartily, the first time any of them laughed like that in quite a while.

"So what happened to the third nun, Reed?" Sierra said, as she reached over and played with Ravel's ear lobe.

Reed shrugged her shoulders.

Time to earn that Oscar, she thought.

"Little shit somehow got out of the stretch cuffs," she said. "She just vanished into the darkness."

"Hmm, how convenient," Ravel said. She wasn't buying any of Reed's story.

This time, Reed glared at Ravel, who clearly was enjoying her role as a trouble maker. Nothing pleased Ravel more than to rile up Reed and Jake.

"Now don't start acting out, little missy," Reed said.

"Oh, I'm just getting warmed up," Ravel answered.

"What does that mean, exactly?" Reed said.

"I'm having a psychic surge right now," Ravel said, as she looked over Reed's right shoulder. "I'm envisioning a young hottie with long fuchsia hair with black tips, exquisite make-up, wearing a slinky black dress and stiletto heels."

Sure enough, a woman bearing that same description walked up behind Reed and approached the club owners' table.

"Sierra, I can't believe we left the front door unlocked," Andre said.

"We didn't," Sierra said.

Reed turned in her chair and looked at the woman, who wore a tiny gold cross on a necklace around her neck. She was indeed very attractive, and she walked with a strong, confident air about her.

It took a few seconds, but Reed appeared to recognize the woman.

Reed smiled warmly at her.

Well, I'll be damned, Reed thought.

"Ms. O'Hara, my name is Chenoa. We've met once before," the young woman said. "Can we talk?"

Author's Notes

First, the all-important disclaimers, which here are rather fun and informative. Please do not rush through this section, as there are some engaging details that will add to your enjoyment of *Bad Habits*.

The vast majority of the names and characters in *Bad Habits* are the result of this writer's imagination. If there is any resemblance to actual people, it is entirely coincidental — for the most part.

Regarding these exceptions, I wish to thank heartily Judi Ploszek, Nat Doliner, and Chenoa Jenks for allowing me to use their names and their personalities in *Bad Habits*.

Let's start with Judi Ploszek. She is the former Chief Financial Officer at Tampa General Hospital. She was, in fact, one of the first women to attend the University of Notre Dame. Judi is a wonderfully dynamic person — brilliant, hardworking, kind hearted or severely tough, depending on the situation. She probably is the least self-absorbed person I know. And that is saying something, as I am surrounded by intelligent, educated, and very successful people. Judi's knowledge and analysis of movies, particularly *film noir*, is so impressive. We have had many fine discussions about film, and what a pleasure it is to have an actual discussion with give and take, rather than endure yet another clash of egos. A crucial sidebar: Judi does not pack a pistol in her trouser sock. At least I'm fairly certain she doesn't.

Now on to Nat Doliner. Though in real life Nat is not a neighborhood watch captain, he is a highly regarded corporate attorney with the prestigious Tampa law firm of Carlton Fields. Nat is a true intellectual, as comfortable with the subtle nuances of an offering agreement as he is with the rococo prose of James Joyce. Though Nat and I could not be farther apart politically, we always have had a shared passion for the printed word. It has been an honor to be Nat's friend for almost thirty years.

The next character in *Bad Habits* who is based on an actual person is a little trickier scenario. Sister Chenoa in *Bad Habits* is based on the colorful and animated Tampa hairstylist nonpareil, Chenoa Jenks. The real Chenoa, of course, is not a crossbow-bearing avenging nun. Yet the literary Sister Chenoa bears a physical and attitudinal resemblance to Chenoa Jenks, who really does have bright fuchsia hair with black tips, a porcelain complexion, and a temperament best described as feisty. She's also a kind soul. And a vegetarian.

On to Reed O'Hara and Jake Dupree, easily the most exciting and dynamic couple in all Western literature (As you will soon learn, that claim amounts to shameless self-promotion.)

One might wonder if I based *Bad Habits*' Jake Dupree — so handsome, sophisticated, and mysterious — on myself. Why yes, yes I did. At least, Jake represents who I'd like to be on a fantasy level. And what the heck, since I am the writer in charge of this narrative, I get to goose things a bit. For comparative purposes, I am not some sort of former field operative, as Jake is. Rather, I am a former journalist and college-level writing instructor. I earned an associate's degree from St. Petersburg College, a bachelor's degree in English from Florida State University, and a master's degree in English from Purdue University. Like Jake, I am French American, as I was born in upstate New York, to where many French Canadians migrated. And Jake and I have shared passions in baroque music, in French Impressionist paintings, and in our wives.

And speaking of wives, as I wrote in this novel's dedication, the inspiration for Reed O'Hara is my beautiful wife, Linda Fleming, who is indeed as Irish American as they come. Linda is one of the finest health care attorneys in the nation. Like Reed O'Hara in *Bad Habits*, she holds a black belt in tae kwon do. Linda also has ran the white water rapids on the Nantahala River in North Carolina, rode horses all day in the Sonoran Desert in Arizona, flew on a trapeze in Jamaica, climbed a mountain in pitch-black darkness in Maine (out of necessity, not by choice), and snow skied both in the Colorado Rockies and in the Swiss Alps. Also, Linda is an enthusiastic feminist as well as a graceful bearer of the roughhewn cross that is her husband. (If you think I am in awe of this woman, you would be correct.)

Next, regarding the Tampa Bay restaurants, bars, hotels, and museums I reference in *Bad Habits*, the vast majority are real. However, the funky El Castillo is fictional. Also, I wanted to pay homage to one of my favorite restaurants in Tampa Bay, Fleming's Prime Steakhouse. Since it'd be problematic for me to use the restaurant's actual name, I changed it to Kennedy's. (Linda's maiden name, after all, is Kennedy.) By the way, the Namaste club in *Bad Habits* is entirely fictional, though Tampa really could use a cabaret of its quality.

As you can tell from reading *Bad Habits*, I dearly love Tampa Bay. Here's proof: Linda and I have been married forty years; we have two adult daughters and three granddaughters; all of us live in Tampa Bay — it's truly a paradise.

So it makes sense that the Exodus program in *Bad Habits* would get its start in as lovely a place as Tampa Bay. However, the Exodus program is entirely fictional. At least I hope so. Oh yeah, to the best of my knowledge, I'm not aware of any vigilante nuns.

Finally, keep an eye out for the next installment from the Tampa Bay Tropics Thriller series: <u>Don Coyote</u> focuses on the ever-increasing problem of human smuggling and trafficking in this county. Only, <u>Don Coyote</u> has what I believe to be a fascinating twist.

Overall, my goal is to publish twenty installments of the Tampa Bay Tropics Thriller series in the next twenty years. Wish me luck.

Until we cross paths again, be well and keep an open mind.

— George L. Fleming
gfleming4@tampabay.rr.com

Coming soon:

DON COYOTE

A Tampa Bay Tropics Thriller

By
George L. Fleming

Made in the USA
Columbia, SC
19 June 2021